The following stories have previously been published:

"SS Attacks!" in *The Lifted Brow* (*The Fake Bookshelf*); "My wife denies being my older self." in *Reinventing the World*; "Sweet William, don't even bother denying it." in *Avery Anthology*; "The Champion of Forgetting" in *Torpedo* and *The Best of Torpedo*; "Wake up body!" in *Sleeping Fish*; "Rules and Regulations" in *Ninth Letter*; "Rules and Regulations" [a different one] in *Lamination Colony*.
Thanks to the editors.

Published by
featherproof books
Chicago, Illinois
www.featherproof.com

First edition
10 9 8 7 6 5 4 3 2 1

Library of Congress Control Number 2009936110
ISBN: 0-9771992-9-0
ISBN 13: 978-0-9771992-9-7

Design and Illustrations by Zach Dodson at Bleached Whale Design

Set in Gentium

Printed in the United States of America

the awful possibilities

Christian TeBordo

featherproof BOOKS

Several of these stories would not have been started,
most would not have been finished,
and almost none would have been published
without the support and intervention of Adam Levin.

Which isn't to say these awful possibilities are his fault.

Thank you, Adam.

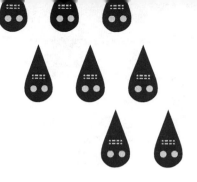

Dearest,

I booked this trip w/the Endless the Continental card Travel Agency because you said getting there was half the fun. How much more fun if I thought when getting there takes so much longer than necessary?

The 3 hour layover in Zembla alone added 2 weeks and 7 pages to our itinerary! who knew all the culture we've absorbed in the airports these last months. Who knew they had Sbarro in Swangri-La?

I'm watching you sleep as I write this. You look beautiful even though you haven't bathed since Xanadu.

Tomorrow you will awaken with a chloroform headache. I'm sorry my love, but what's one more flight delayed?

post card

—— FEATHERPROOF POSTCARDS AND BRIC-A-BRAC, CHICAGO, ILLINOIS, USA ——

U.S.A.

BLEACHED WHALE DESIGN

PERFECTLY BANAL - Postcards I sent home when we were last on vacation together so that you would have something to look forward to on our return.

60647

SS attacks!

①

Imagine you're planning your own school shooting. Imagine you have good reasons, and it's none of that I-play-too-many-video-games-and-listen-to-Marilyn-Manson-because-no-one-likes-me bullshit. You're in tenth grade and you do okay in classes and you've got plenty of friends for what it's worth but it's not worth much to you. You live in Brooklyn. Brooklyn, Iowa. There are no Jews in Brooklyn, Iowa. Keep that in mind.

Imagine your brother's two grades ahead. He does a little worse than you in school but not bad. He's got friends, not as many as you, two in fact, but he likes them more and they all live together in the apartment above your mom's garage. They're in a rap band and call themselves the Mongreloids, but they only have one song and it isn't very good, for lack of inspiration, they say. They've got ideas but no inspiration.

Imagine they are perfectly good at expressing these ideas when they aren't rapping, especially Wallace, your brother, which is not his real name but his rap name, but the ideas are not perfectly good. They're a weird mixture of Nuwaubianism and the *Wu-Tang Manual* with a dash of the *Da Vinci Code* thrown in for balance. Your brother and his friends believe the white man is the devil, but they don't feel like the devil and they all feel in their very cores the call to throw around the word nigger casually.

Imagine your brother won't let you up above the garage except to listen to new mixes of their one song, which always sound the same and never any better, and for indoctrination sessions which he calls Right Righteous Teaching. Right Righteous Teaching is a combination of esoteric and problematic racial/religious philosophy and horrible word play. White stands for With Hell I Triumph Evermore; black for Belief, Love, Action, Knowledge. The missing *c* is the white man's Cancer. Miscegenation is the only hope for humanity. Hence, Mongreloids.

Imagine you find the ideas ridiculous at first and still but there isn't much to do in Brooklyn and you like hanging out in the apartment above the garage which they call the sanctuary, the lab, the thirty-sixth chamber, and eventually start enjoying the teachings, not because you believe, but because it's a very involved and imaginative mythology developing before your eyes and the eyes of the internet, though no one out there seems to be paying much attention. Statcounters don't lie.

Imagine you're there when your brother has the revelation, and though you don't see the connection, you can see that it's utterly spontaneous and that your brother truly believes it. A man will come, a boy really, and he will terrorize a school with the white man's weapons and the black man's sense of style, none of these trenchcoats, shiny black fingernails, combat boots, and hockey player haircuts, and this will trigger the revolution, the new era, the tupacalypse.

If you think for a second that this is reason enough to plan
your own school shooting then you're a fucking idiot. But it's
interesting at least.

Imagine some asshole grad student finds the Mongreloids on
MySpace and decides to do some kind of dissertation on them.
You are suspicious, but your brother, who, despite his naiveté,
is actually a pretty skeptical guy, agrees to go along with it.
Because the grad student lived in Brooklyn, the real Brooklyn,
not this Iowa bullshit, for a year before grad school, so he
probably knows what's up, he says.

Imagine the next thing you know the grad student's moving
into your brother's old room in your mother's house because
he's too good to sleep on the couch in the apartment above
the garage but not too good to spend all the rest of his time
with them in the lab, the sanctuary, the thirty-sixth chamber,
smirking behind his hand like the devil he is, and he might be
fucking your mother for good measure. You don't know it then,
you're not even suspecting it, but keep it in mind.

Imagine you know this, the smirking part, because you're still
allowed up there a couple of times a week for Right Righteous
Teaching, though it's more performative now, less freestyle,
and your brother tones things down, i.e., is suspiciously silent
on the once world-historical issue of a school shooting, but still
you can see Chris Nelson, the grad student, the motherfucking
devil biting his tongue 'til his eyes water like it's the funniest

thing he's ever heard. Like your brother is a joke.

Even without the motherfucking you have your reasons now, right? The only choice is between grabbing the grad student by the back of his blond head and pounding his pale face in until it's red, and throwing your set in the air as you walk down the hall between homeroom and first period. Chris Nelson lived in Brooklyn, the real one, for a year after college, your brother says. What do you do?

If you can get beyond imagining, if you start dreaming of strutting through school in slow motion with a gangsta lean, arms extended and guns blazing, your black hoody barely covering your thousand-yard stare, nothing but your erection keeping your jeans above your ankles, and all those faces begging you to stop, to spare just me, but you can't hear them because the soundtrack shuts it all out ("Sound Bwoy Bureill," Smif-N-Wessun), and all those faces are the face of Chris Nelson, though sometimes they're your brother—if you can dream that, you can understand.

Now imagine you're in the backyard trying to dig a hole deep enough for a backpack full of guns, but the ground itself is buried beneath a foot of hardpacked snow, and the dirt at the surface is practically permafrost and taking forever to break. You're freezing and sweating and aching, and your only hope is that you can get it done before anyone notices you're missing.

Now imagine how pretty soon parents all over the country are going to be digging through their children's things looking for exactly what's in that bag, or even less—plans, drawings, journal entries, rap records—and you know your mom will do the same, will call in the cops for your own good or because she needs some attention too, more than she's getting from Chris Nelson if she's getting any yet, and even though you don't give your own motherfuck about the cops, the last thing you, the Mongreloids, your brother, want is for you to be called a copycat.

Now imagine what everyone else is doing as you pack the earth back into some approximation of its former self. Wonder what Wallace and the guys and Chris Nelson are doing that very moment. Imagine what your mother is doing. Think quickly back to the Mongreloids and wish you hadn't. Remember the look of your brother as you watched the school shooting unfolding the hour before.

Now imagine you can remember watching that grainy cellcam footage yourself. Maybe you can. Everybody else can. Everybody else did. But can you imagine watching him doing exactly what you'd imagined yourself doing, from costume to posture to facial composure. It's exactly like you thought it would be. It's scarier than you thought it would be. It's like watching your imagination of yourself, but cooler and a thousand miles away, a thousand miles ahead, just one fucking hour. Fuck.

Now imagine yourself crying as you bang the snow back over the spot you've dug and filled. It's cold enough to freeze the tears to your face but your face is so hot with rage it never will. Your brain won't stop telling you that whatever the Mongreloids are doing, they're doing it above the garage, and they're happy about it, and you're not allowed to join them now. You'll never get the chance to join them. School's closed. Go to bed little bitch.

Now imagine that—what are the Mongreloids doing?—could be one of your concerns for the next month or two, in fact your only, minus the first couple of days. The first couple of days school's closed, like shooting is a virus likely to spread through the country unless the kids are quarantined at home, and you're in your room like all the other kids. What the nonkids don't realize is everything's a virus nowadays and the kids in their quarantines are downloading videos the shooter made in the hours before the shooting within hours of the event. Four more kids in three separate states catch the sickness before the quarantine's lifted, though they won't know it 'til a few months have passed with a dozen more dead.

You probably don't have to imagine having watched the videos yourself, so remember instead. Remember the way the kid, his hood already up, stood in front of the camera, in front of the cinderblock wall of his dorm room, talking calmly, deadvoiced, about accounting like it was more death sentence than major. Remember the haunting way he told the story of his high school aptitude testing. Remember?

It says here you'd make a good tax assessor.

What does a tax assessor do?

Assess a tax?

Assess a tax. Okay, I'll assess a tax.

Do you see my point now? It's a parable for the generation after metaphor died. It's the Mongreloid creed. Don't forget to remember. You'll be doing more remembering than imagining soon enough.

But before you remember again, imagine school reopens and you give up on shooting and feel about the same about school qua school as you ever have. Your brother and his friends don't. They don't go back to school. They don't even leave the lab or don't seem to, though they must, sometimes, because they have to eat, right, and neither your mother nor your motherfucker seems to be catering to them. Sometimes when you creep around the perimeter of the garage trying to hide your tracks in the snow you can hear their rhymes and drums bouncing like machine-gun fire off the low winter sky, but you can't make any of it out.

Now imagine you still see Chris Nelson pretty regularly. You still see your mother pretty regularly. You don't see any signs of any funny business and you never hear any creaking or moaning creeping through the groaning wooden walls of the old house. But you could be missing something. You're at school all day most days and neither of them ever seems to have anything to say to you anyway, even when you say something to one or the other, even when you interrogate. That's the way it all goes until spring.

Now imagine spring comes to Brooklyn and the snow thaws and the grass greens and what trees there are start to bud. But instead of emerging from the garage, your brother invites you, through Chris Nelson, to inter yourself in the lab, for one night only, where the Mongreloids will perform, live and in its entirety, the concept album they've spent these last months composing and recording and preparing to perform, a concept album full of Right Righteous Teaching with a through-line about the first hip-hop school shooting and how it changed the world forever.

Now imagine that you accept the invitation, but grudgingly, and with low expectations that have less to do with the grudge than with your memory of how bad their first and for so long only song was. But as the music begins it becomes clear that something has changed, and drastically. In fact, it's maybe the greatest, most unexpected jump in quality since The Fugees scored. By the time the final anthem, "Assess a Tax," explodes climactically and decays to static leaving the silence crackling in your ears like wax paper, you're left drained, and you find yourself weeping softly.

Now imagine you have no words to offer your brother, and at first that makes you feel frustrated and guilty and like a fraternal failure. Then you realize, you can see on his face, that he doesn't need them now. Your brother has become a god, a mongreloid god, and he knows it.

Now imagine you go to bed, and despite the night's excitement you sleep well and soundly, assured that you've witnessed the beginning of something new, a renaissance with roots in Brooklyn that will change the world like a virus, the good kind if there is one, the kind that will cure the world of the white disease. Chris Nelson and your mother could be having screaming farewell sex in the room next door and this would not effect much more than a moment of your peaceful dreams of a new era, a new America, completely reversed of its curse.

Now imagine that while you sleep so well, sex or no, Chris Nelson and the Mongreloids are loading their things and themselves into the band van and stealing out of Brooklyn under cover of night, headed east to Philadelphia where the motherfucker knows some people who know some people, the tracks in the gravel driveway the only note they leave for you. To date it's the last time you've seen your brother in person, and you can't decide even now whether to be crushed or fucking furious or both from one day to the next.

Now remember. Remember what you already know.

③

Remember how within weeks Chris Nelson had turned from grad student to rap impresario, how with the guidance of some stupid or unscrupulous advisors the album was released, not as an album—the record industry was dead, they said—but as the soundtrack to an 8-bit first-person school shooter, maybe the worst, stupidest video game ever underdeveloped.

Remember how the game was released without so much as a tracklist much less a lyric sheet.

Remember how the news media, controlled as it is by the forces of the white devil, with its obvious investment in not having a revolution bent on the overthrow of precisely itself, heard, or pretended to hear in the lyrics what it wanted to hear, despite my brother's repeated insistence that the song was called ASSESS A TAX!.

Remember how within weeks everyone involved had achieved a level of notoriety, infamy even, usually reserved for petty African and Middle Eastern dictators, but how, despite the protests of the Anti-Defamation League, the Congressional Hearings, the emergency session at the United Nations, the game sold like crazy, and my brother really seemed to be enjoying himself, at least on the screen.

Remember how the news crews descended on Brooklyn to investigate what kind of evil hamlet could breed such a virus.

Remember the headlines: The Real Children of the Corn. Hitler in the Heartland.

Remember that stupid article in the weekly magazine of the national newspaper of record suggesting a few possible insinuations for why there are no Jews in Brooklyn.

Remember how you watched the screen as the clueless townies, the shit I grew up through, in order to clear a good name they'd never had, because they'd never had a name of their own, because their name was Brooklyn, announced their intention of clearing Brooklyn of the remnants of the virus it had gestated and incubated unaware for so long, with pitchforks and torches, and how you did nothing, never considered that those remnants were more than my house, were my mother, her fetus, myself.

Now it is now and you can neither remember nor imagine now.

Now I'm in the apartment above the garage, but it isn't like I'd imagined it would be because I'm alone, because my brother's in the city of brotherly love forgetting me and getting turned into nothing but Marilyn Manson with better clothes and dope beats, and because the goyim of Brooklyn, Iowa, have my house surrounded. Lucky or not for me they don't know about the apartment above the garage. So they're standing around the house waving their weaponized farm implements and demanding that the sins of the Mongreloids be visited upon the brother and the mother and the fetus of the mother and the motherfucker. They're demanding retribution and the restoration of a reputation of no repute, and all I can do is pray they get tired of it before they realize I'm up here, pray they go home.

Now when I'm not praying, I'm sleeping. It isn't as peaceful as it was the night my brother left—how could it be?—but you'd be surprised. The chanting of the angry villagers, the glow and crackle of their torches, can be soothing enough that I fall asleep despite myself, and though I only nap for minutes at a time, I dream, and I remember my dreams. In the dreams I'm strutting through school in slow motion with a gangsta lean, arms extended and guns blazing, my black hood barely covering my thousand-yard stare, nothing but my erection keeping my jeans above my ankles, and all those faces begging me to stop, to spare just me, but I can't hear them even though there's no soundtrack now, or maybe just the static at the end of the Mongreloids' album, or the crackle of torches in the distance, and all those faces are the face of Chris Nelson, though sometimes they're my brother. And I know now that dreams aren't reality. I know now they're a stand-in for something else, something bigger than a school shooting, like a nudge from God himself, that complicated motherfucker. So when I wake I go back to praying, that they'll go away, burn the house if they have to, my mom, whatever, so that I can head out for the back yard under cover of night, and dig up my bag of guns, and head out east. I could use some Right Righteous Teaching. I need to assess a tax where a tax is due.

the Continental card

post card

Darling,
In the Gallery of Redundancies in Lucy,
we were arrested by the lifelike sculpture
of Dirk Diggler embracing the lifelike
sculpture of Marky Mark.
"They're both Marky Marky" you said.
"No," I said, "only one of them is Marky
Mark. They're both characters played by
Mark Wahlberg."

But Punkinhead, what I want to know
is, which is more redundant —
redundancy or the act of calling
something redundant when it's
redundancy has already been
acknowledged?

FEATHERPROOF POSTCARDS AND BRIC-A-BRAC, CHICAGO, ILLINOIS, USA

BLEACHED WHALE
DESIGN

PERFECTLY BANAL. - Postcards I sent home when we
were last on vacation together so that you would have
something to look forward to on our return.

60647

three denials

My wife denies being my older self.

"I'm not your older self," she says.

Everything was going fine until the vows. Everything always goes fine until the vows. I find someone to love. I find someone I can find no wrong in, another self. And then comes that part in the vows, my other self.

"But we said in the vows my other self," I say.

"It's a metaphor," she says.

"And you're older than me," I say.

She's got six months on me. Six months less four days, leap year notwithstanding. It's one of those April-December things—myself one of them, herself the oldster—if only April and December weren't so far apart.

"You're the one who insisted we write our own vows," she says. "You wrote my other self," she says.

"If only April and December weren't so far apart," I say.

"What the fuck do April and December have to do with anything?" she says.

"It's a metaphor," I say.

"For what?" she says.

Here comes the explaining. I hate having to explain this, having to explain myself to my older self, the possibility, the inevitability that in six months I could be so dense as to need a statement like if only April and December weren't so far apart explained for me.

"It means you're six months older than me," I say.

"April and December are eight months apart," she says. "Or

four months apart," she says.

"I said it's a metaphor," I say. "For how you always get there first and then you ruin things for us," I say.

"Neither of us was born in April or December," she says.

"You don't understand," I say.

Try explaining anything to my older self. Sometimes I think she's willfully misunderstanding, though, to advocate the devil for only a moment, it could be the restricted blood flow.

"Maybe we could work this out if you'd just untie me," she says.

"I've heard that one before," I say.

And I have. There were a couple of times I even fell for it. Don't imagine this one's my only other, older self. Or imagine whatever you want. What are you, my judge? No seriously, are you my judge? Then maybe you can understand why I do what I do?

My neighbor denies the very shit on my shoes.

Believe me when I tell you there is shit on those shoes.

They're sneakers, gray, with Courage on the heels just above the plastic that makes them for running, the plastic above the shit.

I meet my neighbor—not as in rendezvous—I bump into her without physical contact in the stairwell where I have my cigarettes. She's having a cigarette with her daughter who isn't having a cigarette.

I'm wearing sneakers when I meet my neighbor, just not the sneakers in question. The sneakers in question are outside my door, up the stairs first on the left. They're not allowed in for the shit on them. And they aren't in question until my neighbor says your shoes.

"Your shoes," my neighbor says.

I look down at my shoes. They say New Balance, but I'm several exchanges ahead of ourselves.

First she says: "Hello. I am a woman who is divorced from Georgia. Don't ask me why."

"My wife is from Georgia," I say.

"Actually Louisiana," she says. "I'm also an epileptic."

I don't know whether she means that she's actually from Louisiana, as though she'd forgotten for a moment where she was born and raised, or that my wife is actually from Louisiana, that she's met my wife before and can hear through the Georgia accent to the Louisiana one smothered underneath, which I have not detected if it's there to detect.

"Which is why I get confused."

"Have you met my wife?" I say.

"He was definitely a man," she says. "He was making inappropriate remarks while folding my laundry. I became flustered and couldn't find my way through this large building to the apartment where my daughter awaited me with clean pajamas."

It's not such a large building. Four stories and a basement, the whole thing shaped like a horseshoe.

"These ones," says her daughter.

Nothing special—fuzzy and blue with a zipper running from left ankle to only gullet—though there are those who get nostalgic about the footy ones.

"She's like my older self," I say.

"My daughter?" says my neighbor.

"My wife," says me.

"My daughter," says my neighbor, "was awaiting me, being patient. And her pajamas. But how could I know that she wasn't getting frantic with my epilepsy?"

My wife is probably getting impatient, though frantic I doubt. I'd told her I was going for a cigarette and she knows how long a cigarette takes. Not this long. My cigarette is an inch of ash swerving slightly from the filter between my fingers.

"I was standing in the middle of the hallway getting more and more unrecognizable," says my neighbor.

"To whom," I say.

"To me they all look the same," she says. "All except for your shoes."

I look down at my shoes. I say: "They say New Balance."

"They said Courageous," she says, "and gave me the courage to find my way back."

"I should be finding my way back to my apartment where my wife is awaiting me being patient," I say. "Besides, there's a doormat on the first floor embroidered with dolphins frolicking in a moonlit sea."

I take a step toward the stairs. I didn't notice how close she was until I took a step toward the stairs. Her arm, the one that isn't holding a cigarette in its hand, crooked across her chest, hooked by hand on the opposite shoulder, presses into my belly.

I take a step back, and another. I rest my ass on the ass-level windowsill of the window I sometimes stare out of, when smoking and alone. I light a new cigarette, turn my head, and stare out the window. Or into the window where my neighbor's reflection floats.

"I know what you're thinking," she says.

I'm thinking: I was waylaid by the new neighbor. Her features are reversed in reflection, but her voice moves ever in the same direction.

"You're thinking this would make more sense if I wasn't so pretty," she says.

I'm thinking: she's an epileptic. She will have been teetering on the verge of convulsions.

"How do you think it makes me feel," she says as she drops to her knees.

"Courageous?" says her daughter.

She's sitting a few stairs down with her back to us, ignored and feeling ignored. I turn and look down at her, then down at her mother, her mother's eyes about level with my lap. Her mother reaches out both-handed, takes my left foot, and brings the sole to her lips.

"Wrong ones," I say.

She drops the left and lifts the right, brings it too to her lips as though I meant wrong one, as though I were talking about foot.

I say: "What do you think you're doing," but I'm thinking: Do they measure the distance between Louisiana and Georgia in dollars or years and either way, which one is inside? Which is out?

Sweet William, don't even bother denying it.

There is a thing I should tell Sweet William which is: "Sweet William, do not do the come-hither fingers to a man's neck, especially when he has recently shaved, leaving his skin feeling naked and vulnerable."

"It's Wee-yum," says Sweet William.

"OK Sweet Wee-yum," I say, "Where'd you get a name like that anyway."

He's skinny, with bad teeth and finger-waves à la Nat King Cole, but his clothes don't fit right and he's always on his way back from the grocery with several soft packs of the long thin cigarettes, menthol, in a little plastic bag. Kind of sweet, all in all, but you'd have to be perceptive to see it. I never notice anyone perceiving him but me.

"I didn't," Sweet William says, "only you call me that."

"Sweet Wee-yum," I say, "are you suggesting that we have some sort of special relationship, something more intimate than just saying hi when we pass each other in the lobby and then forgetting each other completely until the next time? Do we use pet names on each other? Because don't test a man, Sweet William."

"Wee-yum."

"Sweet. Wee-yum. Shit," I say. I say: "I've had about enough of you. Go back to your room. Get out of my sight."

He pops-eyes like I just demanded his first born if he'll ever bare one, and waves his long, skinny cigarette in my face, this way, that, metronomic, whining: "But I just lit this."

It's almost hypnotic.

"Are you trying to hypnotize me, Sweet Wee-yum?"

I slap it from his mouth, but I don't hit him, not even close. The cigarette tumbles down the steps of the stoop and into the grass. He gets up and scurries after it, following the smoke signals and retrieving it with a smile. It sounds pathetic, but if you saw it, it's the kind of thing that makes him sweet, the kind of thing you're not perceiving.

He takes a victory drag, exhales practically glowing, and says: "These things are expensive."

Those things are nothing but poison wrapped in a combustible tube dipped in acid to make them kill faster. Strictly ghetto.

I think Sweet William's Section 8. That's my only problem with this building. We get spacious apartments with hardwood floors and high ceilings at a decent price, but we also get the toothless hag in fourteen who says she's waiting on an inheritance if you can understand a word she says and the British accent's probably fake anyway, a fat kid named Porkchop practicing his piledriver on the lawn with the neighborhood kids in case somebody from the WWF drives by, and tranny hookers brandishing salt-water balloons any time anyone comes around thinking gentrification.

I wonder what Sweet William thinks of gentrification.

"Sweet William: what do you think of tranny hookers?"

I used to imagine Sweet William hustled himself. Back then I thought of him as Sweetback, maybe even called him that a time or three before he told me his mama named him Wee-yum. Then I thought what kind of hustler name is Sweet William, and besides how are you going to hustle when no one but me talks to you.

After that it was Sweet William, the gentlest hit man in the world, appropriate for a loner like him. But you'd think a hit man worth his Ray-Bans could afford to smoke something a little better than the black death, even if he did have a three-pack-a-day habit. Anyway he's never gone long enough to assassinate anyone of importance, even if he took the Concord, which he couldn't. It's been retired. Probably doesn't even have a passport.

"I don't have any problem with them," says Sweet William.

"Hit men?" I say.

"The tranny hookers," he says, lighting another.

"That's exactly the problem with you," I say.

That's exactly the problem with Sweet William, but try convincing him of that. I don't. I just knock another cigarette out of his mouth. Or try to.

"Missed me," he says, grinning stalactite. Stalagmite. I don't fucking know. I don't know anything about him.

I'm thinking about going back inside when he slips another cigarette halfway out of the fresh pack with a half-slick flick of the wrist. I take it no thanks and pop it in my mouth. He offers me a light, but I've got my own. I pull it from my pocket and get a little buzz from the first drag.

We smoke our cigarettes in silence. It's past dusk now, but not quite night, the sky like the cover of a romance novel, except it's blocked half-out by the factory up the hill that I never found out what it turned out because it hasn't turned anything out as long as I've lived here, and the moon is beaming on a Malibu with only one hubcap instead of some shirtless shepherd and his maiden if that's what this romance was supposed to be about.

Sweet Jesus, the romance of Sweet William.

I finish first because I'm fast without trying. I flick my butt to the curb and wait button-lipped to see if I can get anything else. Sweet William catches me looking at him, but it takes him a while to catch the meaning. He kind of rolls his eyes, which is the exact thing that you don't want to do to me, and if you don't believe me ask anyone who's ever done it, or worse for you try it yourself. So when Sweet William does the wrist flick again and three cigarettes fly out because the pack's starting to loosen up, and I snatch them one two three before they ever hit the ground, he's getting off easy.

This time I say thank you: "Thanks," because I figure it'll piss him off.

"Why don't you just ask?" he says.

I wave all three of them in his face like I'm trying to hypnotize him and say: "Because these things are expensive," like you're getting very sleepy, and I go inside because three should be enough.

But then I want another one right away to keep the buzz going, so I pull out my lighter and it flicks a spark but doesn't burn anything and I try it again and nothing so I go in the bedroom to borrow my wife's but she's tied up making false claims and you know how that goes: no use trying.

I have no alternative but to use the stove which is dangerous but desperate times are calling "just don't singe your see-through eyebrows." I turn the knob all the way right until it clicks and a great ball of fire flies from the right front burner, then back left to a delicate but deadly blue halo, and squat with my knees pressed to the oven, leaning in until I'm lit, trauma-free.

The buzz returns but the cigarette's practically finished by the time I'm finished standing up with the stove safely off and cooling, and I haven't even had time to lean back in my chair and savor it. They put something in Sweet William's brand to make them burn faster so you smoke more. Excelsior, I think, from the planks of a plague-infested ship.

I take the second cigarette from behind my left ear and light it off the first because I'm not going through the whole ordeal again. I throw what's left of the first into a pot soaking in the sink and flop into my armchair like that.

But it's hard getting comfortable. There's the awareness that I haven't got much time, so I have to choose between shifting around and savoring. I choose savor. I drag deep and release like I'm relaxed, but I'm not because there's something poking at my back from the crack between the cushion and the chair's right arm, and my wife is making a racket howling: "If you untie me I'll tell you the truth of how the balance between inside and out equals blessed assurance," which almost makes me want to change the subject until the only good thing comes to an end which is cigarette number two.

I barely have time to get number three from behind ear number right and lit off two before two goes ash but I do. I get it lit. Then I'm grinding the butt beneath my heel on the carpet because I'm so mad and unrelaxed, and going out saying: "It's too late you had your chance" before the door slams behind me.

Sweet William's not on the stoop anymore, but I want three more cigarettes because the last three were hardly my fault, so I wait there in case he decides to come back out. It's not like I can't afford my own. I can. I'm not Section 8, but it's dark now and I don't go out after dark because of the Killer Bee.

He didn't get a name like that from me. I've got way more imagination than to call a guy with nasty blond dreadlocks striped with the gutter's own filth something he could pass for, though really more of a killed bee if you don't tell him I said it and I didn't.

Instead I said: "Okay," when he said don't follow me even though I wasn't following him, I was just behind him and staying that way. I was on my way into Annie's breakfast place to smoke the cigarettes that I did have then, and drink her coffee but not her greasy water because my wife was getting me down.

He had this stagger that was way worse than drunk, more like four feet in the grave and trying to grow a couple more and I told myself this man will be wanting to smoke so stay back until he's past the door.

When I say told myself I mean in my head where he couldn't hear it, but even so he turned around and said what I told you he said and I responded as reported like let that be that and the world keep turning which wasn't good enough for him and it never is.

He said: "Killer Bee's got eyes in the back of his head," and I said okay again—instead of asking him where he got a name like that, which is a dumb name and less surprising than, say, Our Lady of East Genesee Street—despite all evidence to the contrary, the extra set of eyes, not my okay which is not debatable, plus my perception which told me he'd seen me in Annie's window by virtue of his sideways gaze. Even if he did have eyes in the back of his head they'd be watering all the time and probably stinging from the fumes of his pelt.

Still not enough.

"And all he does is kill and kill and kill," he said, which would not be enough to keep me from going out for smokes, no. It was the way his liver was leaking into his eyes. They were the same color as his hair. There are certain eye colors that I have no problem swatting, but there is no winning against yellow even if you win, no none.

I finally got into Annie's when somebody else distracted him with a powdered donut, but he just stood there in the window pointing at me with the index of one hand and eating the donut with the other like eating a donut is such a tough guy thing to do and I have not been out after dark since.

I try to remember if there's anyone else who would give me three cigarettes and can only think of the epileptic who is divorced from Georgia, and I'm sure she'd do it, but she'd make me repay her by letting her kiss my shitty sneakers which let's face it is demeaning to us all. So there's nothing but to head for Sweet William's apartment.

Sweet William's door is closed, but the hallway in front of it smells like smoke and I can hear some music playing inside though not enough to make out and keep your mind out of the gutter. So I put my ear to the door, just to make sure that I won't be interrupting any God-knows-what, and also maybe to figure out what he's listening to which turns out to be "The Impossible Dream" from *Man of La Mancha* which is about what you'd expect. And just when Don Quixote sings: "To be willing to march into hell for a heavenly cause," the door opens and I fall forward into Sweet William's apartment.

Sweet William reaches out to steady me, and I reach out to knock his hand away.

He says: "What are you doing?"

There is a thing that I should tell Sweet William which is: What am I doing, Sweet William? I'm not the one opening his door wearing nothing but a terrycloth robe and a mud-mask, but remember, there's no point telling him anything, so I don't, which is why I said his name the right way.

I push him back, but his head jerks forward and his mud-mask splatters on my shirt. Not much damage done, but doing the laundry in this building can be a huge pain in the ass due to a man down there who will tell you inappropriate things or so says the epileptic Georgia divorced. I've never seen him, but maybe that's because I minimize my laundry-room time by trying to keep my clothes clean unlike some people.

So I knock Sweet William to the floor instead and I put my foot on his neck but not hard. Just enough to keep him down.

I say: "Sweet Wee-yum, this is not a bad apartment," and it's not. Same layout as mine, but he's got a flair for decoration. For example: the white fur area rug that he's laying on which makes me feel like I'm choking him on a cloud.

"Thanks," he says, squirming a little but not much. "Do you want another cigarette?"

Of course I want another cigarette, but you can't tell Sweet William anything so I say: "No, I want the truth," which is true in a way.

"Which truth?" says Sweet William.

"The truth about Sweet Wee-yum," I say. "The best one," I say.

I can't really tell what's going on down there, but the way his head lolls from side to side and his eyes roll backward, I'm guessing he's thinking.

He says: "I was a little boy who loved his grandfather," and then he stops or pauses.

If stop then okay but it doesn't sound like the best truth. If pause it's probably the beginning of a truth that's going to make me puke.

I say: "Is that the whole truth so help you?"

"Do you want the whole truth?" he says. I really don't think so, but he goes on right away: "He was in the war."

"The great one?"

"Yes," says Sweet William, "Korea."

Don't bother to tell Sweet William that Korea was barely even good if you weren't even there.

"He used to call me his little prince," he says. "And then, one night—"

A pause when I want it stopped. I take my foot off his neck and say: "Stop," and Sweet William gasps half the smoke-stale air of the apartment into his lungs, lets it go and takes the other half. You can feel it. The room has its own weather. He sits up and rubs his neck with his old lady fingers, rests his elbows on his knees.

Maybe I can still get another cigarette.

"What about the rest of the truth?" he says.

"I don't want the truth anymore," I say. "I just want a cigarette."

He reaches into his bathrobe, flicks out a couple of cigarettes. He hands me mine and lights his own, but he doesn't offer me his lighter because he thinks mine still works. He pulls a small, clean glass ashtray from the opposite pocket and uses it accordingly.

"Why didn't you just ask?" he says.

"Because nothing gets through to you, Sweet William," I say, "because you got traumatized by your grandfather."

Sweet William looks traumatized to learn about the trauma.

"It wasn't traumatic," he said. "It would have been if not for the angel Tillie."

Who the fuck is the angel Tillie? Because I have read the Holy Bible cover-to-cover three times if you count the one I skipped every other word in search of codes and the gospel truth is Sweet William is about as sane as Our Lady of East Genesee Street.

"Sweet William, who is this Tillie?"

"He's the angel who told me my grandfather was in a better place."

I say: "Bullshit, Sweet William. Everyone knows that angels are girls."

"Not this one," says Sweet William. "This one was a little boy in a turquoise loincloth who floated around on a little cloud like this."

He runs his ugly fingers across the white fur rug on his way to reclining on this night with one elbow on the floor and his head in his hand.

"That's not an angel," I say. "That's a cherub."

I know because I saw a picture when I was ten, a circle of babies flying around their mom, and when the security guards pulled me from the canvas and got the pocket-knife out from between my teeth, they told me: "Cherubim, not babies." My first and last field trip.

"So I've been looking for the better place ever since," says Sweet William.

"What better place?" I say.

Sweet William scurries over to the end table beside his baby-blue sofa, grabs a book, and hurries back, spreading the book on the floor in front of him wide open. It looks like a map from up here, but a map of what I can't tell. Sweet William does come-hither fingers to the air and you can't do anything about it, it's his apartment, but my squat is hesitant.

"New Jersey," I say.

Sweet William points at a blue line on New Jersey.

"I've been saving up for a car," he says. "They got a thing, the Korean Veteran's Memorial Highway, and when I get there, I'm gonna pull over to the side of the road and shove my hands into the dirt until I got two good handfuls."

I look at his hands and wonder if he's been practicing.

He says: "I'm gonna shove the Korean Veteran's Memorial Dirt in my pocket and keep it with me always."

Sweet William just keeps staring at the map as though he can see the highway, the dirt, his grandfather, the best truth, on it, but really it's just a bunch of pastels trying to cover up nature so thick it smells like cat-piss, an oil slick I saw on an airplane my only time up before the knockouts kicked in, the impossibility of ever really getting anything across to anybody in the ugliest place.

I've got my cigarette and my knees are achy. I stand up to let myself out.

Sweet William stubs out his cigarette, passes me an ashtray, and waits for the pressure of mine. When it doesn't come, he looks up and notices me for the first time since the truth came out.

"Your cigarette's not lit," he says.

I say: "My lighter died."

"Why didn't you just ask?" he says.

But I'm tired of asking.

Cherry Pies

As we laced up our skates to head
out on the frozen harbor, you said:
"This is so beautiful I want to smash
it," as much to the harbor itself as
to me.

It was true. One of the lasting
effects of the latest oil spill.

My Patient Etherized Upon a Table,
you were so graceful out on that black
ice that I wished we had insurance
so that I could encourage you to
smash something more substantial —
an arm, a leg, your husband.

FEATHERPROOF POSTCARDS AND BRIC-A-BRAC, CHICAGO, ILLINOIS , USA

the Continental card

post card

U.S.A.

BLEACHED WHALE
DESIGN

60647

*PERFECTLY BANAL - Postcards I sent home when we
were last on vacation together so that you would have
something to look forward to on our return.*

the champion of forgetting

Here is a list of failures.

I was staying in a hotel room with some people. I didn't know their names. I wasn't their friend. Not the kind where you say hi my name's and hi my name's and then you call each other names.

Before I was staying in the hotel room I was walking down Market and they snatched me into their van so I was kidnapped.

What's that called after you're kidnapped. When you're just staying in the hotel room.

There wasn't tape on my mouth or chains. On my wrist or anything. You could walk around in it and watch television. You could go for ice so the door wasn't locked. From the inside.

The first time I went for ice I had to knock to get back in. That was when we made up the idea to put a thing in the door when I went for ice. Or somebody else for something else. A shoe or ashtray.

One of the men slipped the metal chain from the wall between the door and the frame. That was the only chain unless it was a metal bar. The girl had failed the test anyway. It was a good hotel room. My first.

It wasn't the only hotel room. Sometimes there were others. One at a time. It looked like the other ones we lived in. Two men a woman and me. Four. And yes there was sex.

Sometimes there was sex in the other hotel rooms. On either side of us unless we were on the end.

Sometimes when there was sex in another hotel room a man said a woman's name or a woman said a man's.

Sometimes in our hotel room a man said a woman's name or the woman said a man's. Sometimes when there was sex. Sometimes when there was not. I don't know if it was the real names. Sometimes they were different. Sometimes they were the same which was not often. Or I don't remember because I was the champion of forgetting.

When we got to the hotel room. The first time I got to the hotel room. After I got kidnapped. When I wasn't kidnapped anymore. When there wasn't tape on my mouth. When I was in the van there was tape on my mouth but not in the hotel room.

At first there was tape on my mouth and my wrists. That's when the man who was our leader then said not to say my name. And the woman said better forget your name.

If you don't say your name you don't forget your name and you always want to say it. This is how I was for a while. When the tape was on my mouth. Sometimes I said my name because who even knows what you're talking about with tape on your mouth. But when there wasn't any more tape I bit my tongue. It hurts to bite your tongue.

When you forget your name you don't bite your tongue. Why would you. You don't want to say it and you don't say it. If you do you don't know because it's forgotten. It's suddenly somebody else's and you've forgotten theirs too.

This is the way it works.

One time when it was my turn to register for the hotel room. They give you cash from the box of cash and you say you would like a room for your name and give the man or woman at the desk the money they gave you and the man or woman gives you a key. A key is a symbol of a room to them.

I said I would like a room and the man. I don't remember his name. The man behind the counter said what is your name. I didn't remember my name because I had forgotten it. I gave him the money but he didn't give me a key.

When I got back to the van the man who was our leader then. The leader gives you money from the cash box and says what hotel to drive to or what hotel you are driving to if you ask and whose turn it is to drive and who to kidnap and who's turn it is to register for the hotel room. Also some of the sexual things. That time it was mine.

The leader said that it was a test and I had failed the test.

I almost never knew when I was getting tested. Especially when I was first kidnapped and for the time after that I don't know what to call. An example of this is the first test. The first test they said was a test.

The first test. What I think of as the first test they did not say was a test. One of them said do you think she's a screamer and another one said there's only one way to find out. The one who said the second thing. She was the woman. She dug a little corner of the tape away from the skin of my face. Then she pulled off the whole tape.

I didn't scream. The girl said see she didn't scream but not that I had passed a test.

The first test that they said was a test. There was a needle and the needle went in my arm. I didn't scream but that was not this test. Blood came out of my arm through the needle and filled up the tube of it.

While I was not screaming but there was still blood coming out I said what are you doing. The man who was doing it. The leader. He said it's a test.

When the tube was full he gave it to the woman and the woman took it to the bathroom. I asked if the test was over but it was not. I got nervous about the test because some of it was happening in the bathroom where I couldn't do anything about it and I didn't know how much of it was happening where I was so I let him put a wad of cotton over the spot on my arm that the blood came out of and apply gentle pressure.

It felt good until the woman came out of the bathroom with a look on her face. The pressure became more than gentle for a second.

The woman said her blood is wrong and we can't do sex to her right now.

The man let go of my arm and walked out of the hotel room. He forgot to leave a shoe in the door, so I went and did it for him. Then I took a nap for loss of blood or to forget about the failure.

There were more tests but they only admitted it sometimes. Only when I failed except once.

This is a list of failures.

The other time the door locked when I went to go get ice.

There was a new boy that day so five but not for long. He failed the screamer test by screaming, but they didn't tell him that. Or maybe they did but he was screaming too loud. I didn't hear it.

When they fail the screamer test there are two needles.

The first one puts stuff in and the stuff puts them to sleep. The second one takes blood out for the real test.

Other than being the champion of forgetting my only job was getting ice. This was because of the failures I told you about and other failures.

I would get ice between when the tape got taken off. Sometimes I would take the tape off but that wasn't a real job. And the first needle or second needle if the boy or girl was a screamer or not. It was just in case.

One of the things about getting the ice being your job was you were supposed to be quiet. This is not easy when you're carrying every empty container you can find and then it's full of ice but I never got in trouble for that part. The ice rattled a little but this was not a surprising sound.

When I got back to the door of our motel room. The outside. I had the mini trash can from the bathroom and the mini trash can from the bedroom and the ice bucket and the mugs for the complimentary coffee and the pot that you make the complimentary coffee in all full of ice and I shouldered the door like I usually did to get in.

But someone had closed it and it had locked. My shoulder just made a thud against the door. I don't remember if it was me.

On the other side. The inside. I heard someone shush me but I didn't know who. And I didn't know what to do because a knock is louder than a thud from my shoulder. So I waited to see if they would notice that the thud was made by a person who had not brought the ice in yet because the door was locked.

I waited a long time for them to notice but they didn't. I wondered again if I should knock but I couldn't knock anyway with my hands full of containers full of ice. The ice was cold and my hands hurt from it and my arms hurt from carrying it all so I put the ice down so I could have the choice of knocking if that was the best choice.

I did a pros and cons and decided that because a knock is louder than my shoulder I wouldn't knock. So I waited. I sat down next to the ice with my back against the wall and waited and fell asleep.

I didn't wake up until I heard someone scream what the fuck. The man who was our leader then. I didn't know what the fuck for.

I was only a little awake wiping my eyes when the door opened a crack and a head came out of the crack and it was the head of the man saying what the fuck again.

He looked down at the containers full of ice. Over at me. The ice was turned to water and he screamed that at me too. He screamed at me to get up. The boy had passed the second test and someone else had passed the test of doing sex to him.

I had already failed the test of doing sex with one of those balloon things and a steak. A couple of boys ago. That was a failure that you only get one chance at. At least me.

The steak is a symbol of a boy or girl to them. The meat of a boy or girl. And the balloon is their skin. The scalpel cuts it right or wrong.

We were alone in the motel room. The same one or different. I don't remember. Me and the woman. She was our leader when the others were out kidnapping another boy to get him unkidnapped and just staying in the hotel room because he was no good for sex too.

Nobody knew yet.

The woman who was our leader was in the bathroom and I got nervous because of how I failed a test in the bathroom without being in the bathroom.

I was watching TV with an eye on the ice to keep it from melting. She came out with the steak-balloon and said this is a test.

I asked her if I passed and she said I can't tell you 'til you take it. I took it and said did I pass. She said the test not the steak-balloon. She said this is the skin and this is the meat. She said this is what you use to do it. It was a scalpel.

Now do it.

I took the scalpel. My first. In my free hand. The one that wasn't holding the balloon. I brought the balloon up closer to my face to see the meat through the skin. I held the scalpel over it.

I looked up at the girl who was our leader with only my eyes.

She said not like that. She said you've seen how we do it.

I couldn't remember how they did it but I guessed up was bad so I put it on the bed in front of me and hunched over it.

I acted like I was concentrating but really I was concentrating on how to pass the test.

I looked up with my eyes and she just stood there watching. I put the point of the scalpel to the skin of the balloon. Same.

I stabbed with the scalpel. Through the skin and the meat and into the bed. I kept my eyes on our leader.

I couldn't tell if I had passed or not from her face. She walked over and told my fingers to let go of the scalpel with her hand. She pulled the scalpel out of the bed but the meat stayed on like barbecuing.

I asked her if I passed and she said no. I asked her if I got a second chance and she said that was a failure you only get one chance at. At least me.

Failing was easier when she was our leader. With the other leader. The man. I failed like this.

That's fucking it. I've fucking had it. She's got to fucking go.

Twice. At least for me. The first was a failure I already mentioned.

He said get out. He said this is the last straw.

The woman said shut up. She said it's only forty bucks. She said we told her to forget her name and she did. That's one test she passed. She's the champion of forgetting.

I was the champion of forgetting.

After that they called me champ. Except the leader. The man who was our leader. Or forgetful if I forgot something and failed another test. But that time she called me champ.

We went to another motel and it was not my turn to register for a room. Never again.

The last time. At least for me. At least so far. The leader said that's fucking it. I've fucking had it. You've got to fucking go.

His face was standing over mine and spit and bready breath flew out of his mouth. His hands were fists.

Another hand. The woman's. It came out of the door and put itself on the man's shoulder. The hand's voice said his name. I don't remember. It said calm down.

But he didn't calm down. He threw a fit. He punched the walls and kicked and his kicks knocked over the containers full of melted ice and the water spilled over the carpet and made dark shapes on it.

He didn't care. He kept punching and kicking until he was too tired to punch and kick anymore and hunched over with his hands on his knees.

He looked up at me with just his eyes and said get out. He said that was the last straw.

I was too scared to get out of the way of his punching and kicking. I was still just sitting there with my back against the wall and I didn't get up or get out.

Go he said. He said leave now.

The woman said we'll take care of that later. She said first we need more ice.

A door opened down the hall and a head peeked out. The head said everything all right out there and the woman said go mind your own business.

My business was ice. I started to get up to gather the bucket and the trash cans and the mugs and the coffee pot but she said to just stay there.

She put her hands on the shoulders of the leader and walked him back into the room. She came out with the other man and they gathered up all the empty containers and took them down the hall to fill them and came back with the full containers and went back into the room.

The door closed behind them. They forgot to put something in it. I just sat there waiting until I fell asleep.

When I woke up they were in the room yelling. All of them. One of them said she won't even remember. Because I'm the champion of forgetting. One said but I like doing surgery on her and another one said another good reason not to keep her around.

The woman said let's do it and get out of here quick.

The door opened and I looked up. It was the woman. She said come on champ.

I got up slow and walked into the room.

I was nervous. I didn't know if it was a test. I thought it was a test because everyone was looking at me but what kind of test is come on other than come into the room.

They were all standing there with their coats on and carrying their bags. All except the boy they had done sex to. The bathroom door was closed.

The woman. She had the ice bucket. She said we're going to go.

Do something the leader said. We're going to go do something. He said we have a special job for you while we do something.

We're making you the leader of you and the boy in the bathtub.

I asked if it was a test. The man said yes this is a test. He said make sure you have enough ice for when we get back and remember not to remember your name. The other man said or ours and the rest of them said it again. Or ours.

Then the woman said let's go and they went.

I just stayed there making sure my name was forgotten. The way I did this was to try to remember it and not be able to. It was a test that happened inside me and I always passed once I invented it.

It took me a long time to invent it because first I had to make sure I forgot it. After it was my turn to get the motel room I knew I could pass whenever I wanted. I was pretty sure there was enough ice.

I was about to tell myself that I had passed the test when our leader came back in. He was breathing hard so I guessed he made it all the way to the van before he remembered he forgot something important.

I was afraid he was going to make the boy in the bathtub the leader of me and the boy in the bathtub but he just looked at me and went in the bathroom.

I heard him in the bathroom going through something plastic. The bathroom door was open but I stayed where I was. Maybe a bag. Maybe the mini trash bag in the mini trash can. I couldn't tell from the bedroom.

The sound stopped and he came out. He had a needle and a scalpel in his hand and he was wiping them off with a washcloth one at a time walking toward me.

I asked him if I passed the test. I asked him if I was still the leader of me and the boy in the bathtub. He just kept walking toward me wiping the scalpel and the needle with the washcloth.

When he got to me he held out his left hand. The washcloth

was spread out on it like a tablecloth and the needle and the scalpel were laid out on it like a fork and a knife. Or knife and knife.

He said hold these and I held out my left hand like he was holding his so that I could just slide the whole thing onto my hand like in the magic trick except bringing the silverware with it.

He said no. He said just the scalpel and the needle.

So I took just the scalpel and the needle. It was full of sleep stuff. I took it with my left hand and closed it around them. I wondered if I was supposed to hold one in each hand.

I asked him if I passed and he said the test wasn't over yet. He said remember not to remember our names. Or yours.

I asked him if I was still the leader of me and the boy in the bathtub and he said I've got to go champ and went.

That was the only time he called me champ. So far. It sounded funny. Like it was my name. But I did the test of trying to remember my name and couldn't.

I remembered that champ was short for a job. The champion of forgetting.

By then I thought the ice might be melting or melted. I knew how long it took ice to melt. That was my job. But I didn't know what happened once the ice had melted. We always left after the sex, I didn't know what happened when the boy or girl woke up from the nap.

I went over to the bathroom door and knocked with the hand that wasn't holding the needle or scalpel. The boy didn't answer. I knocked again. I hoped I wasn't disturbing him. There was no do not disturb sign on the doorknob.

I knocked again. I opened the door. I walked in.

The bathroom looked empty. Clean like when you first get the motel room. It made me want to sit on the toilet. Usually there was pee on the seat and trash in the trash and scalpels and towels and needles and shampoo bottles everywhere. The only good time was when you just got there.

The shower curtain was closed but I knew the boy was behind it. I said I'm going to pee so don't look. I pulled down my pants and sat on the toilet but I was nervous the boy would look so I couldn't go. I got up and got dressed.

I said you can look now but he didn't.

I asked him if he was behind the curtain. I asked him if he was decent. He didn't answer so I pulled the curtain open with my free hand and looked in. To check on the ice. And the boy because I was the leader of me and him.

The ice was melting but not melted. The boy was behind the curtain but not decent. He was naked on his back on the ice and I could see his whole front.

I told him it was okay. I told him I was our leader now. For now. But he didn't answer. I reached down and touched his shoulder. I shoved his shoulder but he didn't wake up. He was cold.

As the leader I had to do something about his indecency and his coldness. Also the ice. I had to not remember my name or theirs while I did it.

I was used to being the champion of forgetting so I wasn't worried about remembering but I had to stop and think about the indecency and the coldness and the ice. I wouldn't be able to get his clothes on him or warm him up without taking him off the ice but why would I make sure there was enough ice if he wasn't on it.

Then I thought of a thing that would kill two of the birds with one blanket and it was a blanket. I went back into the bedroom. There were two beds and one cot. The beds had a comforter and a blanket on them but the cot only had a blanket.

I didn't know how long it would be until the others would get back and they would need the beds and the blankets on them so at first I was going to give him the blanket from my cot.

Then I remembered that I was the leader of me and the boy in the bathtub so I did a pros and cons and I made a decision like a leader and I pulled the comforters and the blankets and even sheets off both beds.

While I was pulling everything off the beds the hand holding the scalpel and needle dropped the scalpel and needle but my hands were full so I left them.

In the bathroom I dropped everything else on the floor and picked them up one at a time and put them on the boy in the bathtub. I tucked them in between his shoulders and the ice until the floor was clear again and the boy looked decent and maybe getting warm.

When I pulled my hands away from the last tuck I saw that they were wet and remembered that I was going to get ice. I went around the rooms and picked up the mini trash cans and the coffee mugs and the coffee pot.

They took the ice bucket with them. They always did after sex.

I had to put the mugs down to open the door so I put the mugs down. Then I remembered the needle and scalpel and got worried they would come back while I was getting ice and see that I had got ice without the needle and scalpel so I went and picked them up and dropped them in a mini trash can.

I opened the door and picked the mugs back up and went down the hall to get ice.

It took me a long time to fill all the containers with ice because the ice machine was taking a long time to make the ice and let go of it. So long that I thought about going to the one at the other end of the hall which sometimes worked.

I hoped that everyone would not get back and find the boy alone in the bathtub of melted ice without his leader but then all of the containers were full.

When I got back to the door of our motel room I shouldered it like I usually do to get in but it was closed and locked. My shoulder just made a thud against the door. It was either me or the boy in the bathtub. I didn't hear anything on the other side of the door. The inside.

I wanted to knock on the door to see if the boy would let me in but I couldn't because my hands were full of containers full of ice. It reminded me that there was probably no ice left for the boy in the bathtub and I worried about my leadership skills. I put the ice down so I could have the choice of knocking and do it.

I knocked. I listened. I didn't hear anything. I knocked again. I didn't hear anything.

I whispered into the door. I whispered like a yell. Boy in the bathtub. This is your leader. Can you hear me. If you can hear me let me in.

I don't think he could hear me. He didn't let me in. I didn't remember if I left the bathroom door closed or open. If I left it closed he couldn't hear me through two doors. But if I left it open I did not know why he didn't answer me.

I was scared he woke up while I was taking a long time getting ice and left because I was taking such a long time. That he got mad at me because he woke up without enough ice. That it was all a trick to see if I was a good leader and I was not a good leader and I had failed another test.

I whispered into the door. I whispered like a yell.

I don't remember my name.

I said I don't remember our names.

I yelled I am the champion of forgetting.

I am the champion of forgetting.

I am the champion of forgetting.

A door opened down the hall and a head peeked out. The head said everything all right out there. I turned to the head and stopped yelling.

Everything was not all right out there but everything had not been all right out there before and the girl had told the head to go mind its own business.

I did a pros and cons and told the head to go mind its own business but it didn't go mind its own business. It peeked out more to its shoulders and an arm. It said what's all that stuff.

Because it didn't mind its own business I didn't know what

happened next so I told it to go mind its own business again. I told it it did it before but it was a body now and it was coming toward me looking at all the containers full of ice like it was very curious about them.

It said your ice is melting. It said what do you need all that ice for.

I said mind your own business. I yelled mind your own business.

Mind your own business. Go.

But his arm reached out and grabbed my arm and pulled and I was in his room with the door closed behind us and him between me and it almost right away.

I screamed. A little bit nothing and then let me out.

He said shut up. He said I only took you in here to get you to stop screaming. I'll let you go when you stop screaming.

I stopped screaming.

He put his hands in his long hair and turned around and walked away from me. Then he walked back toward me. He looked like I failed another test. I started to worry that this was another test.

He said now what was all the ice for.

I said is this another test.

He said I asked you first.

I said you said you'd let me go if I stopped screaming.

He said first tell me what all the ice is for.

Fuck it if it is a test. And was it a test.

I tried to run past him but he was too big. He just pushed me back and I fell over. I got back up and tried to run past him again. This time I ducked his arm and when he tried to block me with his body I shoved the needle into his belly and pushed the button and pulled the needle back out.

At first he just looked surprised. Then he fell over face first.

After the stuff puts them to sleep the second needle takes out blood for the real test. I didn't know what happened in that test. What the girl does in the bathroom. But I had seen them do the sex and I had a scalpel.

I squatted down and sat on him like a horse and used it to cut open his shirt. His back was hairy and even though there was nobody around I got nervous that someone would find out if I failed this test so my hand shook and I scratched him a little with the scalpel in the wrong place.

Then I put the scalpel in the right place. The skin there was the balloon and the meat was the meat. I poked through the balloon but not as hard as before and slid it down like I saw them do. Then I pulled the skin apart and pulled out the meat. It looked like the others.

I almost cried I was so happy.

Instead I looked around for his ice bucket. It was right on the counter. I went and got it but it was empty. I put the meat in anyway and the top back on.

I went to go get the ice which was melting. This time I remembered to put a thing in the door to keep it from locking. It was his shoe.

I brought back the ice and put a little of the ice in the ice bucket with the meat like they did and dumped the rest in the bathtub. There wasn't much so I went back with all of the containers and filled them all which took a long time again and dumped them in the bathtub.

Usually when they put them in the bathtub they were smaller and two or three of them did it but there was only me. At first I tried to wake him up so we could do it together.

I said I am your leader. Wake up and help me get you in the bathtub. But he didn't wake up.

I tried to lift him up but he was too heavy. I tried to pull him by his arms but they slipped out of my hands. Then I tried his hair. He had long hair for me to get my hands in and I got my hands in and when I pulled, he budged. I pulled again harder and he budged a little more but not enough.

I did a pros and cons and realized I would never get him in the bathtub at this slowness so I went to the bathtub and filled all the containers with its ice and dumped them on him. On the floor. I hoped it would keep him cold enough.

Then I remembered the other boy I was the leader of. I took the ice bucket with the man's meat and the empty containers and went to go get more ice for him but I left the man's shoe in the door in case I needed to lead him anymore.

When I got back to the old room with all of the ice I put the ice down but kept the covered ice bucket in my hands. I knocked and said are you awake yet but the boy didn't answer. So I waited. I sat down next to the ice with my back against the wall to my right of the door and the bucket in my arms and waited and fell asleep.

When I woke up there was a cart with garbage bags and towels in front of me and a maid standing over me saying do you want your bed made. I remembered that she could not make the bed because all of the makings were tucked around the boy in the bathtub if he was still in the bathtub.

I looked up at the door and saw the do not disturb sign on the doorknob. Do not disturb I said.

She said did your mom and dad lock you out.

I tried to remember their names for once and were the names Mom and Dad. I pictured the boy in the bathtub and thought Mom. I kept the picture and thought Dad. I didn't think he was Mom or Dad but I didn't know if he locked me out. Even if he did I was still his leader and I had to get back in to lead him.

Nobody locked me out or I don't know his name I said. I think I would like my bed made after all.

The maid put her key into the lock and the door opened. I slipped by her into the room. I heard a groan and saw that the bathroom door was left open.

I said I don't want my bed made anymore. I pointed to the do not disturb sign with the hand that wasn't holding the ice bucket and said do not disturb. The maid shook her head but walked away and stopped disturbing me for then.

I kept the door open with my foot and dragged the other containers full of melting ice in by ones and twos then let the door close and slid the bolt.

I heard the groaning again and went into the bathroom through the open door. The boy was still in the bathtub but he took off his blankets because he didn't want to be warm. The ice under him was mostly melted and the water was pink. He was indecent.

I told the boy I'm sorry but you would have plenty of ice if you had responded to the commands of your leader. I told him now the ice I got for you is almost as melted as the ice you already have but not as pink. I told him now I'm going to have to go get ice all over again and it will take a long time and you will probably just keep groaning and not cooperating because that's all you have done and not done.

There was a knock at the door. It was you but I didn't know it yet. I don't know you.

I went to the door and peeped through the peephole and saw you. You couldn't see me but you said to let you in.

I didn't know if it was a trick. I didn't know if you were the new leader or if we would lead the boy together. But then I thought that you might ask my name which I can't remember. I'm not supposed to remember. And I decided to be quiet.

I walked away from the door and into the bathroom through the open door and told the boy in the bathtub to be quiet but he groaned.

You knocked again. Louder now.

I did a pros and cons and told him shut up. I told him I can't get anymore ice because someone. It was you. Was at the door.

You knocked. He groaned. You tried to turn the doorknob but it was locked. I told him to shut up. He groaned. You tried to unlock the door with a key. Was it the maid's key. I think it was the maid's. The door unlocked and the handle turned but the door didn't open because I had slid the bolt and you can't unlock the bolt from where you were. The boy groaned.

I said you've left me no choice. If you refuse to obey the

commands of your leader. And you were at the door. I have to put you to sleep.

The needle was empty but I thought there might be a drop or something in it. Enough to put the boy to sleep since he was weak from the sex. I pulled back the button and poked the needle through his balloon and into his meat and pushed down on the button.

I heard you kicking the whole time. You were kicking and kicking and then you took a break to go get the axe you came in with and then you were axing. The boy jerked around for a little while but then he stopped groaning and went back to sleep.

I could hear you axing still and I had just enough time to get the sheets and blankets and comforters back on the bed. They might look made but they are not.

And then your axe came through the door. Then you. And you started pounding on the boy saying what did you do to him and somebody get an ambulance and I'm sorry I cut you with my scalpel but all I wanted to know was am I still the leader of me and the boy in the bathtub and who is the leader of me and you and did I pass the test.

U.S.A.

Private Dances

Is it possible my confusion has been semantic all along? That I'd rather see inside you than be inside you?

Today we met the invisible man and the visible women in the guise of visible people. After we invited ourselves into their homes, we found them standing... perfect from each other in the middle of the room. The whole time we were there they didn't argue, didn't speak, didn't sweat. I think they never do. Their stillness so complete that they don't even gather dust.

You said: "They are the happiest people I ever know." I... watchman, if you and I were surrounded by a hard chair-shell, maybe I could stop having the dream where I pry open your ribcage and claw my way through to your intentions. They're probably nestled somewhere between the warmth of your heart and your spleen.

—— FEATHERPROOF POSTCARDS AND BRIC-A-BRAC, CHICAGO, ILLINOIS, USA ——

BLEACHED WHALE DESIGN

PERFECTLY BANAL - Postcards I sent home when we were lost on vacation together so that you would have something to look forward to on our return.

60647

wake up body!

Sometimes we like to imagine that our bodies know what's best for us, big cuddly shells about the thumb-sized selves located in the intangible crevices between the gullets and the spleens, like the earth, which dares not wobble on its axis or stray from its orbit about the sun, for the sake of our bodies for the sake of our selves.

If we're thinking straight, then what is this man thinking.

What is this man thinking when we imagine that our bodies know what's best for ourselves. What is his body thinking as his self slips softly to sleep. What are his eyes thinking as his lashes interlock and lids meet across four lanes of highway, as his wheels slip to snowy shoulder.

Better shoulder than we, we like to think. But if we're really so smart, then why don't we speed past this accident patiently waiting to happen. If the body knows best, why does the foot not push the pedal to the floor and lead our bodies to a place where they need not concern ourselves with windshields, asphalt, and insurance claims. Or are these concerns diverting our attention from the matter at hand.

See his tail lights shimmering on the horizon like a man-made mirage. Mirages are for daylight. This is more like a fireworks display. We are feeling that child-like anticipation, awaiting the finale, the spark of side-panel against guard-rail. But we aren't children, and these sparks spark conscience, the spark of why are we trailing this man at twenty-five miles per hour from half

a mile back, this man whose body does not know what's best
for him.

This is the sound of the hand on the horn, as of a man wailing
on a continuous loop until the wail becomes a chorus of wails,
until the ear can not differentiate between sound and sound
from one moment to the next. In the car ahead of us, the sound
of the horn increases as we accelerate, in volume and in pitch.
The horn wails, Wake up body! Wake up and tell your man to
save himself.

Either the body does not hear or its man is not listening.
We know this from a distance of less than a car length, our own
ears ringing with the wail of the horn. The finale is but a tease,
because these sparks will spark for miles, a cacophony of horns,
rumble strips, and guard rails that can only end in a whimper.
One of our bodies whimpers, and we understand this to be a
prophecy.

Which is not to say that our faith in the body is not a bit shaken.
There is a tension in the air, a sense of the impending failure of
everything. We're driving on eggshells. And the bodies are not
exempt. Your upper lip is dotted with sweat. As I fidget, my ass
sticks and re-sticks to the seat. There is a smell, a mingling of
smells, a mingling of smells of uncomfortable bodies, sticking
and sweating and tensing on eggshells.

Our own horn sounds closer with the window rolled down.
The air sounds louder, more immediate, like the place where
thunder happens. Our hair whips wildly about the cold dark

night pouring into the car. And above all of this, the screech of side against rail flits about the smog of sound competing for the bodies' attention.

As in the celebrations of our youth, the finale becomes the tease and the tedium long before the pop hiss whimper, and our bodies abandon us to imagination of bodies closer to the action, in peril, sacrificing limbs and skins for an evening's entertainment. What force of mind, of will must it take to hold an explosion in your hand. How much more to sit inside the explosion itself.

That's what this man is doing. Worse, his body seems to be allowing, even encouraging it. I think it's you who can't accept this. I think I'm slower than you just now, still stuck in awe, not of the display, but of the body's place within the display. There's an aura hanging over you, an aura of unwillingness to accept it, to accept that this body doesn't know what's best for itself, and I can smell it, even as I smell the cold black air that has driven our body smells out the window or into the back seat. I can smell your resistance. And don't imagine that it isn't pulling me in its direction, up and over, once again beside the accident patiently happening.

I suppose it's possible that the man is simply dead, that his body has given up its ghost, soul from tailpipe slushing freshly fallen snow. From my angle, behind the wheel, I can't see his angle behind his wheel, but I can picture him slumped over it, his self somewhere else, a dead man driving.

If we were thinking straight, this is where we would leave it. Not him, but it. Death behind the wheel does not implicate the body any more than any other death. The body cannot be guilty of death if the body is not guilty of death, a reflexive thought if I've ever had one, but reflexes are the domain of the body. The body doesn't leave the hand on the hot stove. The body doesn't sleep against guard rails at speeds above no speed, and if it did, it would still be yearning for the warmth of its bed.

I feel like weeping. I feel like bawling on your shoulder. I feel like rolling up the windows and taking my hand off the horn. I feel like falling back and following this dead man, against this guard rail, along this exit ramp, your screams an affirmation of all that we have thought, heard and felt together, a confirmation of the body's best intentions.

And loud, too. Louder than the sound of the hand on the horn, louder than the air in the window, louder than the screech of side panel, his or ours now that we have joined him in explosion, against guard rail, louder than anything I've heard tonight. Your screams are overwhelming, overpowering, overjoying, a syllogism proving that this man is dead.

At least in a vacuum.

There is no sound here. No guard rails, no horns, no screams, though I'm sure that if I looked your way I would see you hiccuping the way that you do when the cry is out. But no sound. Just this claustrophobic calm, as though the sky were not a sky but some sort of planetarium, the neighborhood its own little hemisphere, as sterile and dead as the man in the car ahead of us.

He's moving along slowly now. His foot has slipped from the pedal, the car carrying him forward out of habit. And our car has come to a stop. Our doors have opened.

This is the feeling of the air in your lungs, an icicle crammed down your throat. Your still-moist cheeks are burning below zero, and it isn't long before you're falling behind.

Pause for breath. Yes. I can't imagine what you hope to accomplish with this late night jog. I can't imagine what I hope to accomplish either.

As I overtake the car, I am overtaken by the impossible. Behind the wheel, a man who looks exactly as I've been imagining him, with one exception: he isn't slumped over the wheel, dead, but sitting straight up, hands at ten and two o'clock, precisely as prescribed, eyes watching the road so intensely that the belated blinks cause his whole face to wrinkle when they finally arrive.

And I am staring, with equal intensity, at him. I don't notice the enormous snow bank until we both slam into it as the road ends dead.

Maybe slam is not the word. Fall works better, falling into fluffy snow, floating like a boat pushed from gravel into water. We fell into the snow, and feeling returned, a feeling of complacency.

Stand up, says my body.

But I don't stand up. Why would I stand up when I can lie here in this snow bank.

Stand up, says my body, or you'll die here in this snow bank.

I still can't hear. I can hear but I'm not listening. I am listening without believing. I don't believe in bodies, but I stand up.

As I stand up, the man opens his car door and falls again into the snow bank. I run over to make sure that he's all right, asking him if he's all right, looking him over for signs of injury, asking him again if he's all right. He's breathing, his breath forms clouds in the still clear night, but still he does not respond.

Why don't you stand up? I say.

The clouds of breath begin to thin a foot from his face, but leave no evidence of answer.

Look, I say, there's a house behind this snow bank.

It's true, there is a house behind the snow bank, a big brick house with central heating and a fireplace, with beds and sofas and overstuffed armchairs everywhere you look. Inside.

One cloud replaces another at an even rate, and the sound of them is almost no sound.

It's not a very long walk to the house, and it's sure to be unlocked.

Also true. This is a safe neighborhood, out in the middle of nowhere, and people aren't afraid to leave their doors unlocked.

The man's face is less informative than his breath, his breath informing me only that he is breathing.

If the door is locked, I say, you can break the window.

The houses are breathing, too. Above our heads, the houses breathe evenly so we know they're alive.

Go ahead, I say, break the window. Break the window without even checking to see if the door is locked.

Still, he doesn't move. I can't understand why he doesn't move. Doesn't he know that desperate times have been calling for desperate measures. Does he believe in times and measures. Does he believe me when I tell him that the door is unlocked. Does he believe me when I tell him that no one will mind if he breaks the window. He should believe me. He should listen to me when I tell him that he can break the window, that I won't mind, because I live in this house, and even now, my only hope is that his body knows what's best for him.

the Continental card

post card

Sweetpea,
Tonight we attended the Int'l.
Symposium on Health and Parenting — or
excuse for taking this vacation — to support
our parents, who were the featured group
and to witness my high school health
teacher, also a speaker, though I never
was supported. Mrs. Bourgeois.
"Seran wrap is for keeping food fresh," said
my health teacher. "That is all it should
be used for."
"You need life so great," said my father.
You teared, reached for my knees, squeezed
it tight.
Your father seemed embarrassed. My mother
was not there because she is decided to get over
it.
But baby, I just couldn't understand what
your mother meant when she said: "If you
touch your husband like mine at symposia
on health and parenting, people will wonder
why you're locking doors."
"There are so few uses for Crisco that to
keep it in the house seems an unnecessary temptation," said my health teacher.

—— FEATHERPROOF POSTCARDS AND BRIC-A-BRAC, CHICAGO, ILLINOIS , USA ——

BLEACHED WHALE
DESIGN

*PERFECTLY BANAL - Postcards I sent home when we
were last on vacation together so that you would have
something to look forward to on our return.*

60647

took and lost

"Help!" he screamed. "Help! Police!"

The man was already walking away. The man who had taken something from him.

"That man just took something from me!" he screamed, pointing at the man who was walking away.

No one paid them any attention—the man who lost something or the man who took something—but the man who lost something continued screaming. It was a crowded city and the sky was a dark gray and the people were rushing to finish their various errands before the rain began.

"He's getting away!"

Even in casual conversation, the man who lost something had a high-pitched voice, but when he screamed, his voice was positively shrill, high enough to shatter glass, so high that the average human ear couldn't detect it. But that's hyperbole, and hyperbole doesn't suit the purpose here, which is a relation of how the man who lost something reacted to losing something, an important something.

It was a passive loss, as opposed to an active one. He didn't drop something on the ground or leave it beneath a discarded newspaper in a restaurant or even never have something at all. Someone had taken something of his against his will. The man who was walking away.

And the people could hear him. They just weren't listening.

He screamed again, or he had never stopped screaming in the first place, "That man! That man! Stop that man!" and though he was pointing his finger and screaming in the same direction as he had been all along, he was by then no longer pointing at a man, but at the crowd of men and women and children into which the man who took something had disappeared.

Yes, disappeared. However, this disappearance is not the real concern. The real concern is how the man who lost something reacted to this disappearance, this subtraction, this loss, and he reacted by following the man who took something into the crowd, where he himself didn't disappear.

He found himself surrounded by the crowd, and not by the man who took something, who couldn't have surrounded him. One man could have stood beside him or in his field of vision. One man could have attempted to surround him by putting his arms and legs about his body, but this would have been an embrace, not a surrounding, and why would a man who had just taken something embrace a man who had just lost something when this taking and this loss are linked by necessity?

He wouldn't, because not only was the man who took something not a stupid man, he was a brilliant man. When he isn't taking something and disappearing, he is definitely not surrounding people who have lost something as a result of his taking something. No, he's sitting at a table, penning poems with his left hand and novels with his right, while beautiful and scandalous arias drip from his tongue.

Which is more than we can say for the man who lost something. Nothing dripping from his tongue—he'd stopped screaming. It wasn't so much a decision as a reflex reaction—you don't scream in the middle of a crowd that doesn't seem to care what you're screaming about, or even that you're screaming, if you still have any hope of getting their attention otherwise.

For example: "Excuse me."

It was all he could manage. He said excuse me and paused, waiting to be excused. It was a long pause. So long that if you didn't know the meaning of excuse me, or if you were unaware of the context, you might have thought excuse me was all he meant to say, as though he'd spoken it into oblivion and was observing its effect in another dimension, because in this dimension, the men and women and children didn't excuse the man who lost something. They didn't even stop to consider that he might want to be excused. In fact, many men and women and children in the crowd were saying excuse me, excuse me too, and none of them were excusing any of them.

The man who lost something wasn't as brilliant as the man who took something, but he wasn't stupid. He'd known before he said it that excuse me wouldn't work. It was a matter of manners. It was a stalling tactic.

It was with a clean conscience and less hope than he'd hoped for that the man who lost something surveyed the crowd again, this time in search of someone who might have noticed the man who took something lurking among the men and women and children.

You're not as brilliant as the man who took something either, but you don't have to be brilliant to suspect that the man who lost something wasn't ready to confront a grown man or woman about the man who took something. He was looking for children in the crowd, children with smiling, curious faces and bright eyes that absorbed everything, children who might have noticed a man who took something lurking about in the crowd, children who might be coerced into revealing what they might have noticed.

There were many bright-eyed children in the crowd, but one little boy seemed to be more bright-eyed than the rest. A very little boy, practically a toddler. Too little a boy, in any case, to be standing alone in a crowd. No one around him seemed to be his mother or father or sister or brother, and no one, save the man who lost something, seemed to be aware of the little boy's presence. The man who lost something moved closer to him and affected an air of jolliness, what he thought was an air of jolliness.

"Hey there, big fella," he said, like a grown man who's never spoken to a child—he'd never spoken to a child—and then he waited for the little boy to respond, comforted by the jolly nature of the man who lost something, the jolly man who spoke to the little boy.

But the little boy wasn't comforted. His big bright eyes filled with water, and though the tears didn't slide down his rosy cheeks, the man who lost something grew sad and his stomach ached.

"No," said the man who lost something, "I wanted..." but the little boy just kept staring and the tears just kept welling without fall.

The man who lost something crouched down on one knee. He lowered himself down to the little boy's level.

"I just wanted."

Still no change, and the man who lost something felt awkward. He wobbled a little and steadied himself. He switched knees.

"I just wanted..."

"There you are!" said the little boy's big sister—"Mom's been looking all over for you,"—in the bossy way that big sisters have of addressing their little brothers.

Her little brother showed no sign of having heard a word of it. He kept staring at the man who lost something through the swell of tears that wouldn't drop.

"We better go find her," said the big sister.

She took the little boy by the hand and tried to walk away, but the little boy didn't follow. His arm extended and his body jerked. The big sister turned back toward her little brother, his hand still in hers.

"What're you doing?" she said.

He didn't answer. He was staring away from her. She followed his eyes to the eyes of the man who lost something. His eyes met hers, and the three of them formed a triangle of sorts, angles without lines.

"Who's your friend?" she said to her little brother, her eyes still on his friend.

Again, the little boy didn't respond, would probably never respond to either of them, so the man who lost something took the initiative back from whoever had taken it, and responded for him.

"I was trying to ask him a question," he said.

"He's not supposta talk to strangers," she said.

"I understand. I was just trying to ask him if..."

"You're still a stranger," she said.

"Then you," he said. "Have you seen a..."

"I'm not supposta talk to strangers either."

"I'm trying not to be strange."

The man who lost something knew that it made no sense. He was gambling on his ability to frustrate a child into speaking with him.

"I just want to know if you've seen a man around here."

As he was speaking, a drop of rain fell from the sky and landed on the big sister's nose. She looked up as though to assure herself of where it had come from, and, satisfied with her initial impression, said, "It's raining," and the rain fell violently, hurting their heads and hands and faces.

The men and women and children in the crowd ran with shrieks and cries and curses to their homes or to the cover of the awnings that extended from certain storefronts along the street. The man who lost something and the little boy and his big sister didn't move. The man who lost something hoped the little sister would forget he was a stranger in the chaos the downpour created.

"So have you seen him?" He had to speak loudly because of the rain, and his voice became shrill again. "Have you seen him?"

"Yes," said the big sister, already soaking wet.

"Where?" screamed the man who lost something. "Where'd you see him? Where'd he..."

"There you are," said the mother of the little boy and his big sister. "I've been looking all over for you."

The girl grabbed her mother's hand, but the little boy...

"Let's go," his mother said, "You'll catch your death."

She picked her little boy up with one arm and held his big sister's hand with the other, but as they walked away, the man who lost something grabbed the big sister. Her arm extended and her body jerked.

The mother turned around sharply, revealing an expression of shock and of anger. The man who lost something released the little girl, but the mother's expression didn't change. She was no less shocked or angry.

The rain was still pouring down. The mother, like the big sister like the little boy like the man who lost something, was saturated, her clothes sagging from her body, her face distorted by streams of water streaming, and it was a terrifying sight.

"What do you think you're doing!" she screamed.

There was blood in her voice. There was blood and guts, and the man who lost something couldn't answer. He was still crouching in the rain on one knee. A puddle had formed around that knee, and he was getting the chills. He dropped to his other knee. Two knees in a puddle. It was pathetic.

The man who lost something didn't know what to do. He didn't know what to say. He wouldn't have been able to say it if he did know what to say. He wanted to beg forgiveness. He wanted to explain that he was nothing but a man who had lost something. He was nothing but two knees in a puddle. He was the equal and opposite reaction, not to a man who took something, but to the act of taking something.

The expression of shock left the mother's face, and the anger, abandoned or purified by shock's sudden departure, made the man who lost something tremble and swoon. He tried to ask her about the man who took something, but his voice was the voice of trembling and swooning, which is no voice. He tried to apologize, but his voice remained no voice, and his stomach hurt like nothing. He tried to reach out and grab the big sister's arm.

He reached out and grabbed the big sister's arm.

The mother didn't try to say nothing. She said nothing. She ripped the big sister from the man who lost something, and the big sister cried out in pain. The sound was unbearable, blood and guts again. The mother dragged the big sister and the little boy away, almost running, and they didn't look back to see the man who lost something fall face down.

When the man who lost something awoke, there were two police officers nudging him with their boots. He didn't know they were police officers, but it was clear to him that there were boots nudging him—his ribs, his shoes. He decided to play dead.

One officer, the one who had been kicking more than nudging, continued to nudge, or kick depending. The other one, the one at his feet, stopped nudging, and walked, around the man who lost something, to his head.

The man who lost something wasn't very good at playing dead. He was breathing so heavily that, despite the rain, his breath was causing ripples in the puddle near his mouth.

"He's alive," said the officer who was standing over his head.

He squatted down to get a better look at the man who lost something. The man who lost something still didn't know that the two men were police officers, but he couldn't help opening his eyes to evaluate the situation. The officer saw him open his eyes, and tried to squat even further, bending his head so low that his hat fell into the puddle beside the man who lost something.

"He got your hat wet," said the officer who was still nudging the man who lost something.

He poured more energy into the next few kicks.

The man who lost something didn't react. He'd seen the hat in the puddle, and realized that the men were police officers. It hadn't crossed his mind that two police officers might be interested in finding out why a man was lying in the middle of the street on a rainy morning. He knew, or thought he knew, why they were there, and it didn't have anything to do with loss or taking.

He jumped up quickly and took a few steps backward, trying to keep both officers in view at the same time, trying to ensure that he could run if he needed to run. But his movement startled the officer who had squatted down low, and he fell back, landing in another puddle.

"He assaulted you," said the officer who had only stopped nudging the man who lost something because it was no longer practical.

He drew his gun.

"He just startled me," said the officer who had fallen over. "I fell over."

It took a while for the officer who had fallen over to convince the other officer to put the gun back in its holster, but he finally did. When, guns in holsters, the two police officers turned back toward the man who lost something, the man who lost something had partially disappeared.

Partially, because the tips of his shoes were sticking out from behind the mailbox on the corner. The police officers had been trained to find suspicious characters and interpret suspicious behavior, and they were not fooled. They knew the man who lost something was still in the shoes.

"We know you're back there," said the officer who had drawn and holstered his gun.

The man who lost something didn't respond. The kicks in the ribs had been painful, but the threatening of his life was just too much. That officer, a police officer who would draw his gun on an innocent man, was a bad police officer.

"Everything's okay," said the other officer. "Just come on out."

This was a pleasant police officer, a good police officer. If both of the officers had been good, the man who lost something wouldn't have come out from behind the mailbox, because if they'd both been good, he'd never have hidden behind a mailbox in the first place. Good police officers don't pull guns on innocent men.

He didn't come out.

"We just want to make sure you're alright," said the good police officer

"What about the gun?" said the man who lost something.

"He put it away."

"What about that lady and her kids?"

"What's he talking about?" said the bad police officer.

A feeling of relief washed over him, and he remembered—this wasn't about an angry woman and her unhelpful children. He hadn't awakened, face down in a puddle, to the nudges of two police officers because he'd grabbed a little girl's arm, but because he'd lost something, or because someone had taken something.

"Nothing," said the man who lost something.

It was almost a blessing that these two police officers had come along when they had. The trail, if there was a trail, was getting cold, was being rinsed away by the rain. The man who lost something was wasting time behind the mailbox. He stepped out and walked toward the officers.

"Shit," said the bad police officer.

The man who lost something looked like shit. His clothes were dirty and slimy and wet. His face was bruised from the fall. He looked like a vagrant. The two police officers probably thought he was a vagrant.

"A man took something from me," said the man who lost something.

"The guy who knocked you out?"

You know it isn't the case; the man who lost something knew it wasn't the case, but it was such a long and ridiculous story, the losing and taking and screaming and men and women and children, "Yes," said the man who lost something. "The guy who knocked me out."

The bad police officer removed a small wire-bound notepad and a ballpoint pen from the breast pocket of his uniform shirt. He uncapped the pen and flipped the notepad open to a blank page.

"What's he look like?" said the bad police officer.

The question caught the man who lost something off guard, not because he didn't know what the man who took something looked like—though he didn't—but because he couldn't see why it mattered, as though a man who was sufficiently handsome, or sufficiently ugly, had a right to take something.

"I don't know," said the man who lost something.

The bad police officer looked down at his notepad, but he had nothing to write on it. He wouldn't have been able write on it anyway, because the rain had dampened the page and smeared its light blue lines.

"Let's go," said the bad police officer. "This guy's wasting our time."

"Wait," said the good police officer grabbing the bad police officer.

His arm extended and his body jerked. The bad police officer waited.

"Was he short or tall?" said the good police officer.

"Maybe," said the man who lost something.

The bad police officer turned to walk away again, but the good police officer kept hold of him.

"Was his hair light or dark?" said the good police officer.

"I don't know," said the man who lost something. "I don't know what he looks like."

By then even the good police officer was losing patience. He probably wouldn't have stopped his partner from walking away again, but his partner didn't try to walk away.

"What'd he take," said the bad police officer.

It hadn't crossed his mind. The man who lost something didn't know what the man who took something had taken. He didn't have to say it. He could tell from the bad police officer's expression that the bad police officer could tell from his expression.

"I guess," said the man who lost something, "I could go through my pockets and see what's missing."

He began to search his pockets. In the left front pocket of his pants he found the keys to his apartment; in the right, cigarettes and matches. In his back right pocket was his wallet, and in the left breast pocket of his coat he found a stick of chewing gum. He thought maybe he remembered having more chewing gum, but he could never keep track of how many sticks out of a pack he'd already chewed.

"What's missing?" said the bad police officer.

"I don't know," said the man who lost something.

He put the gum in his mouth and chewed.

There was a pause. None of them spoke. The bad police officer didn't walk—or threaten to walk—away. The good police officer couldn't think of any more questions to ask. It was a moment of silence for whatever was missing, an unspoken eulogy for something lost or left out.

And it was making the good police officer uncomfortable.

"Why don't you let us give you a ride home," he said.

"I only live over there," said the man who lost something, pointing across the street at a three story walk-up.

It was true, he hadn't made it very far before the man who took something took something.

"Then go on home," said the good police officer. "Give us a call if you remember anything."

But the man who lost something wasn't listening. He hadn't turned back toward the police officers after pointing at his building. He walked across the street without a word. A car braked hard in order to avoid hitting him, and the driver yelled "Fuck you," before speeding away, unaware that there were two police officers looking on.

The police officers were looking on, but they took no notice of the car and its driver. Their eyes were following the man who lost something, still crossing the street toward the man who took something, whom they didn't yet know was the man who took something, whom they didn't yet know was the man whom the man who lost something thought was the man who took something, whom they would never be quite certain was the man who took something.

"Give it back!" screamed the man who lost something, shrill again, and he pounced at the man who took something, though he was still a body-length away.

He fell short, landing on his face.

The man who took something stood as though waiting for the man who lost something to get up and pounce again. The man who lost something got up and pounced again, knocking the man who took something to the ground, screaming "Give

it back! Give it back!" as he tussled with the man who took
something, who didn't tussle back or give it back.

The good police officer was the first to reach them, and he
pulled the man who lost something from the man who took
something. The bad police officer arrived and helped the man
who took something to his feet.

"Let go! Let me go!" the man who lost something screamed.
"He took something from me!"

The good police officer had to struggle to hold him back
while the bad police officer searched the other man's pockets,
more because it was his duty than because he believed the man
who took something had taken something. He found nothing,
literally nothing, not even lint in his pockets.

"This man has nothing." He had to raise his voice to be heard
over the shrill screams of the man who lost something, and his
own voice became shrill. "He's taken nothing from you."

"He did!" said the man who lost something—"He has!"—
struggling against the good police officer's bear hug.

"Calm down," said the good police officer, "calm down," but
the man who lost something continued to struggle screaming
for several minutes, before calming down, too exhausted to
continue, going limp in the arms of the good police officer.

"How do you know this is the guy?" said the bad police
officer.

"He's been watching the whole time," said the man who lost
something.

"But how do you know this is the guy?"

The man who lost something had no answer.

"Then we're gonna have to let him go," said the bad police officer, and he let him go.

As the man who took something walked away, he looked over his shoulder, an inscrutable expression on his face. The good police officer assumed it was a look of fear, fear of being pounced on again. The man who lost something saw a knowing look, a triumphant look. The bad police officer didn't catch it at all. He was trying to be unobtrusive while checking his pockets, his belt, his holster to see if anything was missing, and his stomach was beginning to ache.

You know the feeling by now. The same one the man who lost something had as he walked up the stairs to his apartment building. He was dirty and slimy and wet. His face was bruised, his muscles were sore, and he could taste the blood in his throat from all of the screaming he'd done. He opened the door to the awful possibilities of a life with meaning.

Cutie booty;

After we worshipped at the Temple of the Continental card of the Low sincerity we purchased an inflatable monkey and a colorful bandana from the gift shop, then enjoyed a lunch of macaroni and cheese and jell-o in the cafeteria.

And as we were finishing up, you excused yourself, and while you were gone I decided to surprise you by inflating the monkey and wrapping the bandana around its head. When you returned, I said: "It's you when you returned, I said: "It's inevitable."

It seemed kind of inevitable.

You didn't seem to have seen the inevitability, which our child and our child and its our child and its our child—

We can't pretend it's our child, "you said.

Careless? I worried even that you had picked up the sincerity syndrome, and I wanted to carry you out of that place, this city. I wanted to go home. The feeling didn't pass until I was deflated our child so that it would fit in your bag.

Go 'on.

FEATHERPROOF POSTCARDS AND BRIC-A-BRAC, CHICAGO, ILLINOIS, USA

BLEACHED WHALE
DESIGN

PERFECTLY BANAL - Postcards I sent home when we were lost on vacation together so that you would have something to look forward to on our return.

60647

post card

U.S.A.

oh, little so-and-so

A man about my age sees a little girl standing in the middle of a busy intersection, blowing a whistle and flapping her arms like a marionette. He assumes she assumes she's directing traffic. Traffic is flowing smoothly. No accidents are happening.

It isn't a matter of whether he wants to move toward her, to help her. He moves toward her to help her whether he wants to or not, as though there are strings attached to each of his limbs, strings so fine that they can't be seen by the eye that doesn't mean to see them, unless they catch the glare of the sun just so, and even then the eye that doesn't mean to see them doesn't know what it's seen.

The little girl doesn't see them, doesn't mean to see them, or just doesn't care. She's got other things on her mind. Something to do with the traffic. Standing before her in the middle of the intersection, strings slack, the man still thinks she thinks she's directing traffic.

She blows her whistle. She flaps her arms. Traffic continues flowing smoothly, though now that he's in the middle of the street, the man can see that the cars that make up the traffic are slowing as they approach the intersection, the drivers trying to avoid hitting the little girl, and now the man, or to see what they can see.

"Directing traffic?" the man says.

The girl points a finger at him. She blows her whistle at him. She keeps on directing traffic, or whatever it is she's doing, with the arm that isn't pointing its finger.

"What?" he says.

The little girl opens her mouth. For a moment, the whistle sticks to her upper lip. Then it falls downward and dangles from the string around her neck. The girl takes a step forward and her finger pokes the man in the chest.

"You're in my way," she says.

"I'm in your way," he says.

He wants to get out of her way, to turn around, get out of the middle of the street, go back to whatever he was going about, but something—let's say the strings—won't let him.

"Directing traffic," he says.

She drops her finger-pointing arm to its side. She stops flapping the other arm, and lets it fall to the other side. There is no noticeable change in the flow of traffic. Still the same slowing at the intersection for the same reasons.

"I'm hitching a ride," she says.

The man would really like to leave.

"That's not how you hitch a ride," he says. "You hitch a ride like this."

The man stretches out an arm, stretches out the thumb at the end of it, but he's standing in the middle of an intersection, and even if a driver were inclined to pick up a hitchhiker while driving smoothly if slowly through, the driver wouldn't know which direction the man hoped to go, and probably wouldn't take the trouble to find out.

Who knows what their inclinations are. No one is taking the trouble to find out.

"That's not how I hitch a ride," says the little girl. "I hitch a ride like this."

She puts the whistle back into her mouth, blows it at him, and begins to flap her arms like a marionette.

"Good luck," says the man.

But he doesn't turn to leave.

The girl speaks around her whistle: "You got a car?" she says.

"What's your name?" she says.

He tells himself not to tell her. He tells her his name.

They're in his car now, but they aren't going anywhere. He hasn't even put the keys in the ignition.

"Buckle your seatbelt," he says.

The seatbelt barely fits around her backpack. Her backpack is on her lap. It covers her entire lap from the top of her thighs to the tip of her knees, with maybe a little overhang depending on whether she's slouching or sitting up straight. He hadn't noticed how large it was when they were standing in the middle of the street, because when they were standing in the middle of the street, she'd been facing him the whole time. He hears the seatbelt click and starts the car.

"Where are we going?" he says.

"The cemetery," she says. "A funeral."

"You mean a burial?" he says. "They usually have the funeral at church."

He puts the car in gear and pulls out into the busy intersection where traffic is still flowing smoothly despite the little girl's absence.

"Or a funeral home," he says.

He doesn't know why, but he turns left at the intersection, heading for a particular cemetery even though the little girl hasn't told him which particular cemetery the funeral, the burial, is being held at.

"Not Will," she says.

"Who's Will?" he says.

"Will's having a funeral at the cemetery," says the little girl.

He assumes Will is a friend. Her use of his first name—he assumes Will is a first name, assumes Will is a he—leads him to assume that Will is a friend, rather than a relative, a teacher, a neighbor, and he is overcome with feeling for the girl. Something pulls a tear from one of his eyes.

"I'm sorry," he says.

The little girl looks at him as though she doesn't understand why he should be sorry and says: "Yeah you are."

Now the tears flow freely from both of his eyes. No one has to pry them out. He's incapacitated by his own weeping. The car swerves right and harder left while the man tries to steer through the blur of his tears.

The little girl yells at him: "You trying to kill us?" and the man stutters "No," through sobs and around hiccups. Finally he manages to pull over to the shoulder, slam on the brakes, and cut the engine.

"Put it in park," the girl says.

He puts it in park just as the car is beginning to roll backward down the mild incline. The little girl opens the front pocket of her backpack and rummages through it.

"I might have to find someone else to hitch a ride with," she says.

"N-no," he stutters, still sobbing.

"Then clean yourself up," she says, pulling a wad of napkins from the pocket.

The man accepts the napkins and wipes the tears from his cheeks and eyes. He blows his nose as the sobbing slows then stops altogether. His breath comes shaky and shallow, and he feels weaker than he usually does.

He blows his nose again, throws the soggy napkins into the back seat, and inhales deeply until he's sitting upright with his chest puffed out. He exhales, inhales again, and forgets to exhale. He sniffs, deeply, as though something stinks.

"Something stinks," he says.

"Yeah, you," says the girl.

The man sniffs the air again. Again, sniffing in directions, his head rolling as though he's having a fit.

"No," he says. "Something stinks."

"Something stinks," the girls says in her most mocking voice.

She rolls her head, sniffing and sniffing around the car like a cartoon. The man stops sniffing and watches her. He'd like to smack her upside the head, but he doesn't, he can't. The little girl, seeing she's made her point, stops rolling her head, rolls her eyes, and smacks him upside the head.

"Drive," she says.

But he doesn't drive yet. His eyes have landed on her backpack, at its open front pocket. He sniffs again, but doesn't move any closer to her, to it.

"What's in the bag?" he says.

Suddenly she doesn't seem so defiant. She doesn't have an answer. She reaches quickly but awkwardly for the zipper, and it gets caught halfway. She tugs and it doesn't budge. She tugs again but nothing. She's tugging and tugging her way to a tantrum.

The man reaches over calmly and peels her fingers from the bag. He pulls the zipper back an inch or so in the direction of open, and closes it smoothly.

The little girl flashes him a look—something like a pout, but with an I-could-have-done-it-myself anger, or maybe frustration, behind it. He's seen that look before, but he can't quite remember where. It doesn't make him want to cry, though. He can't remember what it makes him want to do.

"Can we go?" she says.

"Is that it?" he says.

They're at the cemetery now. The strings have pointed his finger toward something just beyond the windshield—a party of mourners standing around a casket, mourning, while a priest stands at the head of the casket, chanting or incanting.

The little girl doesn't say anything. She hasn't said anything since asking if they could go, but she unbuckles the seatbelt, hefts the bag, and opens the door. The man cuts the engine.

"So this is it," he says, and the little girl slams her door on his affirmation.

None of the mourners seems to register their approach. No, oh little so-and-so made it to her friend Will's funeral, or who the hell is that man with little so-and-so, or who the hell is that little so-and-so. They're a staid group of mourners, not a moist eye in the bunch.

The man would prefer some tears, a sound or two beside the priestly drone, so he provides it himself. The tears flow again, freely from his eyes, incapacitating him with weeping. The girl punches him to stop, tells him to pull himself together, but he can't hear her through the sobs and hiccups.

The girl takes off her backpack, rummages through the front pocket, and pulls out another wad of napkins. She shoves them into his hands, and his sobs die down. He begins to clean himself up.

As his eyes clear, he looks around to see if his outburst has startled anyone, or sparked any other outbursts or potential outbursts, but the mourners still look like they're lost in themselves. The priest says his ashes to ashes and the mourners file away by ones and twos.

"I feel better," says the man. "Don't you feel better?"

He brings the soggy wad of napkins to his nose and sniffs inconspicuously while he awaits an answer.

"I thought they put the coffin in the ground and throw dirt and flowers on it," says the little girl.

She looks up at him. He yanks the napkins from his nostrils and shoves them behind his back as though the napkins were what he meant to hide.

"Yes," he says, looking around for some physical manifestation of what he's affirming.

His eyes land on the casket suspended above its final resting place and covered in flowers, alone, as the last of the mourners straggle from the grave site, get into their cars, and drive away.

His fingers fiddle with the napkins behind his back. He doesn't want to look at the little girl, but he does. Her physique manifests confusion over the contradiction between his confirmation and the facts before their eyes.

"I mean no," says the man. "Only in the movies."

"What about the guns?" she says.

This time he has no idea what she's talking about.

"Movies," he says.

"Will's funeral's gonna have guns," she says.

"It's over," he says. "There were no guns."

"I'm talking about Will's funeral," says the little girl.

"You're sure that wasn't it?" he says.

They're walking now, through the cemetery, ever further from the site of what he'd thought—because the little girl had done nothing to deny it—was Will's grave, and far from the sight of it.

"It wasn't it," she says.

"Because I don't see any others," he says.

The girl ignores him and keeps walking up the gentle slope. He follows, pulled along by something like a string. The cemetery is larger than he would have guessed driving past it, they've been walking longer than he would have guessed they'd be able to walk without ever retracing their steps and moving in circles, and the sun has just dropped behind the gentle slope a few gentle slopes over, leaving them to hike by dusk-light.

"It's getting dark," he says.

"Don't you ever shut up?" says the girl.

He shuts up. He concentrates on staying that way, but they've been walking for a long time and the less he talks, the more he tries to concentrate on not talking, the more he concentrates on how tired he is, and hungry, the more tired and hungry he becomes. It's like there's another string pulling him in the opposite direction, creating a near equilibrium.

The distance between them isn't so big—a pace or two—but when he falls back another pace or two, the girl, who hasn't looked back in a while, looks back. Another pace or two and the man stops, too exhausted to go on without a break. He bends over with his hands to his knees, stares at the grass around his feet and pants a little. The little girl stops with her back to him.

"What?" she says.

"I need a second," he says.

She slips out of her backpack and pulls it around to the front of her, easing it down to the ground. She bends over, unzips the backpack, and rummages through it.

"Hungry?" she says.

She pulls out an open, half-full package of orange peanut butter crackers, and holds them over her shoulder. The man hears the wrapper crackle, looks up from the ground, and sees it glinting in the half-light. He walks toward her, around her, taking the package from her upstretched hand as he goes. The man stops in front of the little girl and withdraws a cracker from the wrapper.

He shoves the cracker whole in his mouth and hands the package back to her. She accepts, withdraws and nibbles away while putting the package back into her bag and trying to close the zipper one-handed.

It gets caught halfway. She tugs and it doesn't budge. Again, but nothing. The man reaches over calmly and pulls the zipper back an inch or so in the direction of open, then closes it smoothly.

"Ready?" he says.

The girl tries to lift the bag, but its bottom doesn't leave the ground. It's gotten about ten pounds heavier in the course of their break. Not the bag itself but the bag in relation to the girl, its liftability.

"Let me give you a hand," says the man.

He reaches for the bag, lifts it by a single strap, and slings it over a shoulder.

The girl screams: "No."

She pounces. She grabs the bottom of the bag with both hands tightly. She lifts her legs from the ground, allows the bag to lift her in hopes that it will fall with her too. The man spins left, trying to see what's happening behind him, but the girl's ungrounded legs fly out behind her and she remains behind him, though the location of behind him changes from one moment to the next.

Faster now, until her body is perpendicular to yours and her grip starts to slip from the bottom of the bag, until her screams of no and stop and give it back blend into something a little less intelligible and a little more primitive, until her body flies away in the direction of centrifugal force and, of course, gravity, and she hits the ground dizzy and whimpering and empty-handed, but otherwise unharmed.

He stops facing her. He bends over and vomits at the ground between his feet, splattering his sneakers and smearing his face with what little there was in his stomach. The little girl sits up with her head between her hands and her elbows on her knees like she might do the same herself, but she suddenly stands, walks around behind him, unzips the front pocket of her backpack, and rummages through it.

She pulls out another wad of napkins and hands it to him over his shoulder. He takes them, splitting the wad in rough halves, using the one to wipe his shoes, the other his face. He stops mid-wipe, and looks over his shoulder at the little girl.

"What the fuck is that smell?" he says.

She gives him the look again, but he still can't remember what it makes him want to do. She reaches down and zips the front pocket of her backpack without any struggle.

"Can I have my bag back now?" she says.

"I see something," he says as they crest another gentle slope.

It's been a long time since he's seen anything but dark shapes, the dark shape of the little girl in front of him, the bag like a huge, head-hiding hunch on her back. It's moonless night now. They've been relying on their feet and the feel of the ground.

"It's a light," he says.

A fire of some sort, radiating pale-orange a few feet every way but down. A scraping sound comes from the same direction as the fire, slow and faint. They move toward it and the light grows more bright, the scraping louder but just as slow.

The light resolves itself into an old camping lantern. The lantern rests on the ground in front of a large pile of dirt, a pile of dirt that grows imperceptibly larger as more dirt flies out of a hole in the ground—a hole that they still can't see—in counterpoint to the scrapes.

The little girl runs on ahead. The man tries to run, but lags.

"We're here," yells the girl, dime-stopping with swinging arms at the lip of a hole the man can see now, though he's still a few yards back.

The little girl steadies herself, squats, lets the backpack slip from her shoulders to the earth behind her, and disappears into the hole—legs, torso, head and hands. It gives the man the scare he needs to lunge the last few feet.

Looking down into what he can see now is a grave-in-progress, he finds the little girl, arms thrown about the neck of a short, sinewy man of indeterminate age, dirty from digging in his work-wear, face shadowed by the dark of the pit and the stuffed-down brim of a baseball hat, a spade resting against his thigh. They look the portrait of a father and daughter, the portrait of a sinister father and daughter.

"That's him," says the little girl to the gravedigger.

"Who," the man says.

"You," says the gravedigger, lifting the girl by the waist

back to the edge of the hole, and seating her there with her legs dangling over the side.

The gravedigger then puts his own hands on the edge and lifts and pulls and kicks his way up, with grunts and strains and popping veins. He manages to get a leg, crooked at the knee, onto flat ground, and crawls his awkward way out.

"I don't know which is harder," he says, wiping sweat mingled with dirt to mud from his face with the back of a forearm, "getting in or getting out."

The man stares at him as though he doesn't know to chuckle because he doesn't.

"Depends who you are," says the girl with a giggle.

"Depends who you are," the gravedigger laughs.

Something forces a forced chuckle from the man—there's no string that can force a chuckle—then forces a joke as well:

"What man dost thou dig it for?" he says.

The gravedigger rolls his head as though he's rolling his brim-hidden eyes as though he's heard it a thousand times. He digs in his pockets, pulls out a match, and strikes it against his dirt-crusted shirt. It flares, releasing a sulfurous smell and illuminating everything but his face. He pulls a cigarette from behind his ear and lights it with the match.

"There isn't much left," he says. "You can help."

He hops back into the hole and beckons the man. The man steps closer to the edge and looks down. He squats, sits, and slides into the grave. The gravedigger hands him a pickaxe and tells him to watch where he swings it. The gravedigger sets to work. The man too, eventually and reluctantly.

Between swings and scrapes, he can hear the little girl running around above them, digging through her bag, removing things from her bag, placing the things she's removed at some distance from her bag.

He swings, the gravedigger's shovel scrapes, and the thumps of the little girl's feet carry the message that her feet are moving, down through the earth to him. Swing scrape thump. It goes on like this until he swings, the gravedigger's shovel scrapes, and the little girl wails:

"Will!"

The man stops mid-swing. The gravedigger hops from the pit in one quick motion, shovel in hand. The man drops his pickaxe and tries to climb out too, but it's easier getting in than getting out.

The edge is about level with the top of his head. He places his hand on the earth above him and tries to lift himself upward, gets far enough to see flat ground, the legs of the gravedigger with an arm around the little girl, their backs to him, before falling back down.

He swings his arms as far as he can over the edge, grabs a clump of grass with each hand, and tries to worm his way up and over, swiveling his hips and kneeing the side of the grave. He's got his shoulders out on flat ground and his face buried in the dirt when the gravedigger finally turns, sees him, and grabs his wrists, pulling him into the open. He lies there a moment, face down, spitting dirt from his mouth, smelling the grass and something else. Something that stinks.

When he lifts his head he sees it—a fishbowl of average

size, and in it, a goldfish the size of an average fishbowl, dead, bloated round like a cartoon or a bath-toy, and staring at him with sunken, glassy eyes. Beside it, a gun, and several feet away, the bag, a withered crumpled shell of its former self. He'd say something, but something's got his tongue.

"Ready for the funeral?" the little girl whimpers.

She's crying. He reaches into his back pocket, and pulls out the crumpled wad of used napkins he'd put there. He hands them to her. She blows her nose as the sobbing slows then stops altogether. Her breath comes shaky and shallow, and she looks fragile.

"How'd he die?" he says.

Her face twitches on the brink of something, of crying or that look.

"Ate himself to death," she says.

A fish in a bowl can't eat himself to death. The man gets up on his palms, all fours. He stands, breathes in the fresh air. A fish in a bowl has to be fed to death. He looks down on her, her face lit from below by the orange glow of the lamp.

"You killed him," he says.

"That's enough," says the gravedigger.

He reaches a hand out to keep the man from moving any closer.

"I gave him a choice," says the little girl.

She reaches for the gun. The man freezes. He looks to the gravedigger for an explanation.

"For the twenty-one gun salute," says the gravedigger. "She's only got the one."

"She killed him," says the man.

He turns back to the gun, to her. She's got that look on her face again, and suddenly I remember what it reminds him of.

He was about her age, under the sheets late at night reading a cut-rate comic book by flashlight. There was an illustration. It was supposed to teach a moral. Two little kids, a boy and a girl with huge heads, tied together by a rope, one end knotted around the girl's waist, the other the boy's. They were running away from each other, toward milkshakes larger than they were and just out of their reach, stretching the rope taut. This was represented by loose fibers at the center of the rope, and the look on their faces. That was the look.

The moral was in the next panel. They took turns standing on each other's shoulders and enjoying the milkshake. But he didn't learn the moral. He couldn't get past that look on their faces.

It made him want to swing the rope over one of the gigantic straws protruding from the gigantic milkshakes and dangle from their legs, listening to them scream as the rope slipped up their bodies to their scrawny necks, to swing as their bodies spasmed spaghetti western style. He wouldn't let go until every last drop of life had been squeezed from their cartoon bodies.

But I think I'm starting to get the hang of him.

She's got a gun. There's a full-grown man with a shovel standing next to him.

the **C**ontinental card

post card

—— FEATHERPROOF POSTCARDS AND BRIC-A-BRAC, CHICAGO, ILLINOIS , USA ——

BLEACHED WHALE
DESIGN

Sweety,

At the Museum of Futile Gestures we
pretended to appreciate the retrospective
juvenilia of that mid-career artist whose
name I can never remember, but whose
work we both agree transcends the
hype. We stopped before the installation
entitled Do Not Comment on the Size of
This Thing.

"She's really grown as an artist," I said.

"Will you look at the size of that thing?"
you said.

The screen said Will you look at the size of
that thing.

Love & My Life, for the last time, does
it, or does it not, matter?

*PERFECTLY BANAL - Postcards I sent home when we
were last on vacation together so that you would have
something to look forward to on our return.*

60647

moldering

I was growing moldy of wallet from hoeing down and the sweat therefrom. My wife, who does not hoe much anymore, down or up, though her business is fancy-dancing and her body hard in all the right places and soft in the others, liked to remind me that it stank repulsive and caused me to scrub my hands upon handling it.

Now I am faithful to her in all things, and I still enjoy the pleasure of her flesh and hers only as much as I would have on the day I met her if she'd have allowed me to lay hands on her during our five episodes' courtship, but a man has his pride, and so I did my best to ignore her cold-shouldering all the way to rejection-outright until the fourth straight evening of unfulfilled marital duties when I felt myself about to explode, and I burst out with a "What must a man do to regain your affections?"

"I do not know," said my wife, "for no man but you has managed to gain my affections, and therefore no man but you could ever have lost my affections, ergo, there is no man but you who could hope thus far to regain my affections.

"As for you," she said, "your hopes of regaining my affections hinge upon three simple tasks: first, you must secure a new wallet for yourself and my affections by proxy. Then you must destroy the old, moldy wallet now in the seat of your dungarees after transferring its contents to the new. Finally you must lather your hands as you've never lathered them before and run them a minute under the hottest water your skin can stand. That accomplished, you will find me upon this very bed, warm of shoulder and spread of legs, so long as I sense that you will never think on these last days again, except as a reminder to be vigilant against molding the new, and as a warning."

My wife is a reasonable if stingy woman, and I would have been more than willing to fulfill each of these obligations daily, but for the part about the sense of what I would and would not think on, not because I was resistant, but because the senses of people about things or thoughts can be unpredictable if not fickle, not least so my wife's, so I knew that some kind of preemptive gesture was required of me.

Without further consideration, that is, without enough, I told her: "My darling, it's so like you to ask so little of me that it shames me when I fall short."

I leapt from our bed and proceeded to dress myself in the clothes of that day, beginning with the dungarees in whose back pocket the old wallet moldered, saying: "I am even now dressing myself with the intention of marching to the tannery, where I will purchase, not just a new wallet of immaculate hide, but a pretty little handbag for you, cut from the same animal as the wallet, as a token of my dedication to our oneness."

By the time I had finished my modest oration, my shirt was buttoned and tucked, my boots were on, and my hat was in hand. My wife was already sitting up, a look like concern upon her face.

"At this hour?" she said.

I glanced at the clock on the night table. It was midnight, but my brain was aflame, and the lamp behind my wife showed me the shape of her beneath the lacy gown she favored, redoubling my intention of redoubling my efforts on our respective behalves.

"Woman," I said, "my passion knows no midnight, and besides, the tanner was a friend of my youth."

I placed the hat atop my head and tipped it to her, not daring to attempt to rustle a kiss from a woman of such will as I left our bedroom and then our cozy home.

The tannery's neighborhood is not quite as cozy as ours, but I am no stranger to it having grown up there, the son of a preacher man and woman both, and the respect of the residents of the old neighborhood for the memory of my dear departed parents, not to mention my own knack with bootstraps, has earned me the reputation of a local boy made good. The old folks look upon me with homespun admiration. Witness, for instance, the repulsive vagrant who approached me as I strolled the night-dark streets, the same man we used to torment as boys, offering him at times a sandwich or some stale pastry laced with gravel from our lots, others, something a bit more sharp.

He approached me beneath the rare functional street lamp and I recognized him immediately. He was older and might have had even fewer teeth if that was possible, evidence that boys keep being boys, but it was the same ugliness as ever.

He said: "It's kind of late for a guy like you to be wandering these streets," and I thanked him kindly for his concern as my heart's cockles warmed at the thought of the intense loyalty of my downtrodden brothers and sisters, especially as I had not always been so generous toward this particular brother. I offered him a Marlboro Red from my just-opened package, but he refused, most likely out of humility, though possibly he associated free cigarettes with some small explosion in the past.

I lit one of my own, told him to suit himself, and said: "I'm off to the tannery."

"Tannery's closed this time of night," he said.

Again with that almost childlike eagerness to help. I hesitated to tell him that he wasn't saying anything that I didn't already know, but, as he was bound to see me continue on in the tannery's direction, it being only a few blocks off, I feared he would panic if I didn't set his mind at ease.

"I'm aware of that," I said, "but the tanner was my closest boyhood companion."

"Things change," he said, imbuing those two words with all of his pride in my accomplishment, as though he'd had some small role in them, and I grew watery of eye, but decided it would be gauche of me to inform him in so many words that his role had been larger than he could know. Instead, I tossed the remains of my cigarette into the street and offered again. He accepted this time, and I walked on toward the tannery waiting for a bang that never came.

The tannery was closed as expected, but I could see inside by the light of the neon signs in its windows, signs that advertised a variety of tobacco and alcohol products, another reminder that things had changed, but the sign above it still said the tannery. I supposed it made sense that a craftsman in the old neighborhood could no longer sustain himself on fine hides alone, what with the wide variety of mass-produced and artificial textiles available for much lower prices.

It saddened me that someone as skilled as the tanner, someone who had, as a youth, demonstrated the potential to craft chaps for the thighs of the crowned heads of Europe (and no less an authority than Mr. Bedell, our YMCA camp crafts instructor, had suggested it), had sunken to hawking perishables to pay the rent. But a gift is a gift, and gifts don't go away. I reasoned that my friend would be made as glad by the commission as I would by the results, even at this hour.

If things hadn't changed too much, then he still lived above his shop in a cramped, vermin-infested efficiency that was not without its bohemian charms, and I dared to hope that the small workshop where he did his finest work was still there, in the corner by the stove, for I meant my new wallet and my wife's pretty handbag to be his very finest work.

I went to the small door at the side of the tannery and pressed the buzzer's button with a sense of anticipation I hadn't felt in ages, then waited impatiently for the door to open and my old, dear friend to greet me with surprise, then brotherly warmth, a warmth that I hadn't experienced of late, a byproduct, I suppose, of this hectic modern life and of my vast responsibilities.

As it turned out, I would have to be more patient than expected as my friend the tanner did not answer the door at all, and neither did anyone else. While I waited, I thought back on my last trip to the tannery, the time I had purchased the wallet moldering in my back pocket. That had been years ago, shortly before I took my bride, and if memory serves, I had arrived at a similar hour and waited another, periodically pressing the buzzer, only to find that my friend's bell was broken.

It seemed unlikely that a man of my friend's dexterity would not, in the course of these many years, have attempted to fix the bell, or at the very least to engage a repairman, but the urgency was great, greater now that I needed a pretty handbag to match the wallet I would request, and I could not afford to waste an hour standing in the street until my friend came down to take the air and smoke a cigarette as he had before.

I didn't bother knocking on his door as I knew that the street door merely let into a stairway, and at the top of the stairway was another door which led into the tanner's studio and which would block even the loudest of knocks, so I raised my leg and brought my boot down upon the door's knob with great vigor, and the knob came off and fell to the sidewalk with a clang and I raised my leg again and kicked at the hole in the door where the knob had been, and the door splintered and gave.

I ran up the stairs, hoping that I hadn't spoiled my chances of surprising my friend with the racket produced by the door's destruction, and in hopes of maintaining any element of remaining surprise, I crashed through the door at the top of the staircase announcing myself as follows:

"I am come in fulfillment of ancient prophecy, for though I have no need of riding chaps and my head is unadorned, is not the celebrity the new American royalty, and am I not, in all modesty, a celebrity?"

I would not have stopped there, but would have gone on to flatter my friend with my opinions of his abilities if he had been there to hear them, but he was not and I did not, as I am no great admirer of the sound of my own voice and try to use it only when it can be of some use to my fellow man.

My fellow man, as I said, was not there, but there was plenty of evidence that he had not been gone long—the coffee in the pot was still lukewarm—and that he meant to return shortly— the lamp above his kitchen table had been left on.

There were also signs throughout the place that the place was still, in fact, his. The butts in the ashtray were of the brand I recall him favoring, and, mounted on his wall, in a deep frame behind glass—a frame not particularly well-wrought but of great sentimental value because I had made it in the same crafts class at the same YMCA camp in which my friend had fashioned his first wallet—the wallet was even now on display in the very frame I had given him as a gesture of respect for his gifts, and because, even at that tender age, I knew that I wasn't meant to work with my hands, and Mr. Bedell's reaction to the frame had confirmed as much. Most encouraging, though, was the work table, crammed, as I'd remembered, into the space between the couch and the wall.

Whatever was on the table was covered by an oilcloth. I was tempted to peek beneath it to see what dazzling new heights my friend had attained, but the years have taught me nothing if not respect for the sanctity of the artist's sanctuary, be the artist a lowly worker in leather, like my friend, or an artist of personality and entertainment, like myself, so I resigned myself to waiting in a chair at the kitchen table, heartened by the idea that I had retained the element of surprise, and passing the time by imagining his reaction to finding me awaiting him at his kitchen table to offer him the commission of a lifetime.

Naturally, even the most patient of men can only occupy himself with such thoughts for so long before the excitement that they provide peters out and finally becomes a kind of repulsion, but I am a resourceful man, and so I pulled my wirebound notebook and a pen from my pocket with the intention of taking notes on the evening's events to that point, convinced that they could be worked into something revelatory and motivational if recited at one of my many speaking engagements.

However, when I placed the notebook upon the table, I found that it had become, not moldy like the wallet, but warped of page and still damp from the last night's hoedown, and when, undeterred, I put pen to paper, I found that the pen would not make its mark. It was then that I hit upon the idea of ordering a hide-bound notebook to match the new wallet and the pretty handbag, and I made a note of it on the back of my hand with the pen, so that I should not forget about it in my excitement over the reunion and my eagerness to please my wife.

By then I had been distracted from thoughts of the reunion long enough that they were again capable of producing in me a sense of anticipation, although less intense than previously, the type that need to be rationed out lest they become repulsive, so I alternated imaginings of the reunion with imaginings of my wife's silhouette backlit by her bed lamp, and of all the glorious favors she would grant me upon my successful return, which thoughts can never become repulsive, even if the acts themselves might seem somewhat distasteful when put into words.

I won't put into words what I was imagining when I first noticed that I was hearing my old friend staggering up the stairs because I put it quickly out of my mind, lit a fresh cigarette, crossed my legs, and gave myself a sharp slap to the face to clear my head.

I had left the apartment door open in order to hear him staggering up the stairs, being well aware of the difference between surprise and shock, and knowing that when he found it that way, he would be prepared to find someone awaiting him, and would therefore not have a heart attack when I began my speech, but that he would never in a thousand lifetimes expect that it was I who awaited him.

He stormed through the door with the jagged neck of a glass bottle in his hand and thrust it blindly about him screaming, "What do you want motherfucker!"

I realized I hadn't taken enough care to consider the effect that returning home to find both of his doors splintered and open, in the old neighborhood no less, would have upon my friend's delicate and artistic constitution, and he was obviously deeply intoxicated to boot, so I labored to set his mind at ease post-haste.

"I am come in fulfillment of ancient prophecy," I said, "for though I have no need of riding chaps and my head is uncrowned, is not the celebrity the new American royalty, and am I not, in all modesty, a celebrity?"

As I finished my introduction he seemed to notice me, as me, for the first time, and I saw in his inebriate and bloodshot eyes, a look of recognition. He breathed a sigh of relief and let his improvised weapon fall to the carpet, relieving me, not of the fear of injury but of having to injure.

"I thought you were a cowboy," he said.

It was only when he said that, that I realized how true the vagrant's words had been. I'd been thinking of my separation from the tanner in terms of years, whereas the vagrant, in his ignorant intuition, had hit upon the greater changes that the years had wrought. My friend, who, in a sense, I'd left behind even before I'd actually left him behind, had stayed behind to make his way in a much slower universe.

I tried to explain: "Years ago, I did consider the IT professional to be the new cowboy, and cyberspace the final frontier, but, though I still enjoy hoeing down and consider myself something of a proverbial outlaw, for some time now I have supported myself and my family through speaking engagements and television appearances."

The tanner struggled back toward the doorway, indicating it with the hand that had held the bottleneck. "Well, it was an honor getting reacquainted with your highness, but I'm exhausted and drunk and need my rest," he said.

I didn't move from my seat, not wanting to give the impression that I agreed completely with the vagrant. Yes, things had changed, and yes I had moved on to better things and places, but I didn't want the tanner to think for a moment that I had merely stopped in to lord it over him.

"Please," I said, "don't stand on formality. Pretend that we last saw each other only yesterday, because I assure you, the warmth of my feeling for you has only grown as it would have if we'd remained in contact all this time."

My friend didn't move either, but said: "As happy as it makes me to hear that, I do have to open the shop in a few hours."

As certain I was that he was as happy by my attentions as he suggested, his tone contained a certain amount of what I took to be resentment, particularly toward the end of his response, the part about opening his shop, and I realized that he was making a certain assumption, common enough among people of his station, but mistaken nonetheless, about the relative difficulty of our lives and livelihoods. This assumption, that I am successful because I work less, is both absurd and hurtful, and my anger, when faced with it, has been known to get the best of me, but, in this case, my tender feelings toward my friend won out without much struggle and I brushed it off, though I still didn't move.

"But friend," I said, "my visit is not just about pleasure but business too, a matter of business lucrative enough that you could choose not to open the shop tomorrow or the next day or the next week, and still have more money than you would if I left right now."

Perhaps it was crude of me to speak so blatantly about matters financial with someone of his meager means, but it seemed to get his attention and his response was no less crude. He let the hand indicating the door drop to his side and said, skeptically: "Oh yeah?"

I decided that this was the right time to get down to business, so I stood up and made my way over to his work table. He watched me with a combination of friendly curiosity—I was always a bit unpredictable—and an artisan's awareness, but

when I placed my hands upon the oilcloth to remove it with
a ceremonial flourish, he ran to the table and placed himself
between myself and it.

"What do you think you're doing?" he said.

"I respect the sanctity of your studio," I said, "and will follow
your wishes in the way that I treat it, but the workshop will
have to be unveiled if our business is to be transacted."

He didn't move, but he said: "What business are you talking
about, exactly."

"I've come for a wallet," I said, "of the finest hide and
craftsmanship, and a pretty handbag to match."

The tanner smiled inscrutably and said: "You've come to the
wrong place."

I stepped backward from the table, wondering just what he
meant by that, worried that his circumstances had caused him
to abandon his dream, angry at the way the neighborhood, the
world, crushes that hope out of people, of us. And I don't just
mean him. Do you think I dreamed, when watching him work his
magic on that wallet back in YMCA camp, of finding fame and my
wife through *Which Rich Cowboy Wants to Marry a Frigid Virgin*™?

"Please," I said to him, "please tell me you haven't given up."

He laughed again and nodded affirmative, a nod so careless,
so flippant as to stir in me anger, despite our past closeness and
my hopes for our reunion. I clenched my fists and bit my tongue
to avoid another outburst. I turned my back to him and began
counting to ten, allowing my eyes to wander the room in an
attempt to distract myself from my disappointment, but instead
my disappointment was exacerbated when I glanced again at

the poorly crafted frame with the beautifully crafted wallet inside. My eyes welled with tears, and it was well beyond ten seconds before I was again ready to turn and face my friend.

When I did, I found him flipping the oilcloth back over his worktable suspiciously, but I didn't get a chance to see what was beneath.

I asked him: "What are you doing?" and he answered: "Nothing."

I knew he wasn't meaning to raise my suspicions, but he was raising my suspicions. What I couldn't decide was why he was trying to hide whatever was beneath the oilcloth from me. Was he lying about having given up? Was he, in fact, working on his masterpiece beneath that cloth? And if so, who had commissioned it? Someone more important than me? Didn't he know who I had become? Or did it have nothing to do with tanning? Was it something so shameful that he couldn't allow me to see it?

I asked him: "What have you got beneath that oilcloth?" and he answered: "Nothing."

I took a step toward him and another until I was staring directly into his eyes.

I said: "I demand to know what you've got beneath that oilcloth," and he said: "None of your business," but he must have seen from my expression how serious I was, because he reached behind him slowly and slid a hand beneath the oilcloth.

He pulled his hand out and held it up between us. My eyes focused slowly, but when they did, I saw a thin white tube between his thumb and forefinger.

"A joint?" I said.

He laughed nervously, put the joint in his mouth, and lit it. I shoved him sideways and pulled the oilcloth from the table, like a magician, before he even had the chance to exhale. There were scales and bricks and piles of weed and joints and papers and bags scattered across the table. I averted my gaze.

"Do you know the kind of trouble it would make for me if anyone were to find me here, in this apartment with," I waved an arm in the direction of the table without looking back on it, "with this?"

"It's just pot," said the tanner.

"Pot, heroin, child pornography—I don't care," I said. I said: "I'm a role model!"

"Not around here," he said.

I knew he was just speaking in anger. If I was a role model anywhere it was there, where they needed me. I knew it was best to ignore it. But then I worried that his outburst could be a symptom of a greater problem, something more than envy.

"I can get you help," I said, pulling the joint from his mouth and stomping it out on the floor. I put a hand on his shoulder. "We could say I was only here for an intervention. And then, when you're clean, I could take you with me, to my appearances, as an example."

"Like a trained monkey," he said.

"Yes," I said, "like a monkey. Like a cleaned up monkey with a gift."

I was too busy pointing at the frame on the wall to see his wind-up. His fist hit my jaw and I fell backward into the wall behind me. As I slid down the wall to the floor, the frame teetered above me and then fell, its glass shattering to shards beside me, the wallet coming loose from the mounting, landing on the carpet like a spent rag.

I picked it up from the floor and looked it over. It wasn't as perfect as it had been in my memory—there were some uneven stitches and some warped seams—but my memory had been built on potential, a potential I thought I could still see in the thing itself, its smooth surface, its intricate folds. I held it out toward him with both hands.

"You had such a gift," I said, "when did you give up on your dream?"

He shook his head at his sore knuckles. "The store was called the tannery before I ever owned it," he said. "The previous owner's name. I was never a tanner."

"All of the greats feel that way sometimes," I said. "Do you think I always feel like a successful public personality?"

"No," he said, taking a step toward me, "I was never a tanner." He snatched the wallet from my hands and said: "This is the only wallet I ever made."

I was certain I had him there. I pulled the moldy wallet from my back pocket and waved it in front of him. "What about this?" I said.

He winced as though prepared to admit defeat and said: "You made that one, technically."

We had agreed, on my last visit, never to mention the fact to anyone. I was happy with the wallet and he had been handsomely compensated, and I would never have admitted that I had had a hand in making it if he hadn't insisted on bringing it up, if only in front of me.

"That's just a technicality," I said, "and don't mention it again."

It's rare and unfortunate that I have to address my fellow man in this manner, and it always brings me pain to do so, but my manner in such situations is commanding and serious enough that the person I address knows not to raise his voice again. Or usually he does. My friend seemed to have forgotten.

"I'll mention whatever I want whenever I want to," he said.

I stood up slowly and ominously, and each step that I took announced the gravity of my intentions. I left an arm's length, the length of one of my arms, which are longer than his, between us, and said: "Go ahead and mention it."

He laughed again. His laughter was becoming as irritating as his words.

"You think I haven't already?" he said.

He started to add something else, no doubt some petty, childish expression of underclass envy that he would have regretted had I not knocked him unconscious with two blows before he'd had the chance.

As he lay there at my feet, I found it hard to accentuate the positive. All I could see was the sniveling brat whose messes I'd always had to clean up, whose debts I'd always had to pay, whose fights I'd always had to fight, and I said aloud to him: "You will never be a tanner without me," in hopes that it would haunt his sleep, that he would awaken after I'd finished and take it for truth. And to drive the truth home, I pulled down his dungarees, far enough to expose his bare ass and thighs.

I saw straight off the mark from my previous visit, a long and uneven rectangle of pinkish scar tissue across his left buttock. I felt around behind me for a sliver of glass large enough and sharp enough to suit my purposes. I pressed the point to his flesh and punctured the skin. He awoke with a shriek.

"Hold still," I said. "Struggling will only increase your pain."

He went limp in my hands and I continued, dragging the shard slowly downward, across, up and back. When I pulled back the hide, using the glass to cut the skin from the gristle, he began to squirm again.

"I'm not finished," I said, pressing him flat to the floor. "I need a handbag yet."

I lifted his shirt and used the pen in my pocket to create a template over the better part of his back. And then I cut. And then he began to squirm again.

"Go on," I said. "Lie down on the bed."

He made his way to the bed, slowly and shakily, with whimpers and yelps. I went to his icebox and, finding no cube trays, pulled several packages from it. I went over to the bed and placed the frozen peas and beans and such upon his raw flesh.

"Do you still keep the needles and thread in the drawer?" I said.

He didn't reply, unless you count a pathetic groan as a reply, so I opened the drawer and found them right where I'd left them, as though they hadn't been touched since my last visit, and given the tanner's abandonment of tanning, it was likely they hadn't.

I spent the next several hours trying to stitch his hide into a wallet and handbag with a number of false starts and backtrackings and plain old mistakes. They did not shape up to look as I'd imagined them, but that's so often the case with any type of art, and besides, the act itself, the monotonous process of stitching the seams had a calming effect upon me, and soon I was remembering the good things again—my wife, who would overlook the imperfections and see through to the potential and also the vast effort I had made on her behalf, and then my friend who, despite the difficulties we'd had that evening, due, I was sure to his substance abuse, would, I was sure, remain my closest friend, and who, I hoped, might be inspired, after this latest lesson in his craft, to take it up again.

The dawn sun was beginning to peek through the windows as I knotted the thread on my wife's not quite pretty but lovingly crafted handbag. It illuminated the note I had made upon the back of my hand, reminding me that I'd intended to procure a matching notebook.

My friend whimpered again from the bed. I pulled out my old wallet, pulled all of the cash from it, and dropped it on his table. He whimpered again. I looked at the back of my hand. I brought it to my mouth and licked it, rubbing the note into a light blue shadow across my skin. I counted to ten and then tried to decide if a notebook was really necessary.

Sugar;

I'm only noticing now that there's
something wrong w/ the mirror in the
bathroom. Either that or my pores will
eventually be large enough to create a
suction effect between myself — I
mean my face — and anything I might
bump my face against. A wall, for example.
Pony pants. I worry that you won't be
there to help me disengage myself — I
mean my face — from the wall or whatever
I might bump my face against.
Worse, I'm afraid that you might use
such an unfortunate situation to make
we agree to things I would not
otherwise agree to.

the Continental card

post card

—— FEATHERPROOF POSTCARDS AND BRIC-A-BRAC, CHICAGO, ILLINOIS, USA ——

PERFECTLY BANAL - *Postcards I sent home when we
were last on vacation together so that you would have
something to look forward to on our return.*

60647

U.S.A.

*i can only hope that
he still believes
in redemption.*

An old man yelled: "Give it back!"

It was early. Not in the morning, but in general. It was too early in general, for me, for the boy, for the old man who was yelling at the boy: "Give it back!" Again: "Give it back!"

It was already turning out to be a bad day for redemption.

The old man couldn't see what the boy wanted with it. True, it was a bright, shiny penny, but that's hardly enough reason for a maybe eight-year-old kid to tangle with a somewhat able-bodied and in any case full-grown man. Pennies are everywhere. He'd seen a penny—a slightly-less-shiny one—a block up the street from where they were standing, and stepped right over it without a thought. There hadn't been anybody scrambling for that penny.

All right, it wasn't slightly less shiny. It was dull. It was tarnished. But one penny is worth one one-hundredth of a dollar regardless of gleam. Unless that penny carries sentimental value, and it's no coincidence that the penny the boy wouldn't give back was shiny. The old man had spent hours polishing it, and the others, even the freshly minted pennies, the ones that didn't look like they needed it. Yes, there were others, and every one of them was threatened when any one of them was threatened. They were a confederacy of bright, shiny pennies.

The old man set his box down on the sidewalk, cautiously, or arthritically, and walked toward the boy, cautiously or arthritically, with one hand outstretched.

"Please," he said, "just give it back."

The boy probably couldn't understand why the old man wanted the penny so desperately, which is probably why he wouldn't give it back.

"There's a penny back there a block," said the old man.

He gestured over his shoulder in the direction of the other penny.

"On the sidewalk," he said.

The boy didn't respond.

"So you might as well give me mine, since there's another one back there," he said, gesturing again so the boy could go claim the other one for himself.

Still no response.

"I could go get it for you," said the old man. "We could trade," he said. "We could each have one."

The boy's silence caused him to continue.

"Of course," he said, just to be fair, "mine would be shinier cause I spent so much time polishing it."

The boy finally spoke: "Why would I want that when I got this?"

He held it out between thumb and forefinger. The old man's own thumb and forefinger were only inches from the penny. The proximity made things seem even more hopeless.

"Because it's mine," said the old man. "That's why it's shiny," he said, "because I polish it."

The boy didn't seem to understand the politics of polishing and ownership.

The old man took it upon himself to explain: "The one back there belongs to whoever picks it up," he said. "It hasn't been polished in a long time. You could go get it. You could polish it yourself."

The boy let the penny slip into his palm and closed his fist over it, dropping his arm to his side.

"Maybe I will," said the boy. "Maybe I'll keep this one, and go get that one, and polish that one and have two."

"Not two," said the old man. "One for each of us. Two people, two pennies."

"Then why don't *you* go get the other one?" said the boy.

"I don't want the other one because it's not mine," said the old man. "There's no redemption in it," he caught himself, "for me. My redemption's in the one you're holding," he said. "Part of my redemption."

He glanced down at his box, at the other polished pennies pasted to the top to form the word redemption. There was just a spot of glue where the penny that dotted the i—the penny the boy was holding—had fallen off.

"Redemption?" said the boy. "It's just a penny," he said. "It isn't worth any more than the one back there."

"That's what I'm saying," said the old man. "So why don't you give me mine and go get it?"

"Why don't you?" said the boy.

The old man finally gave up trying to convince him. He needed another angle. He lunged at the boy from another angle, taking the boy's clenched fist between his much larger hands and trying to pry his fingers open, yanking and pulling and pushing and scraping the boy's hand with his nails.

"Get off," the boy screamed, his legs running out from under his torso, his torso tugging his arm, but the old man wouldn't get off.

"Let go," the boy screamed, "let go," but the old man didn't let go.

He was lost in a cheap imitation of redemption, afloat the gentle waves of physical struggle. The penny was back in its proper place atop the i, his redemption redeemed by lop-sided violence. As he bit into the boy's flesh, the old man's eyes were dotted briefly by bright, shiny pennies. The boy was still screaming, the old man still biting the hand until it fell open empty.

The penny wasn't in it. The old man released him and the boy stumbled backward, nursing his hand, holding it tightly to his stomach and bending at the waist. He wasn't bleeding. The bite hadn't broken the skin.

The old man watched the boy as he performed a little boy ritual of moans and grunts and a seizure-like shaking of the hand. He knew the boy wasn't really hurt anymore, had never been hurt very badly. The old man wasn't the sharp-toothed strong-jawed predator he'd once been.

The little boy's seizure slowed to a nervous jitter and then stopped altogether. He let out a deep breath, stood up straight and looked the old man in the eyes, which suddenly seemed tarnished.

"You bit me," he said.

The old man pointed at the hand he'd bitten. The boy was still holding it, now more gently, to his stomach. He lifted his hand to show the old man his empty palm, a faint bite-mark on the webbing between thumb and index finger.

"This one," he said. "You bit this hand," said the boy.

"The penny," said the old man.

"No, my hand," said the boy.

"What'd you do with it?" said the old man.

The boy grinned. He held out his other hand and revealed the bright, shiny penny.

"It was a trick," he said, forming a fist.

The old man was dealing with a much craftier opponent than he'd imagined, but the old man wasn't as simple as he'd pretended to be. He knew that if you wanted a penny—a specific penny that you'd polished yourself, that was part of your redemption, a penny that carried sentimental value—from a boy, all you had to do was offer that boy a nickel. It didn't matter if the nickel was shiny. Nobody polishes nickels. Nickels don't carry any sentimental value.

But the man didn't carry any nickels because nickels have no sentimental value. No dimes or quarters for the same reason. There's no redemption in the higher denominations of pocket change. Copper is the color of redemption.

So the man reached for his wallet, opened it, and pulled out a one-dollar bill.

"Here," he said.

You could see the boy's lips working to hold back a smile.

"Your dollar for my penny?" he said.

"My penny," said the old man.

"Your penny," the boy said, opening his hand again.

The old man hesitated, not because he'd changed his mind,

but because he hadn't expected it to be so easy. He took a moment to consider what sort of new scheme the boy might have up his sleeve. Or in his other hand. Would the penny disappear again when he stepped toward the boy? Had the boy switched his penny with another equally shiny penny during the assault?

He needed to assure himself of the penny's authenticity, of its redemption quotient.

"May I?" said the old man.

The boy nodded and the old man stepped closer, bending his head down toward the boy's open palm, reaching out his finger to touch its smooth, polished face.

"Look, don't touch," said the boy.

The old man stepped back and didn't come forward again until the boy nodded permission. He bent down and stared so hard you might have thought he was trying to lift it with his brain.

He could make out the date on the penny. To the best of his memory it matched the date on the one that had dotted the i of redemption, but in order to be sure, he removed a slip of paper from his breast pocket and unfolded it.

There was a diagram on it—it spelled out the word redemption—and on the diagram, a list of dates that corresponded to pennies. At the end of the diagram there was a period, but there was no date on the period.

The old man looked back and forth between the diagram and the penny, and, satisfied, folded the slip of paper and put it back into his pocket.

The boy, no more or less patient than any other boy his age, was getting impatient. He was ready to finish the transaction and get away from the old man forever.

"Come on," said the boy. "We trading or not?"

The old man jumped back again. The boy rolled his eyes as the man baby-stepped forward holding the bill behind his back with one hand and reaching out toward the boy's hand with the other. He snatched the penny and smacked the bill into the boy's palm, then jumped back. He kept his eyes on the boy, not his re-acquired redemption.

The boy was examining the dollar bill with what seemed like genuine happiness, pleased with his ten thousand percent profit, though his math probably wasn't quite so exact. The old man looked down at his part of the bargain, and saw that all was well with redemption—the head where the head belonged, the tail where the tail belonged. He rolled the polished penny over and over in his hand.

He laughed: "Ha! Ha! Ha!" as he rolled.

It was a forced sounding screeching laugh, slower and more rhythmic than the real thing, approximating or faking the unchecked hubris of the redeemed. It didn't sound right. It didn't feel right.

"Never try to con a con, kid," he coughed through the screeching. "Don't try to hustle a hustler."

He kept coughing and laughing and screeching. The boy looked frightened, more frightened than when the old man had bitten him. Or differently frightened. This was his first real glimpse of redemption.

"I am redeemed," said the old man. "I am almost redeemed. And what do you have to show for it?"

He snatched the bill from the boy's hand and waved it in front of the boy's face.

"A dollar?" he screeched. "This?"

He was breathing heavily. The boy was on the verge of tears. He didn't care so much about the money anymore as about escaping before the old man could do him any harm. Any more harm.

The old man stood still and quiet until his breathing steadied.

"This," he gasped. "A dollar."

A dollar that he held between thumb and forefinger of each hand and ripped in two, then in four, then into hundreds of uneven little bits and shreds, each worth less than even the most tarnished penny, until they were sticking to his sweaty palms and flaking to the ground like ugly olive snow.

The old man rubbed his hands on the seat of his pants and said: "I hope you've learned as much from this as I have."

The boy wiped a tear from his cheek with the back of his arm. For a second, I thought he was going to hit the old man. Instead he ran past him, picking up the old man's box and running down the street in the direction of the other penny. The old man didn't even try to follow.

I yelled: "Hey. Up here."

The old man stood staring at his penny. I thought he might not bother looking up at me, but then he did, he bothered.

"The boy lives in this building," I said.

I didn't know where the boy lived, but I'd seen him before. Often, in fact. From my window, I'd seen him go in and out of the building. So he might live here. Or maybe he's only visiting a friend.

"You could wait for him here," I said.

I was standing in the window.

I said: "I'll make coffee. It'll get you out of the cold for a while."

It was cold, an autumn day, crisp as a new one dollar bill, with a wind blustery enough to blow a skinny old man into oblivion without redemption.

I watched him walk in from the street. I heard him walking up the stairs. I closed my window, walked across the room, and opened the door for him. He walked in without acknowledging me, and went over to my window.

I introduced myself. He didn't introduce himself. I'm not sure whether he heard me or not.

"Coffee?" I said.

It took him a minute to say: "No."

No thank you, I wanted to say, but I didn't. I'm a gracious host. I started a pot of coffee.

I walked around the room as though *I* were the visitor, picking things, my things, up and looking at them through my impersonation of his eyes: a puppy-shaped paperweight, an empty tea-tin, a pen with my accountant's name and address on it.

He was staring out my window as though the boy might be hiding anywhere in the scene, as though the culprit, who they say always returns to the scene of the crime, couldn't have actually left the scene of the crime in the first place. As though all he had to do was wait until the criminal, the boy, peeked out from behind that tree trunk, that garbage can, that blade of grass.

The coffee began to drip into the pot with the sound of sizzling water.

"What's in the box?" I said.

He forced a cough and leaned in closer to the window. His breath condensed on the cold glass, and he wiped it quickly lest the fog obscure his view for even a moment.

I walked over to the kitchen table, and brought him a chair. He didn't notice me behind him. I tapped him on the shoulder.

He said: "What?" without looking back.

"I thought you'd like a seat," I said.

He sat down in the chair still staring out the window. He turned around a moment later.

"Thanks," he said, and went back to watching.

The coffee pot was full and my room smelled like coffee. I poured two cups and asked if he took cream and sugar.

"Do you take cream and sugar?" I said.

"Black," he said.

I placed his mug on the window sill in front of him.

"Thanks," he said, this time without turning toward me.

Which made three responses. I thought he might not mind answering a question or two as long as it didn't require his looking away from the window.

I tried again: "What's in the box?"

"It doesn't make any difference now," he said.

"Then why are you staring out my window?" I said.

"I'll go," he said, but he didn't move.

"What's redemption?" I said.

He coughed again and leaned into the window. His breath condensed on the cold glass and he wiped it away. He hadn't touched his coffee, and it was steaming the window below the level of his eyes.

I walked over to the kitchen table and went back to what I was doing. I did what I was doing until it started to get dark. I turned my lamp on as the sun set, and the man started to see more of his own reflection than the street outside until he was just squinting at himself. From the table, I watched him lean toward the window, wipe his breath off the glass and sit back, over and over until finally he fell asleep. I'd almost forgotten about him by the time he woke with a jump, stood up, and brought his mug full of cold coffee to the sink.

"I'm going," he said.

He pulled his jacket tight around his body, buttoned it all the way up to his neck, and left. I watched him walk out of my room. I heard him walk down the stairs. I assume he went out the front door of my building and down the lamplit street in the direction of the other penny, but I didn't get up to check.

Does he stare out his window at another cold autumn day? The day is crisp as a new one dollar bill with a bitter wind that could blow a skinny old man into oblivion without redemption.

Does he pull his jacket tight around his body and button it all the way up to his neck? Does he look down at his box? It's about the size of a shoebox, but any indication of whether or not it's a shoebox has been worn away.

The word redemption is spelled atop the box. Is it spelled in peeled-paper as though something's been pasted on and ripped off? Pennies. Is there a bright shiny penny dotting the i?

Does he take the box under his arm and walk out of his room, down the stairs and into the street? Cars drive by. Children play. Does he walk up the block toward the grocery store? If he goes to the grocery store he will find relief from the autumn morning in the rotting-produce warmth of the grocery store.

Does one of the clerks say: "It's that guy."?

Does the clerk who says it's that guy pretend to be busy so he won't have to help him?

Does he stop in front of the customer service desk? The customer service desk is on the wall opposite the entrance. Do the rest of the employees pretend not to notice him? Do they scurry away like bunny rabbits? Is it because they know that the last to notice him will have to redeem him?

Is the new girl the last to notice him? She barely looks old enough to work. Does he place his box on the counter in front of her?

"How may I help you?" she says with a smile that says, paper or plastic.

Does he open the box? Are there piles and stacks of colorful coupons inside? Does the girl pick through them, puzzled as to what's expected of her?

She says: "What am I supposed to do with these?"

Does he want to redeem them? Does he say: "I want to redeem them."?

She looks up at him as though he's an idiot. She wonders if he's an idiot, if he really doesn't know how to use a coupon.

"Don't you know how to use a coupon?" she says. "You buy things with them. To get a discount on things. Like this one." She picks out a coupon with a picture of a bottle of green dish detergent on it. "It says you get ten cents off a bottle of green dish detergent when you use it."

Does he respond?

"So if you wanna go get a bottle of green dish detergent I can give you ten cents off," she says.

Does he not respond?

"Except this coupon expired over a year ago," she says. "See this?" She shows him the date on the bottom. "It expired on this date. That's a year ago so I can't give you ten cents off."

Does he point to the fine print below the date? The girl squints to read.

"It says actual cash value: one one-thousandth cent," she says.

Does he nod?

"But we don't have one one-thousandth cent," she says. "You would need like a thousand of these just to make one cent."

Does he point toward the box? Toward the other coupons in the box? Does he make sure she counts every one of them? It takes her more than two hours because she loses track and has to start over several times.

"One thousand," she says, and smacks the last coupon on the counter with a hateful look that doesn't become her young face.

She hands him his redemption. One penny.

Does he take it? Does he rub it against his shirt? A rub against a shirt is a far cry from the rigorous routine of polishings that the rest of his pennies got.

Does he ask her for some paste?

She checks beneath the desk—the sound of clutter being tossed around—and stands up brandishing a tube of rubber cement.

"This is all we got," she says.

Does he cement the period to redemption? Rubber cement works as well as paste, but doesn't smell as good.

Does he say thank you?

"Fuck you, too," she says, not quite beneath her breath.

Does he step back outside? It's still a cold day. Does he head toward home with the empty box under his arm? Do the two pennies on the box reflect the rays of the setting sun? Now and again.

How long before he stops in front of a trash can and drops the box in unceremoniously? Who's keeping track? And does he still believe in redemption? Does he finally believe in redemption?

post card

—— FEATHERPROOF POSTCARDS AND BRIC-A-BRAC, CHICAGO, ILLINOIS , USA ——

BLEACHED WHALE DESIGN

Sunshine)

We were both a little tipsy when the Continental card we got back from the nightclub in the Teutonism Districts, so I don't know if you'll remember how we danced to "Pretty Young Thing."

The swarthy natives dancing besides made us nervous and I tried to break the ice.

"You love the King of Pop?" I said.
"We love the King of Pop," they said.

I turned back to you.
"They love the King of Pop just like we do," I said.

"Everybody loves the King of Pop," you said.

Apple of My Eye, if you want to make the world a better place, take a look at yourself and make a change.

PERFECTLY BANAL - Postcards I sent home when we were lost on vacation together so that you would have something to look forward to on our return.

60647

rules and regulations

Rules and Regulations

Do: restrain the child. Though he is smaller than you, he may be quicker, and if he is not now, he will be, soon and suddenly. So restrain him, with your hands on his arms if the discipline is to be an abbreviated version of the discipline for any number of reasons including exhaustion, illness, general weariness, drunkenness, or, for that matter, sobriety. Remember: that a minor offense on the part of the child does not necessarily call for an abbreviated or lesser punishment since, as the Good Lord tells us: a sin is a sin is a lie is a murder is a theft is a sass. Restrain him with something more efficient and reliable (you will one day be old and shaky, if you are not already), for the more intensive discipline, leaving your hands free to mete out punishment as punishment was meant to be meted out. I prefer: leather belts, but have been known to use: twine, bed sheets, shoelaces and other household devices, as the occasion arises. These materials can be used in a variety of ways, the simplest and most common of which is: in conjunction with a chair. The arms and/or legs and/or neck and/or torso may be tied to their corresponding places on said chair. Other options include: the bed, the banister, and, particularly in the winter months: the radiator. You may tie the child's hands behind his back, his hands to his ankles, his feet behind his head, etc., if no props are available. This accomplished, you are ready to begin the discipline proper.

When disciplining, there is one rule that must always be kept in mind: do not: lose control. When I speak of control, I do not mean control of the child, not in this situation. In this situation, control of the child is a given. He has been restrained, and the odds of his escape, especially in the case of the leather belt are: slim to none. To further ensure complete control, you may wish to: gag the child, but I generally choose not to as his cries can be a good indication of the effectiveness of the discipline. In either case, control of the child is not in question. You must not: lose control of yourself. If you forget this rule, as so many others have: your failure is guaranteed. But it is so easy to do! The disciplining of a weak and whimpering child can drive even the strongest-willed of disciplinarians into a frenzy, and we have all succumbed to it at one point or another. This failure has a wide range of manifestations, from: not getting the point across to: the death of the child which will result in the removal of that sweet burden: discipline. Do not: let the child die. Avoid: losing control. Discipline is an act to be carried out in reflection, not passion. Many an evening, after a hard day of work, I took respite in the meditative bliss of discipline, making it clear to the child that it was for the benefit of the both of us, and that the lesson taught and to-be-learned on such an occasion, was a general, rather than a specific, one about taking respite in the meditative bliss of discipline. Always: be sure that the child is aware of the lesson to be learned. There is no justification for discipline if there is no lesson to be learned, or if the lesson to be learned is not learned, as in the case mentioned above. Without a lesson, the child will be confused, and may even grow, in time: not to appreciate the discipline.

The punishment should fit the crime. If the child is caught with his hand in the cookie jar: discipline should be concentrated about that hand which was in the cookie jar, as well as the stomach which he would have filled with cookies and is therefore a co-conspirator, if not the driving force behind the offense. But it will not always be so simple. The child is likely to do ninety-nine percent of his offending with his mouth. In a perfect world, this would not pose any problems: discipline would be concentrated about the mouth. However, this is not a perfect world, and, unless you are a stricter disciplinarian than I, i.e., one who does not: allow the child to leave the house, for any reason, you can imagine the many problems that such an approach could cause. You must then find a method of discipline which will not become a matter of: public knowledge, or worse: public involvement. Many have opted for: washing the child's mouth out with soap. Since the first time my father washed my mouth out with soap, I have found this to be the most ridiculous form of discipline. As disciplinarians, we need to think like our children in order to ensure that lessons are well-taught and equally-as-well-learned. The symbolism of washing a mouth out with soap, making that mouth "clean," is lost on the child. He is left with a soap flavored mouth, and he will get the soap flavor out of his mouth by marching defiantly over to the cookie jar and eating a cookie, convinced that you will do nothing more than scrub another part of his anatomy as further punishment. And how could you really do otherwise? A child needs consistency. He needs a reminder, something that will stay with him longer than a mouth full of suds. I recommend: choosing another part of the child's body, the right thigh for instance, and renaming it, for the duration of the discipline: mouth. You need not consider the philosophical implications of this renaming, so long as the child is led to understand that, for practical purposes: his leg is his mouth. This may, in fact, kill two birds with one stone, as the boy will, for a time at least, be less prone to committing offenses with either: his mouth or his right thigh. Remember though, that the opposite is not true: the renaming and punishment of the leg in place of the mouth does not accrue to credit for future offenses by the leg. If the child commits simultaneous offenses with the mouth and the right thigh, and for the above reasons, you choose to name the right thigh: mouth, you must then designate another part of the anatomy, perhaps the left thigh: right thigh, and apply proper discipline. Stick to the basics. The most successful disciplinarians stick to the basics. They recognize that discipline is an heirloom which has been handed down to them, and which they must preserve intact for future generations.

Finally, do not: allow the child any opportunity to discipline you, ever. If this entails posting an armed guard at the door of his bedroom, better yet: guarding the door yourself, then do: so. Curbing the child's desire to discipline is a painstaking and time-consuming process. Again, there are various ways of dealing with it. Some have chosen to engineer a crippling accident in an icy driveway. Others have gone with a simple policy of sending the child to live with a distant relative at a predetermined age. These are not corrective, but preventive measures in which there is no real lesson to be taught or learned. The child can be faulted for many of the things he does in adolescence, but it is something of a stretch to fault him merely for being an adolescent. And while the latter method seems fool-proof, there arises the potential that the child may act out his desire to discipline on his unsuspecting grandmother. It is also, in a sense, an abandonment of your duties as a disciplinarian, and it denies you the fulfillment of practicing discipline on a less fragile subject. The more honorable disciplinarian chooses not to transplant, or fully disable the child. If you are not going to complete the disciplinary process, then there is no point in ever beginning it. I would advise you to administer sedatives secretly, by grinding them into powder and slipping them into the child's supper, or by placing the pills in an empty bottle of vitamins. If you decide upon the latter method: you will want to make sure that he takes the "vitamins" regularly, encouraging him to grow up big and strong, so as not to betray your intense fear that exactly that will happen. Should he go even one day without the drugs, his disciplinary instincts are bound to surface, and when they do: the child will surely tear you limb from limb, leaving you bound to your bed, and forcing you, in your old age, to: dictate your rules and regulations to: some fairy college boy who wants to: make a poem out of you.

Rules and Regulations

Do what Dad says, but think what you want. He is a shriveled, jaundiced thing, and his phantom limbs are as corporeal as your phantom sister, the pain of them proof that he will not be outlasting anyone as predicted.

Take dictation—fluff his pillow in the morning, change the channel now and then, turn out the lights when you see he's asleep, enact your revenge with double-knotted bows and dirty linen. Every happy family is as corporeal as his phantom limbs. The unhappy ones are like us. We are tired and angry phantoms. Admit it. Just ask yourself when you do what Dad says. Why are you so tired?

Take dictation—take your vitamins. No, the ones that make you tired. Change the bedpan, bite your tongue. Next time do it before you try to remind him that his arms and legs are attached to his shoulders and crotch, respectively, respectfully enough. Not for him. Bite your tongue again while he berates you for the reminder, but think what you want. Think the bathroom is five feet from his ass. Even his voice is shriveled and jaundiced. Even as it tells you it is going to outlast you all it is falling asleep. The process can take hours. Try not to gag when the process has taken its time. Try not to jitter while trying not to gag.

Take dictation—warm up something from a can, take your vitamins and mix them in, take it to him, spoonfeed, wipe, repeat. Try not to think of the airplane game. Try not to laugh when you think of the airplane game. He is too tired to care, but don't push. Ask yourself while you do what he would say. Why are you so sad?

Be your own dictator—turn him on his side so his phantom limbs don't get phantom bedsores. Ask yourself while you watch him look like a sleeping baby. Will this shriveled baby outlast us all? How will this jaundiced baby last with us all gone? Is this phantom tired or is it another unhappy trick? Tell him you were not talking to yourself. Tell him you were talking to your corporeal sister. Tell him you do so have a sister.

I'm sorry. This has been my fault, but you will have to do what Dad says. Think what you want. Think we all thought he would be more tired than he is. Think who is tricking whom.

Take dictation—put him back on his back, change the channel, go start a pot of coffee, take it to him, spoonfeed, wipe, repeat. Apologize for the airplane game. Apologize for the laughter, all laughter everywhere, and for babies who are children who will outlast their parents. Apologize for being so dramatic. Apologize for spilling about a drop of coffee on his shriveled, jaundiced chest. Try not to spill anymore. Tell him to stop screaming. Ask him to stop screaming. Plead. Try not to notice how he fans the burn site with his phantom arms, but if you do, bite your tongue. You're learning.

Take dictation—go get a bag of ice, notice the ice cream beside the ice cubes.

Be your own dictator—make up for it all with a bowl of ice cream. Take your vitamins, crush them up and sprinkle them on. Don't be stupid, they don't look like sprinkles. Slather the ice cream in chocolate syrup, take it to him, apologize, go get the bag of ice, apply, apologize again, spoonfeed, wipe, repeat. Think what you want. Think how did you ever think that the airplane game was funny. Do not do the airplane game. Don't be so sad. Your trick is working, this time it is. He's tired, so tired that he doesn't stop himself from pushing away your corporeal arm with his phantom arm while dribbling the previous mouthful down his shriveled baby chin. Wipe. Say there, there if you can't resist. Say Dad. Dad? Are you awake? Poke him with a finger. Not in a phantom limb. Poke him on the chest. Say are you awake.

Be the only dictator—turn him on his side. Don't think about the cold, rubbery feel of his baby body. Don't look at all. Don't look back. Do what you want for a while. Sit in a chair at the kitchen table and think what you want. What do you want? Do you want an unhappy family? A family is happiest when it wants what it has. This family has any number of phantoms. Which phantom is angriest, the chicken or the egg. Go be a chicken or an egg. Take another vitamin if you're chicken, but go do it. Do what Dad wants. Think what Dad says. Don't look at him. Don't think about how his skin glows jaundice in the dark. Stop thinking.

I'll be your dictator—reach under the bed for the soiled sheets. They're soiled. All the better. Say Dad you soiled the sheets. When he doesn't respond say my dad is a phantom shit factory, a big yellow armless legless baby with arms and legs, my dad is good for nothing but spoonfeed wipe repeat. Keep it up, not louder but going. Check for rapid eye movement while you lay the soiled bedclothes on the floor beside the couch. It means he's asleep but not too deep. It means your monologue is being the dictator of his phantom dreams. It means just a tweak in volume when the time is right and things will go exactly as you want for once. Don't talk to your corporeal sister. Not now. Say you know as well as I do that I believe in you but I'm in the middle of something that's not going to do itself and if you want to watch you can but it isn't going to be pretty.

You need a new dictator—get back to Dad quick. Tell him you never ever believed he would really outlast you all. Lie. Tell him you hardly expect him to outlast the night. Separate the strips you ripped last night from the mostly intact and in any case corporeal mass of the soiled sheet. Use the strips to tie your father's phantom limbs together, wrist to wrist behind his back, go easy if he stirs. Grin when he doesn't wake up. Say What. What would you do about it anyway, baby Dad? Your sadness is the last thing on your mind now, isn't it?

Try dictating for yourself again—raise the volume slowly as you lift the soiled sheet to his ear. Go ahead and put it down to double check the knots if you must. Continue to raise the volume as you lift the sheet again.

Take Dictaphone—press record and lay it on the couch beside Dad's head. Lower your mouth to Dad's ear and raise the sheet. Talk while you tear. Say Dad this is the sound of tearing, of anything tearing, a sheet, a skin, a limb from a limb. Raise the volume as he startles awake. Tell him you are tearing him to pieces as you start another strip. Throw the first strip in the air and watch it flutter like a long, wrong snowflake to your father's face and laugh as he struggles then whimpers, begs and finally cries saying he wants his arms back, his legs, how he knows you are good and he is bad and how he can fix this. But he can't, because for now you've forgotten your sadness and the memory of his miserable face and the sound on the tape. And the fact that you've left your father's phantom limbs bound on the couch with him will keep you company until you fall asleep and wake to clean up your mess.

Rules and Regulations

Keep a journal but do not write in it such bitch-like things as Dear Diary, You are the only one who I can tell all of my secretest stuff to, for only you understand me and accept me as I am, because fuck that, it's no way to do things, the whimperest cry for help. No need for help much less cries or whimpers when you follow these simple rules, so keep a journal, or a diary, and don't write anything in it that the rules don't tell you to, and for God's sake don't write anything *actual.*

Pretend you have a brother. Don't write this down. Pretend to have a brother who pretends to have a sister, which is you. Pretend to pretend. Get so good at it that you're barely even there anymore, wherever it is you are, until your pretension is so strong that it's true if not exactly real. But don't worry about that, Parmenides, your diary is still blank so *shut the fuck up.*

When you've finally shut up and stopped worrying about inanities such as true and real, you might be ready to disappear, to be the brother, but God help you if you're not, if you're lying to yourself about how good you've gotten. They've got people who can see right through you, who will look you in the eye and hand you the gun, the blade, the pills and laugh at you when you're too chickenshit to pull, slice, or swallow. Or worse. They'll coddle you to your face and whisper to Dad that all girls have a tough time in adolescence, that everything will be okay, that all you really need is some love and attention and maybe a positive female role model when you've already got so much love and attention you want to *puke* from the perfect female role model, Dad, so it's probably best if you just stop here now and come back if you're ever really ready to be the brother. *Go now.*

Don't imagine for a second that just because you're reading this I believe you're really ready or that you have any business believing same. Anybody can read who's not a retard and that book better still be *blank.* If it isn't, burn it and go get a new one. I refuse to be held responsible for your attempt to be the brother, but if you insist, this is what you shall do:

Be the downside of the cycle of violence, re to every action, passive to aggressive. Everything is your fault and you pretend to know this. Not as you, as the brother. You're not pretending anything anymore because you are nothing but the brother's imaginary sister, nothing but the fantasy that somebody gives a shit. But you don't have to care. Just let him believe he believes you do, like you let him believe he believes he's the victim when really he's not. Really he's just another *cog*, a whiny little cipher who manufactures impotent little apocalypses every single evening.

Does this mean anything to you? If not you'd better give up now and forever. If so, open the journal and write your brother's rules and regulations in big, bubbly, pengirlship for contrast. Do it *now.*

I have no way of knowing if you did it right or at all, and even if you did it doesn't mean you're ready to be the dad. First, because you already have a dad and your dad is so nice and considerate and caring it makes me want to scrape off every inch of my skin before I jab colored pencils in each ear simultaneously and don't think I couldn't. *Forget that dad.* This is your brother's dad, and he knows how to handle his business, and his business is ruling and regulating. Can you imagine a dad who knows how to handle his business? Even if you can it isn't enough. You can't pretend anymore. You have to become him so hard that you're suddenly all *gone*, because he doesn't believe you exist, even in your imaginary brother's imagination. It's just him and the boy.

Now you're either dead or alive and I can't tell you which and when. If you're where you're supposed to be you can do anything and you fucking well better. If you're where you're supposed to be, then you don't need these rules and regulations anymore, you're already writing the father's rules and regulations in the son's handwriting, because the father is speaking from his mouth to the ears of the son and from there to the son's hand, and you're all of it, every single one. But don't stop there. If you can be the father, you can be the author of the first and last lines of every story left to the English language and all the others too. You can be Odysseus, Borgia, Faustus, Hamlet, *but fuck him.* You can be Descartes, thinking therefore you are therefore thinking everyone else too. Shit, you can be Descartes' evil genius. You can be God.

Calm the fuck down. Come back. You're going to need me again when the notebook's full.

Ignore that empty feeling when the notebook's full. Everyone, all those who've gone before you have felt that feeling, because those who haven't failed worse than those who failed the brother. *Understand*? Breathe deep. Put the notebook down somewhere nobody can find it and come back when you're ready.

If you're ready, pick the notebook up and put it down where somebody *can* find it, in the living room, where somebody *will* find it, specifically the father. Not the brother's father, he's imaginary again but don't let on. Your father. The one who's going to cry his eyes out over whichever page he lands on first, and the waterworks won't let up until he's read it cover to cover, wishing he wasn't, wishing he hadn't, and ending by asking himself what did he ever do to make you this way, because he won't blame you, he can't, and that's his fault, one of many, and this is your revenge, the only one you'll ever need.

Time it right so that you walk into the living room just as he turns the last page, but don't let him know you're there until he closes the cover and looks up like he's looking up to God but only sees you by accident. Be God. Be God *on purpose*. Laugh at him like God should, not like it's all a joke, but like it's all more serious than he could ever know, so serious it can never be any other way ever. Keep laughing as he stammers trying to say something. Use the foam at the corners of his mouth as fuel for your eternal flame. When he finally gives up, tell him, Did you ever expect that God was a girl my age? Why wasn't it totally obvious to you, even when I was just an X on a sperm that I was the meaning of life, and the meaning was all a trick all along?

Lay it on thick, because his first thought's going to be, This girl needs a psychologist. How did I raise a girl that needs a psychologist *this bad*? He still won't blame you because he'll never have it in him to understand your powers, even when he finally tries to respond and realizes you're not there, because you won't be there anymore, and neither will he or the living room or the notebook. You'll finally be where you wanted, call it what you will. No more brothers, no more dads, no more rocks, no more thoughts, no more words.

the **C**ontinental card

post card

——— FEATHERPROOF POSTCARDS AND BRIC-A-BRAC, CHICAGO, ILLINOIS , USA ———

BLEACHED WHALE
DESIGN

Boo,

This morning in our luxury hotel I had foamy in bed, you told me that I had kicked you during the night in my sleep, and called you Shit Tits.

"It's Shakespeare," I said.

"No it's not," you said.

"Sonnet 130, Line 3," I said. "It's a paraphrase."

"His mistress's breasts are dun. Dun – whuwh," you said. "Not dung."

Ponky monkey, Booger bear, Bucket Brimming with Cold Cold Love, sometimes you are so distant that I'm just a tiny speck, and I am trying not to fall to evoke you before I

disappear

PERFECTLY BANAL - Postcards I sent home when we were lost on vacation together so that you would have something to look forward to on our return.

60647

about the author

Christian TeBordo has published three novels. This is his first collection of short fiction. He lives in Philadelphia.

featherproof BOOKSTORE

this is a CATALOG

featherproof **books** is an indie publisher dedicated to doing whatever we want. This might take the form of publishing an idiosyncratic novel, design book, or something in between. We love paper, but we're not afraid of computers. Our free downloadable mini-books are an invitation to all ten fingers to take part in the book-making process. We also have an experiment in attention span: the TripleQuick Fiction iPhone app. No matter the medium, we see our authors as creative partners involved in every step of publication. We make our own fun.

featherproof
light reading series

 Life Sentence
by Ambrose Austin

 Max and Emily
by Kate Axelrod

 So Little Impression
by Kyle Beachy

 Marmal is the Sometimes
by Tobias Amadon Bengelsdorf

 Peanuts and The Amazing Gro-Beast
by Chris Bower

 Every Night is Bluegrass Night
by Tobias Carroll

 Magic
by Mairead Case

 Dear Michael
by Margaret Chapman

 The Feast of Saint Eichatadt
by Pete Coco

 December 26th, 2004
by Brian Costello

 Donovan's Closet
by Elizabeth Crane

 My Father's Hands
by Mary Cross

 Grandpa's Brag Book
by Todd Dills

 All My Homes
by Paul Fattaruso

 Shooting Music
by Jeb Gleason-Allured

M is for
My Hair
by Abby Glogower

 Anniversary
by Laura Bramon Good

 Women/Girls
by Amelia Gray

 The Stork
by John Griswold

 Flash
Flicker Fire
by Mary Hamilton

 My Brother
by Lindsay Hunter

 Hospitable
Madness
by Jac Jemc

 This Is
by Andrea Johnson

 Witch of
the Bayou
by Rana Kelly

 Our
Pilgrimage
to Dollywood
by Heidi Laus

 By the
Rivers, We
Remember
by James Lower

 My Imaginary
Boyfriend
by Ling Ma

 101 Reasons
Not to Have
Children
by Ryan Markel

 Slave-
making
Ants
by Anne Elizabeth
Moore

 A Fourth of
July Party
by Kerri Mullen

 Saints
by Colleen O'Brien

 Sunday
Morning
by Susan Petrone

 In the Dream,
by Jay Ponteri

 Agee by the
Bedpost
by Caroline Picard

 Keftir the
Blind
by Nathaniel Rich

 The Camp
Psychic
by Kevin Sampsell

 And if I Kiss
You in the
Garden...
by Fred Sasaki

 The Lovers
of Vertigo
by Timothy Schaffert

 Flat Mindy
by Patrick Somerville

 The
Nightman
by Zach Stage

 Letter from
the Seaway
by Scott Stealey

 The
Diagnosis
of Sadness
by Jill Summers

the ENCHANTERS
vs.
Sprawlburg Springs
a novel by Brian Costello

The Enchanters vs. Sprawlburg Springs is a satirical, riotous story of a band trapped in suburbia and bent on changing the world. A frenzied "scene" whips up around them as they gain popularity, and the band members begin thinking big. It's a hilarious, crazy send-up of self-destructive musicians written in a prose filled with more music than anything on the radio today.

SONS OF THE RAPTURE
a novel by
TODD DILLS

Billy Jones and his dad have a score to settle. Up in Chicago, Billy drowns his past in booze. In South Carolina, his father saddles up for a drive to reclaim him. Caught in this perfect storm is a ragged assortment of savants: shape-shifting doctor, despairingly bisexual bombshell, tiara-crowned trumpeter, zombie senator.

degrees of separation

Edited by Samia Saleem

Degrees of Separation features 33 detachable postcards from graphic designers with ties to New Orleans. Each one articulates their experiences and reflections upon Hurricane Katrina. This limited edition volume comes wrapped in a gorgeous customized sleeve.

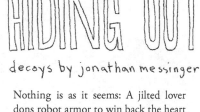

HIDING OUT

decoys by jonathan messinger

Nothing is as it seems: A jilted lover dons robot armor to win back the heart of an ex-girlfriend; an angel loots the home of a single father; a teenager finds the key to everlasting life in a video game. In this much-anticipated debut, one of Chicago's most exciting young writers has crafted playful and empathic tales of misguided lonely hearts. Sparkling with humor and showcasing an array of styles, *Hiding Out* features characters dodging consequences while trying desperately to connect.

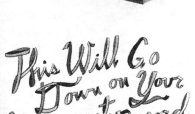

by Susannah Felts

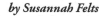

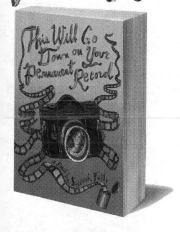

At the beginning of a lonely summer, 16-year-old Vaughn Vance meets Sophie Birch, and the two forge an instant and volatile alliance at Nashville's neglected Dragon Park. But when Vaughn takes up photography, she trains her lens on Sophie, and their bond dissolves as quickly as it came into focus. Felts keenly illuminates the pitfalls of coming of age as an artist, the slippery nature of identity, and the clash of class in the New South. *This Will Go Down on Your Permanent Record* is a sparkling and probing debut novel from a rising literary star.

boring boring boring boring boring boring boring

zachplague.com

When the mysterious gray book that drives their twisted relationship goes missing, Ollister and Adelaide lose their post-modern marbles. He plots revenge against art patriarch The Platypus, while she obsesses over their anti-love affair. Meanwhile, the art school set experiments with bad drugs, bad sex, and bad ideas. But none of these desperate young minds has counted on the intrusion of a punk named Punk and his potent sex drug. This wild slew of characters get caught up in the gravitational pull of The Platypus' giant art ball, where a confused art terrorism cell threatens a ludicrous and hilarious implosion. Zach Plague has written and designed a hybrid typo/graphic novel which skewers the art world, and those boring enough to fall into its traps.

a book by amelia gray

If anything's going to save the characters in Amelia Gray's debut from their troubled romances, their social improprieties, or their hands turning into claws, it's a John Mayer concert tee. In *AM/PM*, Gray's flash-fiction collection, impish humor is on full display. Tour through the lives of 23 characters across 120 stories full of lizard tails, Schrödinger boxes and volcano love. Follow June, who wakes up one morning covered in seeds; Leonard, who falls in love with a chaise lounge; and Andrew, who talks to his house in times of crisis. An intermittent love story as seen through a darkly comic lens, Gray mixes poetry and prose, humor and hubris to create a truly original piece of fiction.

Scorch Atlas

BLAKE BUTLER

A novel of 14 interlocking stories set in ruined American locales where birds speak gibberish, the sky rains gravel, and millions starve, disappear or grow coats of mold. In "The Disappeared," a father is arrested for missing free throws, leaving his son to search alone for his lost mother. In "The Ruined Child," a boy swells to fill his parents' ransacked attic. Rendered in a variety of narrative forms, from a psychedelic fable to a skewed insurance claim questionnaire, Blake Butler's full-length fiction debut paints a gorgeously grotesque version of America, bringing to mind both Kelly Link and William Gass, yet turned with Butler's own eye for the apocalyptic and bizarre.

Daddy's BY LINDSAY HUNTER

You ever fed yourself something bad? Like a candied rattlesnake, or a couple fingers of antifreeze? Nope? You seen what it done to other people? Like while they're flopping around on the floor you're thinking about how they're fighting to live. Like while they're dying they never looked so alive. That's what *Daddy's* is like.

The Universe in Miniature in Miniature

by Patrick Somerville, Author of *The Cradle* and *Trouble*

At approximately two-thirty on the afternoon of June 2, 1980, Gordie Lewis stepped off the streetcar that delivered him closest to Ontario Place. It was a beautiful late-spring day in Toronto, with the kind of sunny vibe that might prompt Gord's old buddy Frank Kerr — more famously known as demonic monkey man Frankie Venom — to lead into a song with his best Linda Blair *Exorcist* impression: 'Nice day for a party, isn't it?'

It sure looked like there was a party in the making. As Lewis, his prized Les Paul Special in hand, made his way through the tidy provincial theme park toward the public amphitheatre where his band Teenage Head was performing free of charge that evening, he saw hundreds of kids. Several hundreds. Thousands maybe. It was like the teen version of that scene in *The Birds* where Rod Taylor and Tippi Hedren notice there aren't just hundreds of angry birds perched on wires from here to kingdom come — there are, like, *millions*.

But the show was hours away. Could all those kids actually be there to see the band Lewis had formed with his high school buddies Frankie, Steve Mahon and Nick Stipanitz back in Hamilton, Ontario, in 1975? And which had now spent nearly three years steadily gigging as part of the so-called punk scene in Toronto? True, by June 1980, Teenage Head finally had hit songs on the radio and an album called *Frantic City* that had gone platinum, but Gordie and the boys had never played to more than a few hundred people at once, tops.

Shit, he thought, maybe they *were* here to see Teenage Head, in which case it was going to be the biggest gig in the band's career. As another hard-rocking, Hamilton-minted Canadian band named Crowbar might have put it in one of their own songs: *Oh, what a feeling, what a rush!*

By the time that day ended, Teenage Head would be firmly installed as a local pop-culture phenomenon and Canada's most notorious rock act. Their biggest audience ever would be estimated to be in excess of 15,000 people. Far too many for the polite government-operated theme park to comfortably accommodate, and enough to warrant the calling in of cops once the overflow of kids started tearing down fences, swimming from the shore to the island where the park sat, overturning police cruisers and generally engaging in what one newspaper would indelibly call a 'Punk Rock Riot.' Ontario Place would ban rock music from its premises for years after the Teenage Head show, and the hard-pop quartet would see its album sales jump stratospherically in the days following. They were the most exciting and well-known Canadian rock band of the day.

June 2, 1980: this was their day. It was the biggest show they'd ever put on, and it was also Teenage Head's peak. They'd never have an opportunity to draw a crowd like this again, never enjoy the same kind of album sales and radio exposure, and never again become front-page news. Instead, they'd soldier on toward long-term cult mythology, all the while hauling behind them the conspicuously tenacious reputation of being the best rock band this country had ever produced.

Introduction
The Endless Party

When I saw the 2013 version of Teenage Head play in Etobi-coke, Ontario, on a hot July night, some thirty-five years had passed since I first fell in love with the band. Two things struck me: the songs that had first seized my devotion sounded as good as they ever did, and so did the band. I mention this because, as anyone who's fallen in young love with a band knows, time can be merciless. Sometimes the music isn't as good as it once seemed, and sometimes an older band just makes you feel old.

Teenage Head still rocks. By which I mean, practices that traditional form of guitar-drums-bass-vocal amplified noise deliv-ery that hits, with irresistible precision, a primal place in your solar plexus and pleasure centres, and makes you want to jump around and holler for more. It's that simple, and that profound. If anything, Teenage Head rocks on record harder now than ever. Even their first album, once so widely denigrated by fans for its murky recording quality, now sounds like a certified punk-era classic. And live, they're still capable of sweetening and shredding your eardrums at the same time.

I've written this book to tell the story of the best rock band I ever saw, period. It was the band I saw more times than any other, the band that gave me more consistent and enduring pleas-ure than most, and the band whose almost-famous reputation sticks in my craw more than any other. While anyone who ever saw them, or anyone into punk rock in general or Canadian rock specifically, knows that Teenage Head had something rare and special and real, their rep remains largely the domain of cult enthusiasm and subcultural fascination. If it tends to bug the surviving members of Teenage Head that they've never been nomi-nated for that dubious achievement the Canadian music industry calls a Juno Award, the same fact simply makes the award that much more dubious. Or maybe plain irrelevant.

Even though the band's outlaw legacy is perfectly legit as far as it goes, it doesn't go far enough. Teenage Head probably inspired more bands and instilled more insane devotion than any other

Teenage Head in full sonic flight.

band this country ever spawned, and the only thing they did wrong was to do it in the wrong country at the wrong time.

'There's definitely nobody in Canada that had more influence on the Doughboys than Teenage Head,' John Kastner tells me of his celebrated Montreal band. 'They had the best songs and they had one of the greatest frontmen of all time, combined with one of the greatest guitar players and greatest guitar sounds to ever be put on record. They're the Canadian Ramones.'

Moe Berg, songwriter and lead singer of Edmonton's The Pursuit of Happiness, tells me about an early-'90s New Year's Eve gig in Toronto where his band opened for Teenage Head. This despite the fact that by that time TPOH enjoyed a far more successful recording career than the Head. Their signature hit was a scorchingly sarcastic pop-punk anthem called 'I'm an Adult Now,' and it might have been transcendently coverable material for Teenage Head were it not for the fact that they hardly ever covered anybody else's songs – save those of such early-wave precursor punks as Eddie Cochran or Iggy Pop – and the sentiment was all wrong. As lead singer Frankie Venom scribbled in a notebook a few years before he died at fifty-one in 2008, 'I don't wanna grow up.' These were lyrics for a song Frankie never finished, and they tell you something about what adulthood meant to Teenage Head.

'Moxy Früvous opened,' Berg says, 'and then it was us and then it was Teenage Head. We were pretty popular at the time and I said, "No matter how much popularity we got, we're still opening for Teenage Head." And I thought I'm completely fine with that. Give them their respect. They work hard for it. And I just remember writing on a piece of paper, "Fuck the Rest: Head's the Best," and I taped it do their dressing room door.'

As a teenager in Kingston, Hugh Dillon, future lead singer of the Headstones and movie and TV actor – his most famous role being that of the intensely Venomish aging punk Joe Dick in Bruce McDonald's 1996 punk-rock road-wreck movie *Hard Core Logo* – saw Teenage Head and heard the sound of his life falling into place. 'The impact the band had on some of these tough little Ontario towns was phenomenal,' Dillon tells me. 'It was liberating. They did something the Pistols or some more hardcore, more aggressive bands couldn't do, because they were so foreign and their message was so nihilistic you couldn't quite catch it. I'm sorry for the Monkees reference, but they were the stepping stone to everything. They changed the face of rock 'n' roll, opened the door to all the American bands, the Ramones and everything else. It was Teenage Head first and then I discovered everything else. I wouldn't be here without them, period.'

Bob Segarini, born in California but resident of Toronto by way of Montreal, has been in the music business since the 1960s. When he came to the city in the late 1970s, he was immediately alerted to a new scene emerging in the underground clubs around Queen West. Despite being older than most of the regulars at the gigs, he was a fixture. He can't remember the number of times he saw Teenage Head, and his band Segarini would eventually open for the Head at the notorious 'Punk Rock Riot' at Ontario Place. Over the years, he had seen and played with some of the most mythologized rock acts in history, and he believes Teenage Head was as good, and often better, than any of them.

'They were one of the few bands that took the stage with authority as opposed to hubris,' he says. 'They brought a sense of professionalism. And of course Frankie was a firecracker. He did some pretty strange shit onstage that in some bands would look like a desperate attempt to get attention, but in this case, this is just what Frank did. Frank would just go over that line every single time they got onstage. And the great thing about the band was that they understood what was going on. They also understood their place in the scheme of things. And their place was to play really well.'

When *Perfect Youth*, Sam Sutherland's history of the birth of Canadian punk, was published in 2012, the book not only culminated with a chapter on the Head, it kicked it off with this: 'Teenage Head is the greatest Canadian rock and roll band.' Even though I wholeheartedly concur, I ask Sutherland to tell me why. 'Teenage Head start playing in 1975,' he says. 'They're playing at the same time that the Ramones start playing and they hit on the same really important ideas musically. They took what was great about '50s rock 'n' roll and played it louder and with a little bit more energy. It was an evolution in rock 'n' roll that I don't think '70s rock ever quite was. And so for that reason alone I think they belong with the Ramones in the upper echelon of punk respect.'

Sutherland also points out that the Head's distinctly Canadian earnestness put them in a different category. 'There was this trend in punk at the time where everybody had to cut their hair,' Sutherland says, 'and everybody had to dress a certain way. You had to have short, spiky hair and straight jeans. Teenage Head kept their hair long, they still had their flared jeans, and there was something truly honest about them that they expressed not just through their music but through the way they didn't change. They looked like these heshers from Hamilton, and when it stopped being trendy to look like a hesher from Hamilton, they refused to sell out that part of themselves because it was such an intrinsic part of their identity. Hamilton – 'the Hammer' – is different from Toronto and has its own traditions with blues and rock 'n' roll and King Biscuit Boy. That combination of a new sound and an original aesthetic birthed from something so completely honest is something you don't see very often in art. And there are few bands that reach that mantle.'

I don't think Colin Brunton would disagree, although he'd put it differently. Now a TV producer and filmmaker who began as a club bouncer and beer slinger in Toronto's brief punk heyday, he saw Teenage Head shortly after they first arrived in the city and played the Colonial Underground. And he saw them many, many times after that. When it came to making his epic subcultural Toronto music documentary *The Last Pogo Jumps Again* (2013), Brunton cast Teenage Head as the most consistent, professional and inspirational band on the scene. In a movie where every surviving veteran of the Toronto punk scene seems to nurture a still-festering resentment, no one speaks ill of Teenage Head. It's the one thing everybody in *Jumps Again* can agree on: Teenage Head were the balls-out, no-contest, we-are-not-worthy, unplug-and-go-home *best*. They were the ones who compelled all the others to be as good. But equally impressive to Brunton was the Head's utterly unfashionable indifference to fashion: they played because they liked playing, and could care less whether or not anybody thought they were authentically 'punk.' You could like them or fuck off. They were in it for the long haul, not the short burst. 'They're the Jack Nicholsons of punk,' Brunton tells me.

When Steven Leckie first saw Teenage Head, he was already notorious as Toronto's first fully formed punk iconoclast. He called himself Nazi Dog and his band the Viletones, and he had a vision that was based on music, fashion, shameless self-promotion and giddy, fuck-it-all disregard for anything status quo. He was Toronto's Johnny Rotten, Malcolm McLaren and Vivienne Westwood all rolled into one skinny southern Ontario teenage package. When he first heard rumblings of the new noise rolling out from Hamilton, he waited like a home-turf street brawler for an opportunity to show these guys how it was done in *his* town. But when he actually saw them, he dropped the switchblade. Instead of defending his vision, he expanded it – it *had* to include Teenage Head. They had to be part of the gang.

'Wow,' Leckie remembers of that first encounter with Teenage Head in performance. '*That's* what you could put at a world level and say, "This is what this team is offering up, this city is offering up."'

As calculating a stylist as Leckie was, he'd never seen anything quite so perfect as the crew from the Hammer. 'I loved the name the second I heard it,' he tells me. Then he saw the band. Frankie knocked him sideways. And Gordie Lewis? Jesus. 'Man, I'll tell you. That stance that Gord had in his prime, from fucking head to toe. Man, oh man. Fucking spot on. Just a look you'd envy. I always loved a guitar player that didn't need to look at his fretboard all the time. He's just kinda looking down. Hair's perfect. He would have been a great add-on to the Ramones. I mean, he just fit that. As concise as Johnny.'

Tom Wilson, currently one of Hamilton's most prized musical progeny, and steeped in the tradition of Steeltown punk and attitude that Teenage Head forged, never misses a chance to pay due respect to the band that inspired him. He has performed with the band often, cites their influence devotedly and even wrote a song, 'Lean on Your Peers,' that includes these words about the long, dark shadow cast by Frankie Venom: 'I still remember the first time I saw him sing/Two black eyes, from a knuckle and a biker's ring/Climbing up the speakers/Hanging from the Bala rafters/Hamilton punk king swinging to his own disaster.'

After Frank's death, Wilson said this to Hamilton's *View* weekly: 'Nobody fills Frank's shoes. I watched more Gord Downies, Hugh Dillons and Tom Wilsons standing in front of the stage at Teenage Head shows learning to put heart into rock 'n' roll, and most of my career I've just tried to be as good as Frankie Venom on a bad night. He was the greatest rock 'n' roll singer I ever saw.'

As Gord Lewis has reminded me more than once, the same year the mob-stirring *Frantic City* went platinum and tore up Ontario Place, Canada's most celebrated recording artist was the soothing college-dorm acoustic troubadour Dan Hill. Teenage Head were called punk when the Canadian recording industry had no idea what to do with a punk band. As a result, the band suffered from too little exposure outside of the country and too constant bar-band exposure within. Their sublime skill at writing, recording and performing some of the catchiest, no-nonsense, two-point-five-minute pop-rock songs ranks with any of those bands they're so constantly – and misleadingly – compared to: the Ramones, the Buzzcocks, the New York Dolls, the Flamin' Groovies or even Cheap Trick or the Clash. The shit they did was their own shit, and it deserves to be credited as the great shit it was.

It's a story that abounds with what-if scenarios, alternative might-have-been speculation and strikingly divergent interpretations of the same events. For instance, when one comes to the intersection where the four boys from Hamilton cross paths with the veteran music promoter Jack Morrow, the story takes on more perspectives than *Citizen Kane*, with the late Morrow being variously characterized as a genius, a crook, a visionary, a hustler, a one-man star-making machine and a southern Ontario Colonel Tom Parker. Some call Teenage Head one of the finest punk bands that ever plugged in, others insist they were punk only by circumstance and that the appellation itself thwarted the wider popularity they might otherwise have attained. Some say you can take the band out of Hamilton but not vice versa, while others see their appeal as a more universal form of pure rock 'n' roll mojo. You'll be told that Gord Lewis's near-fatal car accident in 1980 sunk any possibility the band ever had of breaking out, but you'll also be told that the man's sheer determination to get back up and out in front of the band again is proof Teenage Head simply *couldn't* be stopped. Then you get to the big-picture analysis, the retrospective musings on whether Teenage Head was an unfulfilled failure and victim of industry fumbling, or a resounding triumph, a band that transcended all that was stacked against it simply because they were too fucking good for any of that shit to stick.

But all you need to really do is listen to that first album again, or maybe listen to *Teenage Head with Marky Ramone*, a ferociously good re-recording of a lot of early tunes produced by Ramones studio vet Daniel Rey and released just a few months before lead singer Frankie Venom died. When I hear either recording, all questions of whether the band got big enough melt away. If they did this, if they leave *only* this, there will always be evidence that, once upon a time, Hamilton let some amazing noise loose in the world.

Picture My Face: Monkee Planet

While I don't remember where I saw Teenage Head for the first time — it could have been Ottawa, Toronto, St. Catharines, Hamilton or Niagara Falls — this much is certain: as soon as I heard 'Picture My Face' I was in for good.

I'm not alone. '"Picture My Face" is a perfect fucking song,' Sam Sutherland says. 'It holds up to whatever they're playing on Q107 this very second. There's music from that era that requires context to really be appreciated. "Picture My Face" is every bit as good as any endlessly canonized classic rock song.'

'Picture My Face' was the A-side of their very first single — the B-side being 'Tearin' Me Apart,' the first song Gord Lewis ever wrote — and they played it every single time they performed. Still do. By now, I've probably heard the song a thousand or so times, and it still hits like a jolt of hot liquid sugar in the ear. It might be one of the most flawless pop songs ever, and to hear the band play it was, I'll bet, the steepest tipping point to Teenage Head fandom. Because it stuck in your head, you took it with you when you left an early Teenage Head gig — before there was any radio airplay or records — and you came back to hear it again. If 'Picture My Face' didn't hook you in, your ears were on wrong.

Or maybe you just didn't like bubblegum. Because that's what 'Picture My Face' is: a perfectly rendered bubblegum anthem, sweet and simple, cranked to formidable amplitude. A punk 'Sugar Sugar,' a sonically atomic 'Dizzy,' a Tommy James and the Shon-dells song for the blank generation.

If you've got the bubblegum gene, the magic works like this: a perfect pop song sounds like it's doing exactly what your ears want it to do before they even know they want it. It feels like the fulfillment of a foreordained sensory pattern, the needle slipping into a preprogrammed subliminal groove activated by just the right progression of chords, notes, verses and choruses. It feels like it's always been there — in your ears — just waiting to be tickled to life by the right sonic stimulation. An eargasm.

'Picture My Face' hit my aural g-spot the first time I heard it. It felt perfect from the first instant, immaculate and impermeable.

While the sensation was too purely visceral to bear analysis at the time, later I'd hear all those other songs that rang my ears similarly, songs that 'Picture My Face' reconstituted and rearranged so sublimely and inexorably that maybe they'd always been only one song in the first place. At times it was sung by Neil Diamond and called 'Cherry Cherry,' or 'Windy' sung by the Association, 'You've Got to Hide Your Love Away' by the Beatles, 'We're for the Dark' by Badfinger or 'A Little Bit Me, a Little Bit You' by the Monkees.

Especially, it turns out, 'A Little Bit Me, a Little Bit You.' Whether I heard it first on the radio or on the Monkees' TV show, this Neil Diamond–penned song hit my ten-year-old ears with the *boinnnnggg!* of Cupid's arrow, and when I bought the single I played it over and over and over until my father finally pleaded with me to play something, anything, else. It had That Thing – in his early songwriting years, Neil Diamond was the king of That Thing – and I couldn't get enough of it. If there was a song that made the bubblegum first stick, this was it.

That was 1967, so imagine my sheer atavistic thrill when, some forty-five years later, I'm interviewing Gord Lewis for this book, and I tell him what I tell everybody who'll listen: that Teenage Head had me for good from the first time I heard 'Picture My Face.' One of the most perfect songs I've ever heard, I add yet again.

And then Lewis tells me this: 'It's "A Little Bit Me, a Little Bit You" by the Monkees. That's where it comes from. With a bit of Badfinger thrown in.'

Holy shit. One of the very first bubblegum pop songs I ever insanely obsessed over was the inspiration for one of the very best power-pop/punk songs I ever insanely obsessed over. A link: a sticky sonic string of bubblegum running not only from one era to another, but suggesting a magical chord arrangement that probably informs all those pop songs I have ever become intemperately bewitched by and, finally, a reverberating string between me and one of my favourite rock songwriters and guitarists. For both Lewis and me, it all began with the Monkees. We were brothers in the bubblegum, fellow travellers on the pop highway.

If you were ten when *The Monkees* arrived on TV, you were in an especially vulnerable position to buy into it all the way. Not only was the show goofy and bright, the songs were too, and the guys in the band made being in a band look like the only kind of young adulthood that made sense – one where you're just a grown-up ten-year-old anyway. The boys – Davy (Jones), Mike (Nesmith), Peter (Tork) and Micky (Dolenz) – lived in a funky little apartment with stuffed animals, posters and a fireman's pole, and they never did much more than goof around, get chased by girls, put on silly costumes and lip-sync to their songs in antic-ridden montage sequences that stole from *A Hard Day's Night* and roughly anticipated MTV.

In our different respective living rooms in fall '66 – mine in suburban Chicago, his in Hamilton, Ontario – two things impressed Gord Lewis and me hugely about The Monkees: they were living a life that seemed entirely governed by fun, and their music was catchy as all get-out. Largely composed by Neil Diamond and Tommy Boyce and Bobby Hart in the early days, and then by the Monkees themselves later on, songs like 'I'm a Believer,' 'Stepping Stone,' 'Last Train to Clarksville' and '(Look Out) Here Comes Tomorrow' were instantly sing-alongable, radio-friendly rock-pop tunes, and to hear them as much as they made you want to hear them you had to watch the show or buy the records.

Indeed, for kids like Lewis, myself and perhaps a few million others – born in 1957, the baby boom's biggest year   Monkees albums were our first records. The first single I might have purchased was Billy Joe Royal's 'Down in the Boondocks' (another ace rearrangement of those magical chords), but my first album was *The Monkees*. Although universally denigrated – at first, anyway – as a packaged pop act singing factory-produced Fab Four knock-off piffle, to us ten-year-olds *The Monkees* felt like the first rock 'n' roll phenomenon of the decade made especially for us. It was a band, and music, we could call our own.

If the Beatles really belonged to our older siblings – or, in my case, an aunt only six years my senior – and ditto with the Stones, Beach Boys or Simon and Garfunkel – the Monkees were *ours*.

They were made for the medium we spent most of our time with, they represented our childish aspirations and they sang songs you wanted to hear over and over and over.

If my fixation resulted in a room covered in Monkees pictures – mostly clipped from magazines aimed at teenage girls – Monkees records, Monkees paperback books and a membership in the official Monkees Fan Club, Lewis wanted more. He wanted the lifestyle. The Monkees' TV show, along with the contemporaneous and similarly silly Saturday-morning Beatles cartoon show, made Lewis decide there was only one dream worth having, and that was to form a band.

'I knew I wanted to be in a band since I was like six years old,' Lewis says now. 'I bought my first *Hit Parader* magazine, and I couldn't believe the words to "I'm a Believer" were actually all in there. I'll never forget that. Then I started going down to the record store and actually buying 45s. I knew I wanted to be in a band from a really, really young age.'

Lewis was a bit of a junior jock at the time too – he played hockey, baseball – but being in a band held a different communal promise. For one thing, as he says, on hockey teams there are more people you can potentially like – but also more people you can dislike. Putting together a band, you could choose your compatriots. 'I thought that was the natural way,' Lewis says. 'I was shocked when I heard later that people were hired by the day as session guitarists. Guns for hire. It never occurred to me to *not* be with a group of friends and comrades. That was the way it had to be.'

That settled it for Lewis. He was going to grow up – or perhaps *not* grow up – and be in a band.

Hammered

For their entire career, the members of Teenage Head would identify themselves as a band from Hamilton, Ontario. It was said as purely stated fact, as though you couldn't really know them properly without acknowledging where they came from. Kind of like *Dragnet*'s Jack Webb saying, 'I'm a cop.' *We're Teenage Head, and we're from Hamilton.*

Being from Hamilton, known across the country as a city where steel was made, seemed to mean *always* being from Hamilton, and it conveyed a grounded durability and practicality. One of Canada's other longest-running punk-era acts, the Forgotten Rebels, also hailed from Hamilton and also never really left. Blues are a deeply dug staple bar item in Hamilton, and blue collar is a proud thing to be. There's something about the city that prevents too much delusion from clouding up even your dreams. It might be a little-brother thing, the practical modesty that comes from sharing the tip of Lake Ontario just down the road from the country's biggest city. Or it might be a working-class thing, the sense of proportion that attends people who know they've got a job to do and do it. But it's there. If you come from Hamilton, you always come from Hamilton.

Unlike neighbouring Toronto, a city that has long seemed to wish it was something or somewhere else – New York or L.A. especially – Hamilton has always been happily resigned to being itself. In the simplest Hamiltonian terms, it's a town short on bullshit, but long on pride. There's a saying in Hamilton that Teenage Head made possible: 'The only reason Toronto had any punk rock is because we drove up the highway and showed them how to do it.'

For Lou Molinaro, teenage Teenage Head fan, Hamiltonian and future proprietor of the punk-dedicated Hamilton club This Ain't Hollywood, the fact that Teenage Head hailed from the Hammer conveyed to citizens automatic respect. 'In a city like Hamilton,' he says, 'especially being so close to Toronto, it was like the kid brother that beats up the bigger brother. It was really assuring on a confidence level, and it's major bragging rights to say that Teenage Head is a Hamilton band and not a Toronto band.

'For everything that they did artistically and in terms of attitude,' Molinaro adds, 'they defined what Hamilton was all about. There was a coolness factor to it, there was a fashion sensibility. They epitomized everything the city was about musically. I would hate to think what the city would be like had Teenage Head not been from Hamilton.'

Gord Lewis came from a large Catholic family with seven kids. He was the second oldest, with an older brother, two younger sisters, then three younger brothers after that. As with many people I've known who came from large families, the sense of childhood isolation was actually made more acute by the crowd. It was easier to feel lost with so many siblings milling about.

'I felt outside the family,' Lewis remembers. 'You get that many kids, it's hard to feel close. I had three brothers so much younger, I don't even remember them. By the time they were whatever age, I was eleven or twelve and stuck in my bedroom. I never left. I was just learning how to play guitar or the bass, teach myself the instruments. There came a point where I didn't even know I had a family. I just went straight to my room and tried to learn how to play these songs.'

Lewis nonetheless did well in school. Well enough to skip second grade, in fact, but that only made him feel more out of sync with his peers. He kept himself out of trouble, worked a paper route and played team sports, and generally did his best not to get noticed so he could get back to his bedroom as soon as possible and get to the one thing he never tired of: listening to music and trying to figure out how to make it. He'd put a record on, locate a difficult guitar or bass part, try to play it himself and then – a bit of a challenge in those pre-digital days – try to find it again and repeat the whole process. 'It was a labour of love,' Lewis says. 'And as with any labour of love, you will progress if you keep going.'

Around people, the tall, skinny, generously fair-haired Lewis was introverted, self-conscious and uncomfortable, but in his room with his music, lifting the needle and listening over and over again to the hard parts, he felt right at home. Music took him to a place where he was meant to be.

He'd come out of his room to do everything that was expected of him, and do it well, then return again as soon as it was done. On Saturdays, if he had any money, he'd go buy new 45s and listen to them back in his bedroom. He also drew a lot, mostly pictures of instruments, rock stars and band logos, cool stuff that kept him in that zone of bedroom hideaway bliss.

At the same time, in another part of Hamilton's west side, a kid named Stephen Mahon was experiencing his own version of the rock 'n' roll calling. It was different from Lewis's: raised a Baptist, Steve was discouraged from most of the primary temptations – the life of a rock star was as remote and forbidden as it was intensely alluring.

Being Baptist, Mahon recalls, 'meant Sunday school and church on Sunday, no long hair, no swearing, no going to movies, no fun. The only reason I got to see the Beatles on *Ed Sullivan* was because it was Sunday night, and me and my sister were home with the babysitter while mom and dad were at church, and she was watching it.' For six-year-old Steve Mahon, that appearance suggested a world beyond what was normally permitted, a horizon bright and forever beckoning. 'There was certainly something very appealing for a good Christian boy like myself about being in a rock group,' he says.

As it was for Lewis, the appeal to Mahon of being in a band was as much about living confidently as about making music. It was an alternate universe where everything was cool, especially yourself. That universe became more alluring as Mahon discovered the opposite sex. 'I was a pretty shy kid growing up,' he says. 'Very scared of rejection, so I just wouldn't bother to ask a girl out. I would wait for a friend to say, "Did you know that Debbie likes you?" I was all nerves.'

Looking at the guys in rock bands, Mahon saw the solution to his own timidity. If you looked cool, everyone would treat you like you were cool, and everything would *be* cool. No more complicated than that.

'What I really thought would help me was if I could have long hair,' he says, his hair still rock-star-long nearly fifty years later. 'Guys in bands had long hair, and I figured they had girls ripping their clothes off. Only problem, my dad had a home barber kit, and he made sure my hair never grew past my ears. It wasn't till high school that my mom finally stepped in and let me start letting it grow. She used to say, "As long as you keep it clean."'

Mahon's mom is fondly remembered as a facilitator of forbidden desires – at least of the rock 'n' roll variety. She let him grow his hair. She bought him his first single, the Beach Boys' 'Darlin'.' And when Mahon was about ten, she took him to Toronto's Canadian National Exhibition, the annual agriculture fair-cum-carnival that takes place at the end of every summer. As soon as he entered the gates that first time, holding his mother's hand, he saw a band playing live. Mahon heard the band, saw the band, looked up at his mom, and then she gently let go of his hand.

'It was as if to say, "Off you go,"' he recalls. 'She knew how much I already loved rock 'n' roll. I was drawn to that unknown band like a moth to a flame, and I knew, even before I got to the edge of the stage, that this was *cool*. At that age I didn't even know *why* it was cool.'

Around the same time – fifth grade or so – Mahon met a neighbour kid named Nick Stipanitz, whose older brother, Paul, was actually *in* an honest-to-god rock band. That band practiced in the Stipanitz basement, and Mahon remembers being mesmerized by the amps, guitars and drums. When Paul forbade the younger boys from watching them play, they sat outside the basement window, rapt.

But Nick wasn't content with that arrangement. Watching wasn't his calling. So he learned how to play drums and by Grade 9 had his own kit in the Stipanitz basement. Eventually he was good enough to join his brother's band, and long before he was even old enough to legally drink he was playing semi-professionally.

Stipanitz's passage to pro status had been facilitated in no small way by a friendship he'd struck up with a kid a year older than him named Frank Kerr. Born in Glasgow, Scotland, but raised in Hamilton, Kerr was a black-haired firecracker personality who took bullshit from nobody (including, to the shock of most of the other kids, his parents) and also played the drums. He'd done marching drills for years, a discipline that eventually kicked young Stipanitz's skills up considerably. This mutual passion was discovered in ninth-grade music class, where Kerr and Stipanitz both played trumpet. When Paul Stipanitz left one band and sought to form another, he enlisted both his kid brother and his buddy Frankie to be *dual* drummers in an outfit named Earthmover. It might have lasted only a year, but it forged a bond between Stipanitz and Kerr.

Mahon was transfixed. Stipanitz remembers him hanging out at all their basement rehearsal sessions, and even devising homemade light boxes for the band's live shows. At that point, Mahon's musical education consisted exclusively of the Top 40 radio charts he picked up every week at the Kresge's department store, but more than anything, Mahon wanted to be *in* a band. Like Lewis, he never felt like he had much choice about his future. 'I never really had any other passions, like working on cars or building rockets,' he says. 'And while I'm not sure how old I was when I set my sights on becoming a rock star, once I did, nothing was going to stop me. Even if I didn't own an instrument or know how to play one, I was hooked.'

The Basement Years

There is no Teenage Head without Saturdays and basements. The summer between Grade 8 and high school, Nick Stipanitz got his first drum set and started jamming with his brother Paul. (One of his first gigs was filling in on drums in Paul's band at a YMCA gig. The loyal Mahon served as roadie.) This led to Earthmover and Stipanitz's inaugural pro experience, but it also led Stipanitz to Lewis. The two had lunch and a spare period together, and they talked music. 'Gord knew a lot about new music from New York and London,' Stipanitz recalls. 'So he turned me on to a lot of music and he told me he had a name for a band, Teenage Head, but he had no band.'

Lewis told Stipanitz about bands he'd been reading about in music magazines like *Creem* and *Crawdaddy*. Bands like Mott the Hoople, Iggy and the Stooges, Hawkwind. Bands that were restoring a welcome unholy racket to popular music, bands Lewis thought provided the inspirational ticket. He played Stipanitz some records. Stipanitz agreed.

When Paul eventually expelled Nick from his band, their parents expressed filial solidarity by expelling Paul's band from the basement. This meant Nick had his kit and rehearsal space all to himself, so he invited Lewis, then a bass player fiddling around on guitar, to come over and jam. 'So really the first Teenage Head was Gord and me in my basement,' Stipanitz says. With Mahon standing by.

Lewis was ready. He'd been practicing on an SG-Style bass just the like the one his then-idol, Dennis Dunaway, played. 'Alice Cooper was one of my favourite bands,' he says. '*Love It to Death* was probably the first album that really opened my mind to a different style of music. It wasn't the Beatles anymore, it wasn't just love songs, it was about the dark side of life. It really did something to me.' Although Lewis would later make a name for himself as one of the most proficient rock guitarists Canada's ever produced, the bass gave him both a foundation and a work ethic. He sat in his room with his new bass, a cheap Japanese knock-off of Dunaway's model that he paid for with money made on the Westinghouse assembly line, methodically and meticulously studying songs.

'They were songs where I could understand what the bass was doing,' Lewis says. 'Hawkwind had many long songs, but there were repeated bass patterns, which gave me time to figure them out. Alice Cooper stuff, which was very, very tricky. Anything that made sense to my ears that I thought I possibly could do. I didn't even know it but I was teaching myself ear training by identifying the intervals and progressions. I was teaching myself root motion with chords, and then adding the fifth and adding the third, and finding harmony from the bass. That led me into guitar. The bass really helped a lot.'

It was one step closer to the Monkees dream come true. Now Gord Lewis actually had a band, if that's what you could call Nick and Gord struggling with Mott the Hoople in the Stipanitz basement.

Mahon desperately yearned to join the fun. 'I wanted to be a part of it,' he says. 'I didn't care if I was a roadie or what.' Well aware of Mahon's ambition, Lewis generously handed bass duties over to his friend, went out and bought a ten-dollar guitar, and proceeded to quickly teach himself the same way he learned his first instrument. 'I'd learned a few harmonic things on the bass that I was able to apply,' Lewis says. 'It was pretty primitive stuff, but at least I was able to make noise on the guitar.'

Childhood friend Dave Desroches, also a guitar player and Lewis's neighbour, remembers Lewis's almost preternatural facility with the instrument. 'I always thought Gord could excel at anything he wanted,' Desroches says. 'He was a brainiac. When he picked up the guitar, it didn't take too long.'

Mahon wasn't quite so adept. When he first picked up the bass, nobody noticed that he was holding it upside down. 'I'm left-handed,' Mahon explains. 'So when I first picked up Gordie's bass, the strings were upside down. I never knew anything was wrong until a couple of years later some guy told me I was playing backwards. At first I didn't believe him, then I thought about it and realized why the volume and tones controls kept hitting my strumming hand. When I eventually bought my first left-handed bass, I had to get them to change the nut so I could continue to play upside down. By then it was too late to learn the right way.' In his bedroom with the upside-down bass, Mahon followed the Lewis school of DIY musical immersion. 'The only way I was ever going learn how to play was to teach myself. I'd just put on a record and jump in. I'd put one ear on the body of the bass so I could hear it, and play the record at the same time. The first song I remember learning was "Strutter" by Kiss.'

The classic Gord.

Lewis had read about the Stooges' third album, *Raw Power*, and found a copy – the dark, relentless sonic assault was precisely what he wanted to hear. They tried a little Bowie, a little Iggy and the Stooges, a little Kiss. The music they were attracted to was frequently called glam or glitter, but it rocked hard and popped smartly, and it was the first music of the 1970s to mark a more or less complete break with the folk, blues, country and psychedelic traditions of the 1960s. This was the first music of the late end of the baby boom, and it would prove instrumental in generating the punk explosion on the other end of the wick. This was not your older brother's rock, and that's exactly why Lewis loved it. It was as though the likes of Iggy, Bowie and Alice had been stewing somewhere else in exactly the same pot, just waiting to boil over.

It was a pot that Lewis was eager to add his own ingredients to. 'Even then we were trying to write original songs,' Lewis says. 'The barriers were down as far as material was concerned because we were just goofing off. When somebody had an idea for a song, we'd work on it and play it just for fun. That was always the key.'

Lewis had named their new band after a song by the Flamin' Groovies. But almost as soon as Teenage Head started, it fell apart. Paul Stipanitz's band was going on tour, and Nick, his drums and, effectively, his basement were once again going with him. Lewis and Mahon were devastated. Mahon called Stipanitz a 'turncoat.' How could he possibly wreck the band's initial momentum?

Enter Frank Kerr again, former high school trumpet player and Earthmover. He was a year older than the rest of the band, and barely known to Lewis and Mahon. But Kerr could also play drums *and* had a basement. He wasn't in a band at the moment, but he had actually *been* in bands. Stipanitz, who wanted to help out his buddies before hitting the road with his brother, was sent to see if Kerr was interested. At first he wasn't – he didn't know these kids, didn't understand their musical aspirations and was pretty certain they had nowhere near his experience. But persuaded by Stipanitz's enthusiasm, Kerr finally agreed to jam with Teenage Head in his basement. He even offered to sing – but only while sitting behind the drum kit. 'I used to put a coat hanger around my neck and stick the mike into it to sing,' he told me when I interviewed him for CBC Radio in 1992. 'That's how hard up we were. We'd beg, borrow and steal gear back then. But we did it. We made it.'

Kerr came from a far different world than the one Lewis and Mahon inhabited. Where the younger guys were shy and church-going, Kerr was fearless and came from the other side of the tracks (in reality, just a few blocks away). He had long hair, and a beautiful set of Ludwig drums he bought for himself with the money he'd made pumping gas. Most mind-blowing, he had a girlfriend. And god knows jamming with him wasn't like playing in the Stipanitz basement.

'Frank was a real cool guy,' Mahon recalls. 'The kinda kid who just grew up pretty much doing whatever the hell he wanted.'

Lewis remembers that fact in vivid detail: 'First his mom would come down: "Frank, turn it down! Turn it down!" Frank would tell his mom to fuck off. And then his dad would come down.

"Did you tell your mom to fuck off?" "No, Dad, I never told her to fuck off." And then Frank's dad would say, "You've got to turn it down, Frank. It's the bloody bass. It's the bloody bass! The cat cannae even walk because it's rumbling so much!" I'd never seen that. I came from a very middle-class Catholic background. I'd never seen the Scottish Protestant way of life. The things Frank would say to his dad I would never even dream of saying to my dad. I'd have been killed. This would go on every Saturday and Frank would always win. And nobody suffered any consequences or anything – it was just the way they were.'

'That story sets the tone with Frank,' Mahon says. 'He was running the show there. If his parents said, "Be in at nine," he'd laugh. There weren't really any rules for Frank. He probably started drinking and smoking when he was young and never got told by his parents not to.'

Despite these domestic theatrics, the band was quickly coming together. Lewis, who by that point had only taught himself rhythm guitar, devoted himself to studying lead. 'Because I was the only guitar player,' he says, 'I had to play two notes at a time –otherwise it would sound really empty. I was influenced by Chuck Berry at a very early age, and by then the New York Dolls album was out and Johnny Thunders was doing that same thing. Double stops. And from the harmony that I learned on the bass, I tried different riffs.' Nick Stipanitz returned from the tour with Paul and, rancorous feelings having dissipated, Lewis asked him to rejoin the band as drummer – 'He was our buddy,' Lewis says – and Frank moved out from behind the drum kit to front the band. Dave Desroches, long-time friend and future member of Teenage Head (1982 to '89), had heard Frank sing in purely informal, goofing-off terms, but it was enough for him to know there was something special at work there. When Desroches was rehearsing with his high school musician friends, Frank frequently sang along.

'He would lead us in a sing-song when we'd stop for our break, and we'd go and rehearse again,' Desroches remembers. 'I knew he could sing, and I knew he had a natural voice.'

'You had to think, "Here's our Iggy,"' Mahon says. 'He was meant to be the singer. It wasn't even whether he had a good singing voice. He had the balls.' Stipanitz too was entirely blown away when Kerr moved up front. *This* was a born lead singer – crazy, physical, confident – and *this* was a band. A band that threatened to be as good as its name, the band each of these guys, in their separate bedrooms and basements, had dreamed of belonging to.

There was only one issue: Kerr didn't like the kind of music the rest of the guys were into.

'We stopped with original material once we went over to Frank's,' Lewis remembers. 'Frank wasn't that keen on doing original material. So we were doing more cover songs – the New York Dolls, Sweet, Aerosmith. Stooges – definitely some Stooges. But Frank was more Beatles. Beatles, Rolling Stones, Genesis. He was a combination of classic rock and progressive rock. With the Stooges, he was like, "What the hell is this?"'

'He wasn't into collecting,' Mahon adds. 'It was almost like, "That stuff really doesn't matter. I like music but there's lots of stuff to do to have fun. Let's go steal cars or something."'

'Frank wasn't a big music lover,' Lewis says. 'He was a drummer. He liked being in bands, but he wasn't out to change the world or anything like that.'

'Three-chord rock is a great place to start for any young band starting out,' Mahon says, 'but when we first started jamming with Frankie, we learned that he thought the three-chord stuff was a little lame for his tastes. He actually made fun of our choices, as did a lot of people back then. He was into stuff like King Crimson, Nazareth and the first Rush album! We actually tried to play some of those songs on the first Rush album, like "In the Mood" and "What You're Doing," with Frank on drums, me on bass and Gord on guitar, just to try it Frankie's way, but it wasn't meant to be. Frank had attitude back then. He figured that because he had been playing drums long before any of us had even played a note, we were just hacks. Playing what would soon be called punk rock, he just didn't get it.'

He would, of course, and not only get but *own* it. Considered by many who knew and saw him to be one of the purest expressions of punk force in Canadian music, it says something about the emerging Frankie Venom that he came to punk – a term he never liked – suspiciously and reluctantly, first not even thinking himself a singer, then certainly not a punk rock singer. But that only suggests how natural a certain mode of performance was to Frank Kerr: when the full-blown Frankie Venom finally emerged, he was Canada's unchallenged punk prince, and like all royalty he just seemed born to it. He couldn't help it. He'd have been punk even if the word hadn't existed for it.

Meanwhile, however, the band was kicked out of even Kerr's tolerant basement. The noise levels had reached a point where the cops had come calling, and the limits of the Kerr parents had finally been breached. The band was hauled upstairs and out. It was a blow – for Lewis, if they didn't have a basement to practice in, there might as well not be a band – but a temporary one. In March 1975, a new store opened at the corner of King and James streets called Star Records, and it soon become Teenage Head's world headquarters.

You couldn't have asked for a better location. King and James was at the hub of downtown walk-around traffic in Hamilton, and it was where kids in the mid-'70s did most of their hanging out, on weekends anyway. When Paul Kobak opened Star Records on a second floor at that corner, he began with four boxes of vinyl. Within nine months, Star had an inventory of 5,000. By 1978, there were 25,000 records in the store.

The intersection had history. For years prior to Star's opening, it was the place for Hamiltonians to go for some Saturday-afternoon excitement. Record stores, bars, head shops – all were at or around King and James. Future Teenage Head drummer Jack Pedler remembers hanging around the corner in the summer of '69 when he heard an unholy racket ring out: 'Fuck off!' some kid was shouting. 'Fuck you! Fuck *you*, you fuckin' *goof!*' Pedler, already a pro teenage musician and a former record shop employee himself, swivelled around to find the source of the blue streak. It was a skinny thirteen-year-old kid laying verbal waste to a group of much bigger, much older dudes who'd likely caused the provocation with a gratuitous sidewalk shove. When Pedler looked, they were shrinking from the sheer blast of the scrawny kid's tirade. 'That was my first glimpse of Frank Kerr,' Pedler says.

Kobak's cousin Mike Shulga had opened the original Star Records in Oshawa, and he suggested Paul – who'd been working with him – try his hand at taking the Star philosophy to new territory. The Star approach was born of a music geek's impatience with the way records were sold by the major chains and in department stores, which charged a lot of money for a narrow selection. Starting in Oshawa, Star offered cheaper records, a wider selection, used vinyl and service with expertise. It was a record lover's store run by record lovers, and it was inevitable that Gord Lewis and Steve Mahon would show up quickly after the doors opened.

Star was a bit of a dream come true. All that music, the underground rock stuff written about in *Creem* and *Crawdaddy* that had once been unattainable, was there. And Paul was clearly cool: into the same kind of music Lewis and Mahon were into, and able to point them to stuff they hadn't heard but he knew they'd like. For one half of Teenage Head, Star quickly became a hangout. At some point, Lewis or Mahon mentioned to Kobak they were in a band. He went to one of the basement rehearsals to hear them play. He was impressed. So impressed he invited them to practice in his record store while he looked for a more permanent rehearsal arrangement. So impressed he began to provide the guys with beer, money and transportation to practices and gigs.

Something like an actual manager – or at least a true believing benefactor – had landed. Lewis and Mahon accompanied Kobak on his buying trips to the Records on Wheels warehouse in Toronto. Before it had an actual storefront, Records on Wheels was quite literally that – a bus that parked outside of concert venues and sold records by whomever was performing inside. If Emerson Lake & Palmer were playing Massey Hall, they'd have Emerson Lake & Palmer on the bus. 'Don't go up the street to Sam's and A&A's,' owners and brothers Vito and Don Ierullo would yell, 'come to the bus! You'll get 'em first!' At the warehouse, Kobak would not only grab stuff that sold, like Supertramp's *Crime of the Century*, but also more obscure stuff he liked, such as Captain Beefheart's *Trout Mask Replica*.

'The guy was there for a lot of the start,' Mahon recalls. 'And bless his heart, he gave us the shirt off his friggin' back. He really was into the band big time. He knew that we had something. He was a music lover and knew what was out there. He knew what we were trying to do.'

Teenage Head's first gig was at a high school in 1975. With its members averaging around seventeen years old themselves, the band fit right in. It would be the only gig for the next four years that Kobak didn't arrange, haul the band to and hang around for. As Mahon says, he was an early and true believer, whose passion for the band's music, and belief in their potential, committed him to doing whatever he could to share the noise. 'They didn't have any transportation,' Kobak explains, 'and I guess I volunteered to help them out.' To the band, Kobak was a combination of Brian Epstein and Santa Claus. 'He had the record store, so he had money and an apartment,' Lewis says. 'We had free beer and a place to hang out. At that age you're always looking for a place to hang out, especially at wintertime. We practiced and rehearsed in his store sometimes. He took care of us.'

With the added help of a cousin of Kerr's, the band joined the musicians' union and began performing regularly, doing a blend of covers and originals, at any place an underage band

Steve Mahon and Paul Kobak.

could legally play. This meant a lot of high school dances and so-called coffee houses, and more than one appearance at a detention centre. The detention centre gigs quickly dried up, however, when Kerr got caught smoking a joint with one of the kids housed there. 'That was Frank, right?' Lewis says. 'He thought he was doing a cool thing because the kids wouldn't have been allowed anything. He had already started being the bad boy.'

If Kerr had already demonstrated ample bad boy tendencies offstage and prior to Teenage Head (Lewis, Stipanitz and Mahon all agree that Kerr was one of those kids other kids were magnetically drawn to because he just didn't give a shit), as the band's frontman he channelled it all into one sizzling firecracker of a persona. Using his microphone stand as a combination pole vault and butter churn, he'd jump, joust, jab and generally seem deliriously auto-electrified. Although his signature stunt quickly became a bowstring jump with his heels almost hitting the back of his head – like a man hit by a cannonball in the square of his back – even his regular repertoire of stage moves was cat-on-a-hot-tin-roof antic. Part Iggy, part Elvis, part Jagger and part Jerry Lewis, the total package was 100 percent Frank. Add to this the name he'd adopted thanks to something Stipanitz's mom used to say when her boy misbehaved – 'Son, you're full of venom!' – and the perennially kohl-blackened eyes he copped from Alice Cooper, and a flaming hunk of pure punk charisma was unleashed.

Kobak was undeterred. If detention centres were out, there were plenty of other places to play. No matter what, Teenage Head had to be heard. He found them rehearsal spaces. He held a Star Records first anniversary and hired the band to play it. He knew Delta Dave at the Delta Theatre and knew Dave liked punk, so he got them a show there. The Head quickly gained fans.

One thing that impressed Kobak from the beginning was the fact that, at a time when most of the bands in Canadian bars, high schools and college auditoriums were cover bands, Teenage Head was playing original material. 'They kept inventing songs and dropping songs,' Kobak says. 'They actually had many more tunes than were ever recorded. But they just kept dropping tunes and moving on with the ones they felt were best. Like Frankie's tune "I Want to Get Raped." Something like that. Everyone had their own ideas of fun.'

In 1977, Kobak had begun investing money into the renovation of a former recording studio called Plateau. Before other investors dropped out, ending that dream, Teenage Head had a place for several months where they could practice all day and night, every single day, if they wanted. 'That was when we started really, really writing,' Lewis says, 'and that was the main focus of everything. I started writing as soon as I could figure out how – once I'd learned chord progressions that worked and things that worked for other bands and other music and was able to identify it and then make it my own.'

Both Stipanitz and Mahon see the songwriting process as a key measure of the band's original, essential spirit of all-for-one equal opportunity.

As Stipanitz, who wrote the lyrics for the immortally catchy 'Picture My Face,' recalls: 'The substantial body of our work was written by the four of us. We all got equal writing credit and every-one really did contribute. Some people more or less. Frank and I did most of the lyrics and Gord did the music, but everybody would contribute to the arrangements. It really was a good functioning democracy. If you felt strong about an idea, you could be told to fuck off a few times instead of just once. If you really weren't that strong about it, you'd be quiet after the first "fuck off."'

Mahon insists he was the guy who got told to fuck off the most. 'Nobody's ideas were shot down as much as mine,' he laughs. 'I tried through the years to throw my two cents in, but it was tough because you had three other visionaries.'

The writing process would often begin with a riff, a little something Lewis had plucked out at home or in a basement rehearsal. 'The riff would come from the guitar,' Mahon explains. 'If we liked it, we'd say, "Play that again, Gord." That's what happened with "Let's Shake." Gord just did that little riff not knowing if it was any good or not, and we said, "That's cool. Play that again." Frank was good at that. Frank had a good ear.' According to Mahon, at least half of those early lyrics were written by Kerr and Stipanitz in a spirit of pure collaboration.

The first song Lewis wrote was 'Tearin' Me Apart,' a tune that blended many of his early influences. It took him months of work, but the song remains a staple of the band's live performances, an oft-cited punk classic and a perennial fan favourite. 'There's a Chuck Berry–type intro,' he says. 'There's a riff in there for the chorus, it changes key, it's got a solo that makes sense, there's a theme to it. Lyrically, it's a bit teenage, but as a song it's one of my favourites. When we recorded it in 2003 with Marky Ramone, at the end of the take he said, "I could play that song all day."'

Despite his devotion to the craft, songwriting never came easy to Lewis. He could never sit down and bang something out – the closest he ever came were the chords for 'Let's Shake.' 'But that was again just following a musical pattern,' Lewis says, 'a progression of chords and a sequence that makes sense musically and kinda goes around in a circle and comes back home. And I learned a lot of that from trying to learn other people's songs. I wasn't a good mimic. I would learn close to it, but the musical theory was still there, so I was able to adapt it and write my own songs from it.'

Lewis had a keen ear for precisely the kind of sound and structure a song needed, and these were invariably found in the songs of others that he loved. True to the rapacious and cyclical nature of pop music, his music was the product of diligent borrowing, rearrangement and juxtaposition. 'Tearin' Me Apart,' to cite just one example, fused different riffs from 'What Is Life,' by George Harrison, one of the first 45s Lewis ever bought, and the Badfinger song 'Andy Norris.'

'What I find fascinating in songwriting,' Lewis says, 'is that you can take different ideas, and while their forms and patterns are set, you can take them and mould them and make them into something that's totally original. And one of the keys to good songwriting is to not be afraid to use those rules. They're there for a good reason. They make sense theoretically. '

(Decades later, the self-taught guitarist enrolled in music-theory classes in Hamilton to find out how much of what he'd taught himself in practice held up as theory: 'I wasn't working, the band was split up and I wound up just taking this music course over at McMaster. It's funny, I remember going to that class and talking about classical music and theory and realizing that it's the exact same thing. It's all the same. It all matches, it all mixes and matches just fine.')

From the beginning, Lewis was convinced you weren't a real band if you didn't play your own songs. Even though songwriting was a struggle for him, it was a necessary struggle. And though difficult, he would never feel the same purity of expression he did in his late teens and early twenties. 'That's when I did a lot of writing – eighteen, nineteen, twenty. Which seems to be the age a lot of songwriters do their best stuff. Your brain must really work differently when you're that age. All pistons are going.'

The gigs Kobak arranged for the band made something abundantly clear: Teenage Head connected instantly and deeply with audiences. Fans were made at brushfire speed, and the same people – with more friends and friends of friends – kept coming back. 'We had a favourable audience no matter where we went,' Lewis remembers. 'Joe Strummer's advice to young bands was

"Make sure you've got a following. Find fifteen friends that are going to come to your show."'

For Kobak, Teenage Head became like a second management job. Or maybe a first. He'd take them to Toronto to the record warehouse where he picked up his stock, and let them hang around his apartment and drink as much beer as they wanted. He even bought them equipment: Kobak purchased Lewis's first prized Les Paul. And – perhaps most crucially – he took them to all the important shows in Toronto.

Like the Ramones. The first Ramones album, eponymously titled, landed in 1976, and it was an atomic bomb. Lean, sparse, aggressive three-chord two-point-five-minute rock, delivered by a band that looked like skinny high school biker-boy wannabes and with a tone as tongue-in-cheek as it was loud and snarky. The front cover, a black-and-white shot of these four snotty rockers leaning against a brick wall, wearing ripped jeans, Chuck Taylor high-tops and motorcycle jackets, is not only a classic piece of album art but a manifesto in snapshot: the '60s are over. Good fucking riddance.

Dave Desroches recalls his first encounter with that album: 'It all blew open when the Ramones album finally came out. It sounded like the pictures. That's the most important thing. Elvis sounded like his picture. Eddie Cochran sounded like his picture. The Ramones sounded like the picture. That was the key.'

The release of *Ramones* was a sign the world was ready for a new kind of rock, one that Teenage Head had been practicing for as long as the Ramones. Coincidentally, it should be noted that although the Head would forever be tagged as 'Canada's Ramones,' the fact is they were almost exactly contemporaneous, which merely strengthens the case for punk as a force that sprung in several places at once at the same time, and for the same reason: the kids were sick and tired of that old hippie shit. Time had come to kick out the jams. For the Head boys, *Ramones* was vindication of everything they'd imagined and been working for for nearly two years in those basements.

Jack Pedler, the future Teenage Head drummer who first noticed the thirteen-year-old Frank Kerr dispensing profanities on the corner of King and James in the summer of '69, next saw the kid on the stage in the basement of Duffy's Tavern in Hamilton. It was Teenage Head's very first bar gig, and they played the entire first Ramones album in sequence, song by song and side to side. Pedler was amazed: first, by the fact that the singer onstage was the kid he remembered from that street corner, and second, by the music.

'One of the first songs they did was "Beat on the Brat,"' Pedler remembers. 'And that was the first time I became aware of a different genre of music that was going down. At the time I was getting pretty dissatisfied with rock 'n' roll. There *was* no rock 'n' roll. It was this kind of music you have to sit down in a chair to listen to. So, wow: what's this "Beat on the Brat"? I'd never heard anything like that. I just knew there was something interesting coming around the corner.'

But Teenage Head's ostensible resemblance to the Ramones could undermine them, even in the beginning. The Ramones' Toronto debut was set for the New Yorker Theatre, run by promoter Gary Topp. The New Yorker had once been just a movie theatre, but inspired by *Blank Generation*, Amos Poe's documentary about the nascent New York punk and new wave scenes, Topp built a stage and started booking those same American bands. Paul Kobak, recognizing an opportunity for Teenage Head to take a stratospheric leap forward career-wise, tried to convince Topp to let the boys from Hamilton open for the boys from the Bowery. Topp was not convinced.

'At the time, in my musical mind, they were kind of similar to the Ramones and I wanted something different,' Topp says, wincing at the memory. 'I didn't want to have the same thing. It was a new scene going on and I just wanted something new. So we didn't book them. They were kind of pissed off about that.'

The New Yorker Ramones show was one of those events that's gone down in legend, especially among those who would emerge months later to define Toronto's punk scene. Everyone who was there (and probably some who weren't) call it a galvanizing experience, a call-to-arms and a confirmation of identity and purpose. They all had yet to meet, but Teenage Head was in the audience with future members of the Viletones, the Diodes, the B-Girls and Johnny and the G-Rays. The Ramones show drew everybody who'd been feeling the same sense of restless musical anticipation that Mahon, Lewis and Kobak had, and who had snapped up the first LP like a pop-cultural life preserver. They were the people who'd been reading the music magazines, scouring the more open-minded record stores, ears to the ground for the rumblings of something new, dangerous and different.

The show lasted barely thirty minutes, although in Ramones time that meant somewhere between fifteen and twenty numbers. The house wasn't quite full, and even less so when the gawkers, dilettantes and anthropologically curious were driven out by the sheer sonic force of the show. Legend has it Peter Gabriel, in Toronto to record an album, walked out disgusted after fifteen minutes, and much of the local press coverage at the time expressed the same disdain. But for those who loved and needed it, the Ramones show at the New Yorker was much more than a shit-kickingly good show. In the darkness, it was light at the top of the hill.

Lewis and Mahon still recall the night with a teenaged fan's giddiness. 'Do you remember us running back around the alley?' Mahon says, reminiscing with Lewis just before a Head gig in summer 2013. 'And listening to them talk about what they're going to do for an encore? We literally left when they finished their set. We went out the front doors around the alley behind the New Yorker right to the stage door and you could hear them talking: "We gonna do an encore? What'll we do? Maybe we'll do 'California Sun'?" What did we do then? Run back around and try to get in again? I don't know.'

'I think we wanted to meet them, so probably we went to the backstage door,' Lewis says.

'This was one of their first shows out of New York, so that was big for them too. Migrating out of New York, out of the Bowery. Hey, there's an audience for you guys in Toronto – come on up!'

The members of Teenage Head drove home to Hamilton that night with Kobak, cranked to the moon by what they'd just seen and heard. They'd be back in Toronto very, very soon.

Punk? Yeah. Sure. Why not?

The Ramones' New Yorker show wouldn't have had the impact it did if there wasn't already something in the air. And there was, but it was dispersed. In Hamilton, it floated around the members of Teenage Head, who went home more determined than ever to drive the band forward. In downtown Toronto, it trailed along behind a glammed-up young kid named Steven Leckie, who would later rename himself Nazi Dog and who sought out every show and band he could find that gave off even the faintest waft of danger. At the Ontario College of Art (OCA), it converged around a group of new young bands who, like Leckie, Paul Kobak and the members of Teenage Head, had heard the news from New York and – somewhat more faintly – from across the Atlantic. Rock music was rumbling restlessly with reactions against the old ways of making noise.

This is why, when the Doncasters, the Diodes and the Dishes got together for what was called the 3D Show at OCA, all of the above were present. It is also why that event was just as significant to the emergent Toronto punk scene as the New Yorker Ramones gig. If the Ramones brought those atmospheric cultural ions together, the 3D Show made them converge into a genuine collective force. Even in Toronto, where drinking on Sundays had only recently been permitted and heavy-metal cover bands ruled the rock 'n' roll bar scene, punk was about to break.

Over on Yonge Street, blocks east of OCA and smack in the middle of the strip where Neil Young, David Clayton-Thomas, Robbie Robertson and other big-brother-generation Canadian rock acts had made their bones, was a moderately revered traditional jazz club called the Colonial Tavern. Upstairs, it featured jazz and blues acts for slow-sipping contemplation. Downstairs, it had a room where just about anything went. It was cheap, unkempt and available for rent, and therefore a natural enclave in which punk could flourish, mushroom-like, in the dark. Appropriately enough, booking the Colonial Underground – nicknamed 'the Meat Market' – was the purview of a guy named Jimmy the Worm.

Here's a description of the Underground, on the occasion of one of the venue's first shows, in February 1977, given by Steve Leckie's band the Viletones. It's written by then nineteen-year-old would-be journalist Brad Spurgeon, who posted the unpublished piece decades later on his blog:

> I went to the club where they were to play about two hours before the proposed showtime. I went into the side door and down the stairs into the room which is called the Colonial Underground. It's a dirty room with room for about 200 people. There were only about twenty-five people there when I came in and they were mostly middle-aged and blue-collar workers. It is dimly lit and the walls are plastered and painted a very pallid green. The bar is at one end, the end by the entrance, and it is quite a large bar, for the size of the room.
>
> There's a stage along the wall on your right as you enter and the bar is on the left. The stage is about a foot off the ground and only about twelve feet wide and six feet deep, and there's a hole in the middle of it that hasn't been repaired. The owners of the bar can't afford to repair it.

Later, the bar would fill to capacity. In fact, when the Viletones gave their first gig at the Underground, following months of pioneering, inspired, DIY self-promotional antics – wearing band jackets before there was a band, stapling up band flyers before there was a band and crashing other bands' shows to draw attention to a band that didn't exist yet – the joint was packed. Again, as with the Ramones and 3D shows, everyone was there: members of the Diodes, future members, managers, scribes and stylish proto-punk scene-makers, and Teenage Head.

Steve Mahon, as natively gregarious as Steve Leckie was innately confrontational – at the Viletones' first gig, Leckie walked onstage, put a cigarette out on his arm, smashed a bottle, started lacerating himself and writhed around – remembers approaching Leckie in the spirit of how's-it-goin'-man rock solidarity. 'I said, "Hi, I'm Steve, how you doing?"' recalls Mahon. 'Goofy little Hamilton boy that I am, I went, "So, Steve, how do you spell

Steve and his hair. No other punk band got away with this.

your name? Because I spell mine with a 'P-H.'" He looks at me and says, "I spell my name F-U-C-K O-F-F.'"

Kobak, attuned to a potentially receptive opportunity for his boys, approached Jimmy the Worm to make the pitch for his band. Luckily for Kobak, the din in the bar was such that when Kobak said 'Teenage Head,' Jimmy heard 'Talking Heads.' By the time he realized his mistake, the band from Hamilton was already booked. Opportunity beckoned like that big hole in the Underground stage into which, in a matter of weeks, during one of the Head's first shows, Frankie Venom would disappear like an antic rodent, only to appear moments later from another hole. Says Leckie, 'Like a ferret he managed to find another exit and he came out another place on the stage. It was unbelievable. Kiss couldn't have done that.'

Getting into the Underground was imperative. Hamilton was getting small. Despite the loyalty of hometown supporters, who followed the band like a school of pilot fish wherever they went, the Head and Kobak knew the future – any future – depended on mobility and expansion. The mobility was provided by Kobak's boat-like '75 Thunderbird, and to begin with, expansion lay eastward on the QEW toward Toronto.

Time begins its warp-speed thing here. It's 1977, and the scene Teenage Head are about to enter – which would move from a few pre-punk gigs at the Beverley Tavern to the Colonial Underground, the Crash 'n' Burn (yet another basement), David's and finally the Horseshoe – would end on December 1, 1978, with the Head headlining that latter venue's very last punk night. Less than two years. A lifetime if you're in the middle of it, a whiplash turn of the rollercoaster if you were there and are now looking back. The experiential equivalent of a perfect, two-and-a-half-minute pop song. Punk time.

Before we delve into one of the most electrifying moments in Teenage Head's history – the minute they step onstage in Toronto and ignite – let's consider this 'punk' thing. Because from here on in, like it or buy it or not, Teenage Head will be labelled as a punk band. It's not a label any member of the band was ever comfortable with, nor were any of the more arguably authentic punk bands they shared the sign above the door with. If punk, as it's been retrospectively defined, had anything to do with political dissent, then Teenage Head fits about as comfortably as a stray cat in a dog kennel, for politics – or even dissent – was never part of the band's MO (apart, that is, from a general fuck-you to anyone who didn't get what they were doing). If punk, as it has also been retroactively identified, had anything to do with fashion, then Teenage Head also fires well wide of the strike zone. If you look at any of their pictures, even those taken after Lucasta Ross – visionary fan, fun facilitator and future B-Girl – convinced Frankie to ditch his Bowie shag in favour of a close-cropped shear, they're probably the least punk-looking 'punk' band of the era: Lewis, Mahon and Stipanitz all kept New York Dolls–like rock 'n' roll hair throughout the era, and Mahon even remembers performing at Crash 'n' Burn wearing bell-bottoms.

And musically? Not punk, not really. Teenage Head was primarily a hard pop-rock band, a Monkees-glam-and-rockabilly-influenced outfit with New York Dolls tightness, amplitude and attitude. But this last quality counts for much, at least in terms of proffering any punk claims to Teenage Head that actually stuck: they exuded fuck-it, don't-give-a-shit, love-us-or-leave-us attitude, and that truly is punk. This is why more than one observer of the band, looking back over the decades through the stifling layers of retrofitted punk orthodoxy and purism that has adhered to what was a mostly spontaneous expression of endearingly optimistic anti-fashion, has suggested that Teenage Head was one of the punkest punk bands of them all. Why? Because they truly didn't give a shit if they *looked* punk. And how punk is that?

'They would have been Cheap Trick if it hadn't been for the punk scene,' observes Bob Bryden, Kobak's successor at Star Records and eventual producer of the Forgotten Rebels. 'Frankie looks like a punk. The rest don't, never did. They never went out of their way to look punk except Frankie. If he'd been with three other guys like the other three guys in the Pistols or something, he would have fit right in.'

Bryden wasn't the only observer for whom Teenage Head evoked Cheap Trick, an American power-pop rock band that traded in a visually schizophrenic image, a knack for high-decibel melodiousness and fun to burn. Says Steven Leckie of his early impressions, 'The only band I could think similarly of was Cheap Trick. This certain tightness, the way the melodies went and the fact there's a massive public that love that goofiness.'

Liz Worth, whose 2011 oral history of the Toronto punk scene, *Treat Me Like Dirt*, was the first comprehensive history of the period to appear, agrees that the punk thing for Teenage Head was primarily circumstantial. When writing the book, she says, 'I realized it was really hard to talk about Toronto without talking about Hamilton, and Teenage Head has a very large part to do with that. And while they are definitely a Hamilton band, they're also a Toronto band, and that's unique in Southern Ontario. You don't see a lot of other musicians crossing over into both in that same way and being held on to by both cities.

'So they kind of fit into the scene in a very different way than other bands did, and even though everyone says they were very much a part of Toronto, I also got the sense that they felt very much outside. I do think they were outside in some ways but not in a bad way. It's just that they were so much further ahead than everybody in the punk scene and they just happened to come along at the right time for that scene to be there for them that they could kind of absorb and grow from. But if that scene hadn't been there, Teenage Head still would have existed. There were a lot of bands around at the time where, if there wasn't a punk scene, those bands never would have happened.'

'I almost think it doesn't matter,' Canadian punk historian Sam Sutherland says about the punk purity of Teenage Head. 'They were a punk band, and that kind of speaks as much to the incredibly wide net that was punk at that time. Look at the New York scene. If a band like Television came out now, people would not call them a punk band. Or a band like Blondie. What was punk about Teenage Head was that ethos, that drive, that kind of stripped-down approach that we now recognize as just being a rock band. But I think they were punk by association, and punk by execution.'

The band themselves now groan a bit over the term, although they recognize it gave them a boost they might otherwise have lacked. The punk thing, explains Lewis, 'was such a big influence on us and just encouraged us to do what we were planning on doing. It fuelled the fire, there's no doubt about it.' But, as Lewis says, Teenage Head came at the scene sideways – their songs were rooted in melody and thoughtful songwriting craft. For Lewis, certified perfectionist and dedicated musical self-improver, the most frustrating thing about the movement was its defiant amateurism: 'There's no growing in punk.'

'For me,' Mahon says, 'all the bands that came along during the punk-rock frenzy were 98 percent attitude and 2 percent talent. Mostly just kids ripping their jeans and spray-painting their hair. They all thought it was cool to not be able to play guitar. I hated most of it.'

For his part, Frank Venom wasn't too thrilled about how audiences behaved at punk shows. 'We used to get a lot of people who hadn't seen the band before,' he told me in 1992, 'and because they thought we were a punk band, would come out and slam dance, spit on us, throw beer bottles and stuff. We used to have two security guys travel with the band all the time. If anybody spit on me, or spit on Gordie or Steve, that was it. They were gone. They thought it was like the punk thing down in L.A., where it was just like crazy, bands like Screamer and stuff. We're not that type of band. That was the only part I didn't like. I didn't like being spit on. I still don't.'

On a personal note, permit me to intervene here with a pop-cultural confession. Much as I was drawn to punk, collected punk, dressed (sort of) punk and hoisted the punk torch whenever in the presence of anyone running the music down – much, that is, as I loved the *idea* of punk – I was really a closet power-pop rocker. Too much punk was based in noise, attitude and flamboyant DIY amateurishness for my taste, when what I really wanted – always wanted and still want – are hooks, melodies and tunes that lodge in your head and run around like nesting squirrels. Ergo, Teenage Head sounded like the ceiling of heaven itself crashing down.

If the punk cred debate continues to rage to this day among musicians, musicologists, record collectors and fans, it's because history's passage has only raised the stakes. Punk now stands as white-boy, guitar-bass-drums rock music's last stand. A revolution as much against the mid-'70s ossification of mainstream rock as it was political response, punk's insistence on restoring danger and threat to rock music – as Elvis had once done – was an ultimately doomed but inspirationally idealistic gesture. And that's why it mattered then and matters even more now. No longer the cultural tentpole it once was, rock has now comfortably retired to the boutique sidelines of popular music. But punk was its last gasp, the final spasm before the body expired twenty years after Elvis had first jolted it to mass cultural life. Punk is so passionately argued about because it was the last time – grunge being really only a post-mortem twitch – the music really mattered. And in this context, of restoring to rock music a sense of ballistic urgency, Teenage Head was indeed a punk band.

Kobak booked Teenage Head a series of mid-week gigs at the Colonial Underground. To the crowd of regulars who already gathered there – including members of the Viletones, the Diodes and other bands just starting up or soon to be – they were familiar: the friendly long-haired kids from Hamilton who came to see everything in that huge T-Bird. But no one was really ready when they actually hit the stage. Bear in mind, most of the bands in this embryonic scene hadn't been playing much longer than it took Paul Kobak to pick up the guys and equipment and drive in. The Viletones, who were a concept, a brand and a manifesto before they were a band, were only the most conspicuous example of just how unseasoned, musically, the scene actually was.

But the Head were, in a word, tight. Equipped with a complete set list of original songs – including 'Picture My Face,' 'Tearin' Me Apart,' 'Kissin' the Carpet,' 'Disgusteen' and 'Lucy Potato' – Teenage Head took the stage with a deadly combination of attitude, confidence and authority. Already well-seasoned as live performers and rehearsed to perfection, they were not nervous and they did not dawdle. Based on all recollections of those first Toronto gigs, the band, dressed in their customary collision of glam and punk accoutrements, just plugged in and exploded, Lewis assuming his imminently indelible stance with lowered head, feet apart and cascading hair, Mahon planted sturdily under a beaming smile, Stipanitz pounding away with frenetic precision and Frankie out front glaring, goofing, chest-puffing and generally making like a punk monkey on a Benzedrine splurge. It was loud, relentless and timed to clockwork precision.

The total Head package, however, was only partly sonic. As mercilessly irresistible as the music was, the band *looked* like they were born doing what they did. Four bone-skinny kids in denim and leather, two of them sporting spouting fountains of hair, one of these parted so the bass player could stare down the audience from behind a low-slung instrument with an inscrutably pleased grin, the other cascading fully over the guitarist's face so you had to watch the guy's body and hands, and a drummer who looked about twelve pounding the perfect bejesus out of his kit.

And then, in front, there was Frankie Venom, only three years out from behind his drums: black hair cropped Lou Reed short, black eyes deepened by rings of black, staring a smoking hole down the centre of the crowd, playing the mike stand like an organ grinder's monkey chained to a pole, at any time as likely to jump up and swing from a pipe in the ceiling as – at the Underground especially – disappear beneath a hole in the stage and pop up like a whack-a-mole just in time to sing the next line.

Which, it must be added, he never, ever, *ever* missed. Even if he ran to the back of a room and jumped up on a table – which he did as I was sitting there one night, sending us diving for our hard-earned stubbies – he would always be back up there and behind the mike just in time. It was a cartoon performance in real life, a gravity- and physics-defying demonstration of pure energy. This was perhaps the one thing about Teenage Head in perform-ance that could not be denied. Even if on the remote chance you did not like the music – even if, in the unlikely event, you didn't think the rest of the band was ferociously tight and cool to look at – you couldn't deny the power of Frankie Venom.

Although he's come to be one of the most enduring symbols of 100 percent pure punk spirit, it's generally agreed that Frank never intended to be a punk. He just couldn't help it. Going back to his childhood, Kerr was an irrepressible shit-disturber, impulsive instinct-follower and uncalculated free spirit. He couldn't be contained, didn't care what anyone thought and would do anything for a laugh: properties that would serve his punk persona well, but which were apparently embedded in his DNA long before they synched so magically with the musical ethos. Frank not only had to be constantly coached to look properly punk, he always bridled under the label.

Unlike Nazi Dog Leckie – 'Steven was always looking in the mirror,' Mahon remembers – Venom was barely interested in appearances. 'With Frank we had to say, "Don't wear that,"' Mahon says, '"Try wearing this." He didn't really care. He did care, but in a James Dean cool kind of way, like, "What the fuck, I look good." We had to sort of Doll him up at the start. "How about a little eye makeup, Frank?"'

'He would go up there and he'd perform,' Lewis recalls, 'and even when it was off, it was still entertaining.' During one show, with the band performing 'Take It,' Venom refused to sing the eight lines of the song, and improvised entirely new lyrics. 'What he was coming out with was incredible,' Lewis says. 'It was very creative, made sense and had nothing to do with the original lyrics. But the people that were there were hearing something they'd never heard and would never hear again. No matter what shape Frank was in, that would happen at a show. He would say something or do something that was worth the price of admission.'

Lewis also came to appreciate the professional-development opportunity Venom's goofing around presented. 'When Frank walked off to do something or go into the crowd, you learned to improvise,' Lewis explains. 'You quickly realized the song wasn't going to continue because the singer wasn't there anymore. I remember thinking, "Okay, we got a long break here, we'll just kind of play around." Again, learning the hard way how to improvise.'

And that was it. Out of the gate, they were all there. Perfect, and what most of the musicians watching wished they were. Who *were* these guys?

'Teenage Head were the torch,' musician-broadcaster Bob Segarini says of those first gigs. 'The light in the dark that the kids followed. Because they were an undeniable band. They had an undeniable lead singer, they had undeniable music and they managed somehow to mingle rockabilly, punk, mainstream rock and show business without any of those particular interests taking over. It was like a soup of these influences that made them incredibly unique.'

Filmmaker Colin Brunton, veteran employee of the New Yorker, had heard plenty about the band the time he finally caught them a couple of months after the Colonial gigs. 'The thing that was startling about them,' Brunton says, 'that was different from the other bands, was that they weren't a clichéd, spontaneous let's-start-a-band like the Viletones, and they weren't arty dope smokers like the Scenics, who were around as long as the Diodes. They just didn't surface; when they came on, they could *play*.'

Don Pyle, future producer and musician (Crash Kills Five, Shadowy Men on a Shadowy Planet), was an underage suburban teenage punk fan who always suspected these guys with the long hair he'd been seeing at shows for months were part of a band. At the Colonial, his suspicions were confirmed.

'They could really play and were more advanced than all the other bands, and that really gave them a power," he recalls. "It's funny how you could instantly tell which bands were the stars, and with Teenage Head you just *knew*. These guys were amazing. Just as great as any of the other bands I was listening to.'

Like many present for the Head's inaugural Toronto gigs at the Underground, Freddy Pompeii had also been seeing the guys around for some time. Originally from Philadelphia, Pompeii was the guitarist for the Viletones, the band that played a week or so before in the same basement.

'They were way better than the Viletones musically,' Pompeii recalls. 'They had a great backbeat. That was the first thing that hit me. Frankie Venom's style. He was skinny and had short hair, real arrogant attitude. Gord Lewis with his hair down in his face, the bass player with the long curly locks. They looked like the right kind of band. They did "Somethin' Else," which is an Eddie Cochran song, and they really kicked ass with it. I was very impressed with them and liked them right off the bat. Even got kinda jealous about it.'

Curiously enough, for a guy whose competitiveness was already notoriously established, Steven Leckie was *not* jealous of Teenage Head. He was in awe. Instead of seeing the Hamilton invaders as usurpers, he saw them as validation: that the local punk scene he imagined could be as musically exciting as it was culturally cutting-edge, that it was possible to have the ability to back up the attitude. He wasn't intimidated by the Head, he was inspired by them. Even more remarkable, they were all nice guys who got along with each other and everyone else (including, it would quickly turn out, Leckie). Unlike the terminally squabbling Viletones, Pompeii recalls of Teenage Head, 'They were like family to each other. They were finishing each other's sentences.'

Stipanitz remembers those first Toronto shows fondly and vividly. He also remembers how quickly the out-of-towners were accepted and adopted in Toronto: 'We played so much better and were very tight, well-rehearsed. In hindsight we may have been too good for the scene, but we were accepted. And we knew how to have a good time. That contributed as well. We made friends, gained the respect of the other people and never looked down on them or said, "You can't play worth a shit."'

Promoter Gary Topp, who'd first turned down the band's request to open for the Ramones, was similarly amped when he finally saw the band play. 'They were real,' he says. 'They were real like the Viletones, but in a different way. Frankie had a similar outlandish stage presence as Steven Leckie, but Frankie reminded me of Iggy Pop. But in a more straight-ahead rock 'n' roll kind of band. There was more of a '60s, garagey feel to them.'

In their transition from the basements of family homes to the basement of the Colonial Tavern in Toronto, Teenage Head had rung some ears. Punk or not, they had arrived. With endearing immodesty, Mahon remembers that first night on Yonge Street: 'Our first Toronto show was right around exam time for the boys at Mohawk College, and I think Frank had an exam that weekend or something and he just went, "Fuck it, we're rock stars now." 'Cause when we did that Colonial Underground, we felt like, you know – this is Toronto. *This is Toronto.* And all the other bands were there and they knew that we knew we got it. We were the best thing they were going to get.'

1978–79: The Sweet Spot

Ask Gord Lewis, and he'll tell you things were never better for Teenage Head than during the year and a half following the first gigs at the Colonial. The band had not only stormed the nascent punk scene in Toronto but played a role in galvanizing it, the fan base was crazily loyal and steadily building, the Hamilton kids were liked and accepted, and Lewis and his band felt surrounded nightly by people – both musicians and audience members – who got and loved what they were doing. Enough money was coming in to pay gas, keep drinking and focus on the music, and everything was jumping on a huge shit pile of fun.

'It was really healthy,' Lewis says. 'That was one of the best times of my life, that whole brief little punk-rock scene before we started to get big, before an album came out. That was my favourite time. And we were really focused. Or young. Twenty-one, twenty-two, lots of energy. Lots of fresh young livers. Could drink a lot of beer and still be okay the next day.'

Frankie Venom, almost instantly recognized as the new scene's most magnetic performer, was likewise having a blast: 'We would play for like a hundred bucks then and we were happy, you know? We got free booze and a hundred dollars. What else could you ask for, right?'

I don't remember where I first saw the band, though it was probably in the Rotters Club, yet another glorified basement bar, on Bank Street in Ottawa. I do remember, however, that I was smacked upside from the very first time, and especially by the pop-perfect 'Picture My Face.' I made a point of catching them wherever and whenever I could. I simply *had* to hear those fucking songs again. And again. Even if it meant cranial injury, and I don't mean from Teenage Head's propensity for scalp-lifting amplification. I refer to the night in 1978 or '79 I walked out of the Rotters from a Head show and promptly got the bridge of my nose broken in a beating prompted more or less by the fact that the beaters – who'd just left a country-and-western/classic-rock dive called the Hitching Post – didn't like the look of us middle-class university punk wannabes and thought we'd best be blended into the sidewalk. My nose still bears the mark of striation, a wound incurred in the name of getting my Head fix.

I was hardly alone in my overwhelming affection for the band. Bob Segarini had been living in Toronto for a year or so when he first saw Teenage Head. A founding member of the Wackers, he was an inveterate music lover and player who thrived on energy bubbling up from the underground. It's what had led him to the L.A. strip in the early and mid-'60s, and to Montreal's off-the-beaten-path rock clubs in the early '70s. At the Colonial Underground later that decade, he once again answered the call of the urban wild. 'I moved to Toronto thirty-six years ago because I was so engaged by what was going on musically here,' Segarini says. 'And I remember I used to go on and on about the new wave and punk scene to anybody that would listen to me.'

Segarini had seen a lot of performers go to the edge before – opening for Jim Morrison and the Doors had sealed that – but he'd never seen anything quite like Frankie Venom. 'You never knew if Frankie was going to hit the first sentence in the verse because he was too busy hanging from a pipe over the stage or something,' says Segarini. 'And they learned to live with that to a fault. I mean, you could *not* shake that band. They never stopped in the middle of a song. They never looked at each other like they didn't know what to do. They were like the band on the *Titanic*. "We're going down? Fuck it. Let's keep playing." And that was a real inspiration to a lot of people.'

Venom always worked on two completely different perform-ance levels, Segarini points out. There was the show he was giving, of course, but he was also looking for ways to amuse himself. Always looking to stave off onstage boredom. 'If you watched his eyes when the band played, they'd be roving around the room. *Is there a PA stack I can climb? Somebody whose body I can throw myself at? Maybe I should tackle Gord in the middle of his solo?* His mind was always going,' says Segarini.

Although it was always part of Teenage Head's master plan to play and record original songs, they did make some concessions to doing covers. But even those songs were head-turners. They were songs that rooted the band in a very particular history, less crowd-pleasing retro-solid-gold fixes than a pathway to the past that had created not only them but their own immediate influences. Past the Dolls, that is, beyond Iggy and MC5, to some of the original rock 'n' roll punks.

The covers were also tactical. Aware that the Toronto underground scene was not the same as playing country or classic rock bars in Whitby or Niagara Falls, the band customized their set list according to the perceived local appetite for all-original material. So they picked up a little rockabilly to soften the transition to their own material, or maybe added some classic jukebox rock to orient audiences to their roots. Venom, his radar always alert to crowd vibes, was especially sensitive to what the bar patrons were prepared to hear, and would often make last-minute changes to the song list. The strategy might have been situational, but it only sharpened the Head's versatility. In time, they'd play Eddie Cochran near as blisteringly as Eddie Cochran did, and to this day the band's covers of early rock 'n' roll songs render even the oldest chestnuts as hot as the freshly roasted variety.

'Whoever was feeding Teenage Head,' says Ralph Alfonso, former Diodes manager, 'their choice of covers was brilliant. They're doing Nashville Teens, Eddie Cochran, all this amazing stuff. Where they didn't quite have it together was the marketing savvy that the Toronto bands had. The Toronto bands were a little more worldly wise in that sense. The Head would become more adept at that a little bit further down the line as the right people came into their orbit. But unfortunately for them, because it was so obvious they were the sure bet, some of the wrongish people may have orbited a little earlier.'

The 'wrongish' people Alfonso is referring to may have been of the mendacious managerial variety, but other kinds of wrongish people made appearances on the emerging scene as soon as it started getting some media traction. Moreover, the media attraction itself was frequently wrongish, focused far more on the superficially sensational aspects of the urban-music subculture – ever more frequently being called 'punk' – than the music, its origins or politics. One of the earliest news stories generated by the scene

Teenage Head: Frank and Gord foreground, Steve and Nick behind.

appeared in the *Toronto Sun* in 1977, the night after hell came bursting down the stairs at the Meat Market.

It was a Diodes show and all the usual suspects were there: the Viletones, Teenage Head, Lucasta Ross. Upstairs, veteran bluesman Long John Baldry was settling down for an acoustic set, and he complained to management that the noise coming up from the Underground was too loud. Depending on which account one encounters, this was either a polite request that elicited an impolite 'Fuck you,' or all hell broke loose without warning. Either way, the Colonial Underground was quickly aswarm with large men — reportedly 'from Detroit' — bearing Altamont-issue pool cues (and, by some accounts, baseball bats), which they started swinging. The Diodes fled the stage for the street, and several people in the audience got whacked and bloodied. From behind his tape machine in the corner of the club — he was recording as many gigs as possible — Paul Kobak noticed a bouncer poking his buddy Slash Booze in the belly with a pool cue and ran over to see if the man might listen to reason and cool it. When Kobak came to, he was in hospital. At one point, he was in hospital with his head bandaged looking at his picture — in hospital with his head bandaged — on page ten of the *Sun*. If the subsequently unshakeable association of local punk rock with violence had been made – never mind the fact the violence was perpetrated to protect an acoustic set by a bearded old hippie blues guy – it had also been made with a singularly fortuitous reportorial faux pas: according to the *Sun*, the band making the noise in the first place had been Teenage Head. As Kobak told author Liz Worth nearly thirty years later, 'Oh well. Free publicity is free publicity.'

In the following year and a half, the scene – still relatively contained and mobile – would find homes primarily in three other clubs beyond the Colonial: the Crash 'n' Burn, opened by Alfonso and the Diodes in a warehouse below the provincial Liberal Party headquarters on Pearl Street just south of Queen and Duncan; David's, a gay disco northwest of Yonge and Wellesley that boasted an apparent outsiders' affinity with the new music; and the Horse-hoe Tavern, a venerable Queen Street music institution that handed over new music programming to Garys Topp and Cormier, who had closed the profit-challenged rep cinema cum concert hall the New Yorker to focus exclusively on live music.

But on December 1, 1978, that era would end, mostly, when the Horseshoe held its final, standing-room-only punk show before turning to less contentious, rabble-rousing fare. The so-called Last Pogo was the ending most fondly remembered by all involved (both on- and offstage). The police arrived to stop the show – for rowdiness, presumably – just as the headliner, by then the most famous, popular and notorious of the local bands, was wrapping up the fail-safe crowd-starter 'Picture My Face.'

Teenage Head was closing the door on a few eras that night: on the virginal heyday of the Toronto punk scene, on Queen West as the locus of the movement and on their own moment of being exactly what they wanted to be in exactly the way they wanted it. Things would never be quite the same for the scene or its most dynamic and seemingly starbound band again. Even better times than this lay ahead, but so did worse. For the moment, however, with the crowd spilling out onto the cold sidewalk with 'Picture My Face' reverberating in their skulls, Teenage Head were the best live-rock act certainly in the city, probably in the country and – fuck, why not? – perhaps the world.

Paul Kobak still remembers the morning his phone woke him in bed. It was the summer of 1977. Someone named John Brower from Toronto was on the line, and he was wondering if Kobak might bring his band to a rehearsal space on Danforth Avenue for an audition. Brower had a partner named Jack Morrow, and they were interested in taking on Teenage Head.

The band had already recorded a five-song demo tape in Hamilton – featuring a version of 'Picture My Face' heavy on the tambourine – but it hadn't yielded any of the things Kobak had hoped for: no recording contract, no major gigs, tours or interest in other parts of Canada or, especially, the U.S. He told the guy on the phone he'd get back to him.

Brower, it turned out, was a major player. A veteran Toronto music promoter, he had organized the Varsity Stadium gig in 1969 at which John Lennon had headlined, and brought Led Zeppelin to town for their first Canadian date. Never mind that the Lennon gig had been, for some observers, a clusterfuck, Brower was clearly a connected guy. Despite looking nothing like a punk-band manager – he was an older guy of hippie vintage with a full head of curly hair – he seemed like the perfect person to bump the band up out of basement bars and into the international spotlight. Kobak talked the boys into doing the audition, but only after he'd had a lawyer draw up a contract making him Teenage Head's official manager for two years.

To paraphrase Lennon, they passed the audition. Brower and the even older, even straighter-looking, completely grey-haired Morrow, whose resumé reportedly included some carnival barking and discount TV retailing, took over drawing up the band's career game plan and, for the moment, everyone was convinced the Emerald City was at hand.

The ubiquitous Steven Leckie and the Viletones were also at the rehearsal space that day, and the Nazi Dog had an idea. Why not drive down to New York City and see if CBGB owner Hilly Kristal would book the Head and the Viletones for a Canadian punk gig? It might have been the helium effect of just having signed with Brower and Morrow that helped such a screwball suggestion make sense, but make sense it did, and a few days later Leckie, Lewis, Mahon and a couple of Star Records regulars were driving Kobak's T-Bird toward Gotham. They hadn't called ahead first, for fear of being turned down flat over the phone. Besides, Leckie was a firm believer in the authenticating power of image, so he dressed in full Dog regalia – spiky collar, head-to-toe leather, pointy boots – for the ten-hour drive. When they announced themselves as punk rockers from Canada, they wanted Kristal to know they meant business. 'Leckie said to me, "We're going to go to New York,"' Mahon remembers. '"You guys will be the talent. We'll be the fucking show."'

They arrived outside of CBGB by mid-afternoon. Kristal was there, and agreed to let the bands play, provided they understood they weren't going to get paid. No problem. For Leckie, Mahon and Lewis, who'd been tracking the role Kristal's club had played in the careers of bands like Johnny Thunders' Heartbreakers and the Ramones, simply getting a gig there was payment enough. They piled back in the car and headed home to Toronto to get ready for the big time. When word spread among the other Toronto bands, they scrambled to hop on the wagon. By the time Teenage Head and the Viletones were loading up to return to CBGB, they were followed by the Diodes, the Dents and the Curse. It had become a Canadian punk showcase.

The shows, covered by mainstream press like *Melody Maker* and *Variety*, came off smashingly well, even considering Leckie had to be briefly hospitalized after an especially vigorous onstage self-mutilating stunt, and considering Frankie's mid-set decision to jump up on the amplifiers and use the club's ceiling pipes as a jungle gym. Deborah Harry and Andy Warhol were reported to be among the enthusiastic crowd, and the whole thing seemed to confirm that Canadian punk rock was not only world-class but about to burst through the basement ceiling.

Lewis and Mahon both recall the New York trip, summer of '77, as the highest moment of that sweet season. CBGB was the Emerald City of their rock Oz, where the bands that had inspired and motivated them most had made their bones. And they not only played the legendary CBGB, they played the shit out of it.

Back home, the escalators to the next level all seemed up and running: both the *Toronto Star* and the *Globe and Mail* featured stories about how Canadian punk had invaded and taken New York – proving, once again, that the best way to get Canadian attention is by getting American attention first – and both papers played up the 'punk pilgrimage' big time. *Maclean's* arranged to have the Viletones shot for a cover story on Canada's emerging punk scene, and Kobak's phone was ringing off the hook with offers from agents wondering who the hell this band was and when could they get them?

The newly signed management team of John Brower and Jack Morrow must have felt as though they'd discovered the Beatles just before they finished up that last set at the Cavern Club. Here was Canada's hottest young band, just seconds away from breaking out. But Brower's and Morrow's own connections would also be a boon. After Morrow, who had seen some success as the manager of the Toronto-based early-'70s pop-rock band Abraham's Children, contacted his old acquaintance David Marsden – the renowned Canadian FM DJ who'd left CHUM-FM to start his own alternative music station, CFNY – songs from the Head's five-song demo tape were actually played over the airwaves.

Accounts vary as to how and precisely how long Brower and Morrow were circling the scene before closing in on Teenage Head, but some memories of the time recall seeing both men – conspicuously older than most punk-club clientele – hanging out well before they latched on to Hamilton's favourite prodigal sons. It would probably be sometime around March 1977 that the men's ears might have pricked up punkwise, because that's the month England's already globally notorious Sex Pistols signed with A&M Records in front of Buckingham Palace for a gobsmacking £75,000. With that kind of money potentially on the table, it wasn't necessary for either Brower or Morrow to appreciate punk or even understand it. All they had to do was sign it.

'When the Pistols took down all that money in England,' Mahon says, 'the story was Brower wanted to do the same thing. And word hit the street: who's the best punk band in Toronto?

Brower got back, "Teenage Head." "All right, that's what I want. I want Teenage Head then."'

To demonstrate both his resolve and his tactics, Brower once invaded a Teenage Head show with ready-made posters and banners, and plastered the venue in a manner that told everyone there the band they were watching were already stars. 'He wanted to sign a punk band and get some money from a record deal,' Stipanitz explains. 'He was an opportunist, a businessman. Came on strong. He wanted us to know he knew how to be a manager.'

Don Pyle, the teenage fan, amateur photographer and future musician who'd been present since the first chords came crashing up from the Underground, noted Brower's and especially Morrow's presence in the clubs immediately. 'Once Jack Morrow came on the scene,' Pyle says, 'he was at all the shows, and he would stand and watch them and be kinda like their dad at a party, where he'd go around and ask you, like, "Hey! You having fun? They sound great!"

'I thought that because he was older that he knew what he was doing. I thought, "Okay, he's going to help them." He definitely came across as like a professional. He was flirtatious with the guys and I just imagine it was a Brian Epstein kind of thing where it's like, you know, he probably adored them and saw dollar signs too.'

Brower took to TV to explain to Canadians what all the musical fuss was about. 'Punk rock is the rock 'n' roll of today,' Brower told CBC Television. 'It's this new generation's expression of their frustrations and aspirations. I don't think it's a fad. I think it's the beginning of a new approach to music. I think that very shortly we'll see records in the Top 10 in America by punk rock and new wave bands, and after that the floodgates will be open.'

As for his contribution to this dam-busting, Brower said, 'I think Teenage Head are on the threshold at this point of making it. They've crystallized the audience here and in New York. They have come through with solid music and they'll be recording very shortly. And I think from then on you'll see them as a concert touring act with legitimate recording success. I think that we're right up there.'

Kobak was still the band's nominal manager, but he was willing to relax his grip on the reins a bit in the face of experience and age: 'Jack was twenty-five years older than me and had more expertise talking on the phone to lots of different people. That's what I needed.'

As a smooth operator, Morrow impressed just about everybody. He talked a good game, got along famously with everyone he met, was connected up to the sideburns and understood that the art of creating a standout sensation lay in shameless and relentless branding and promotion. This was how he'd worked with Abraham's Children during that band's brief bubble of pop popularity in the early '70s, and it was how he was obviously going to work with Teenage Head, only that much harder. More than anything, he seemed to have a plan. A map to get the band to stardom.

That August, Morrow, Brower and Kobak tore a page from the Malcolm McLaren promo book and staged an event in which Teenage Head, assembled conspicuously in front of a Rolls-Royce borrowed for the occasion, filed for a $25 million insurance claim. 'We see it as a necessity,' Brower told the *Toronto Star.* 'There's so much violence in punk rock, you never know what's going to happen.'

Or what's *not* going to happen. Despite Brower's boasts and bravado, Teenage Head didn't land a record-breaking label deal, and even radio play proved a tough sell. The clubs were still packing out for the shows, but the escalator had stalled. Maybe this punk thing wasn't so sure after all. I mean, weren't the Sex Pistols dropped by A&M – unamused by the lads' offstage and on-air antics – within two weeks of that blockbuster signing?

'Brower was just looking for a good kill,' says Mahon, 'because it worked for the Pistols. From what I gather, the money didn't come quick. Brower was like, "Okay, now I've got Teenage Head. Let's get them into a studio, let's get a deal, let's get a million dollars, see ya!" Whereas Jack was in it for a longer haul. He obviously wanted to manage us. He wanted to see how far he could take this thing, and it wasn't just to get a cheque from A&M. Maybe he was smart enough to realize that if you're looking for a quick money fix, then maybe that's not going to happen in Canada.'

In the scene, the hovering, persistent presence of Brower and Morrow instilled suspicion in many. Part of it had to do with the men being conspicuously older than everybody else, and some of it had to do with Brower's perceived legacy as a promoter of crisis-plagued music events. But to a lot of people, the two men just seemed wrong for the band, and they said so.

Gord Lewis recalls his former managers with far more harshness than his bandmates. 'If he wasn't so crooked,' Lewis says now, 'Brower would have been a good manager, I think. He had the right instincts. But they weren't trusted by anybody. We were even told, "Don't get involved with these people," and we didn't listen, mainly because there was nobody else who wanted to get involved.'

John Brower eventually walked away. Jack Morrow did not. He would be Teenage Head's manager for the next six years, and his legacy with the band would prove one of the most disputatious aspects of its history. Now deceased and unavailable for first-hand appraisal, accounting or rebuttal, Morrow exists only in people's memories and impressions of him, and there are almost as many of those as there are people who remember him.

Jimi Bertucci had known Morrow for years by the time his former manager signed Teenage Head. Bertucci had been in Abraham's Children, and his experience with Morrow was eerily similar to what would transpire over the next six years with Teenage Head.

'Jack was a selfish person,' Bertucci says. 'A very selfish person. He had a good brain as far as recognizing something that could eventually become something, but again for his own selfish reasons. We had the same ingredients that Jack saw in Teenage Head. He saw four good-looking young guys that were playing something with potential. Didn't matter what it was – Jack didn't care because Jack had tin ears.'

Bertucci's band had put their fate in Morrow's hands for half a dozen years. When Bertucci discovered Morrow wasn't entirely forthcoming when it came to giving the band their contractual due, he quit. As far as he was concerned, Abraham's Children had been working their asses off and not getting paid what they were supposed to be paid. 'You have to understand something about Jack,' Bertucci says. 'He was a great promoter. As much as he did bad things – and I'm sure later on in life he regretted that – Jack was a really good promoter. He could put a band in the right place and sell them. Jack was a salesman. He started off by selling televisions down on Yonge Street.'

Others put a more generous spin on Morrow's talents. 'Jack Morrow was the master,' Diodes manager Ralph Alfonso remembers. 'The guy was a genius. I mean, the stuff he did for the Head was unbelievable. Jack and Paul Kobak created this sort of rolling event thing, where every gig was an event. You got this Teenage Head passport and you got it stamped at each gig. I remember at the time admiring him, like, "Genius at work here." Every conceivable promotion, scam, whatever, to get people in through the door. Eventually they were making thousands and thousands of dollars. Probably making five grand a night. That was a machine.' Morrow opened an office at 526 Queen Street East. One of the first promo items he made were T-shirts that read 'Blow my jets, I'm a Teenage Header.' Lewis hated them.

As a music business veteran, Jack Morrow corresponded to a type Bob Segarini was already all too familiar with. 'I partied with them and they were a hell of a lot of fun,' Segarini recalls, 'but I would never have done business with any of them, for the very reasons that other people have stated. You could sit down with Jack or any of these guys and they could explain to you very reasonably and very rationally why they could take money, and it made perfect sense when they said it. Although I disagree with it, I can understand why these guys didn't feel any remorse or that they were doing anything wrong. Morrow didn't feel any guilt simply because in his mind, if it wasn't for him, they wouldn't be making any money.

'But Jack, I mean, come on,' Segarini laughs. 'Jack was a *playa*. He did do some pretty awesome things for Teenage Head. He fought for those guys. He made sure they got their way. What he did that was not kosher was take advantage of his position.'

If Morrow's reputation preceded him with so many people I spoke with, it hadn't reached Al Mair by the time Teenage Head's manager approached him to discuss signing with Mair's label, Attic Records. It was a bold gambit and looked like smart strategy. Home to acts like Anvil, Lee Aaron and Triumph, Attic was quickly becoming known as the most vibrant and market-savvy Canadian label in the country, and hitching the Head to Attic seemed a logical way to strengthen that springboard to greater stardom and maybe even a leap right over the border.

'When I first met Jack Morrow he was very charming,' Mair remembers. 'And talked a good game. Things like making a special event wherever they played. Jack would go in in the afternoon with the paper banners to dress the bar for that night to make it kind of unique. Very creative guy in that regard. We didn't know his background, so we took him at his word.'

Mair's partner at Attic was Tom Williams. He also remembers Jack Morrow with a special clarity. 'Jack was a con man,' Williams states. 'Let's put it right out there. Jack did everything in his power to make that band happen. And that meant stealing and lying and doing whatever had to be done to get them out there. That's how Jack lived his life. He didn't know how to do anything from A to B; he had to go around in a circle and he had to make it more complicated and he was brilliant, but he was unable to do things in a straight manner.'

Lindsay Gillespie also worked at Attic. He'd known Morrow for years by the time Teenage Head fell under his management. Gillespie also worked at CFNY in the station's early years, and later became Teenage Head's full-time record company promo rep. Much as he loves Teenage Head – whom he calls 'Canada's Clash' – he thinks they would have sunk long before they did if it wasn't for Jack Morrow.

'He was a hustler,' Gillespie admits. 'He was probably hustling Frank Sinatra. And Jack wasn't a kid at this time either, so he knew how to hustle. He knew when to buy beer for someone and how to collect on that. Just a really good manager and promoter. He knew how to work me as a promo guy because the manager is the guy who gets the record company fired up to go out and actually sell records. Any time they had promo wear, I had a jacket and so did the whole record company. The band was groomed to do what it took, but I wouldn't say it ever compromised their integrity in any way as a hard rock or a punk band. They didn't compromise ever.

'Jack was a hustler first and a manager second,' Gillespie went on. 'And I don't mean that in any negative way. He knew how to get things going. He would eat, sleep and drink Teenage Head. Up early in the morning and late at night, always at the shows. He was the total front guy. Everybody had T-shirts, everybody had buttons. You couldn't get within fifty feet of him without getting a button that said "Teenage Head." No matter how old you were, who you were, somehow there was a button stuck on your jacket when you got home.'

During his years spent in rock radio in Canada, Gillespie's former boss David Marsden had crossed paths with Jack Morrow many times. It was only natural then that when Marsden started the alt-rock station CFNY, Jack would alert him to his new prospect.

'Jack Morrow was crazy,' Marsden says with a chuckle. 'If Teenage Head were an assemblage of punk rockers who were over the edge and just went out there and beat their music until some people paid attention, Jack was the manager who did the same thing. Over-the-top and outrageous. And he had a very persuasive way, could probably sell just about anything. He had that ability. He was a guy who just loved what he did, and he loved the bands he had, particularly Teenage Head.

'Jack never cared about what anyone thought about what he was doing or how he was doing it,' Marsden elaborates. 'Very confident. He believed in himself and believed in what he did, and he was going to go out there and make it happen. That was a time before we had a lot of famous Canadian rock stars, but that never seemed to interfere with his concept that he was going to make this band very famous. The fact that we're still talking about them today I believe has something to do with Jack's attitude back then. He set that whole thing in motion.

'Someone in the industry recently said Jack was his own worst enemy. I think that's probably true. I actually believe he meant well. The murkiness comes from the fact that sometimes Jack would go too far in regards to how he promoted the band. I honestly believe his efforts were sincere, but his oddities overwhelmed people.

'But he put the music out there and the band had some pretty solid ideas," Marsden continues. "So here I am in the year 2013, and I'm doing a radio show where the station owners are kind enough to let me pick and play what I want, and I'm still getting requests and playing Teenage Head.'

These conflicting views aside, by all outward appearances, and especially if you were nineteen or twenty years old and it looked like this older dad dude guy was going to get you to the rock-star level you'd always dreamt of, Jack Morrow seemed like exactly the right guy for the job. Particularly when he announced what everyone else had just about given up expecting to hear – Jack Morrow had actually arranged for Teenage Head to record their first album. Finally, the world was going to hear what all those people who'd gathered in all those dank basement bars already knew: Teenage Head was one of the best rock bands of its day.

The Grit and the Glory: Into the Studio

The announcement of an album deal came at a time of buffeting good and bad news for Teenage Head, a kind of hug-and-slap pendulum the band would eventually come to accept as normal – at least for them.

The Head had already recorded a single version of the sublime 'Picture My Face.' That version still remains many fans' favourite recorded Head song and, at least until Ramones producer Daniel Rey re-recorded it, along with other signature tunes, on *Teenage Head with Marky Ramone* in 2003, the closest thing on record to hearing the band live.

Morrow had somehow got money for the single, released by Inter Global Music, from Epic, distributed by CBS. The Epic deal was for only the one 45, and there was no money to package and distribute it.

Packing his T-Bird full of 'Picture My Face' singles and his pocket with a $200 cheque from Jack – money owed to a Vancouver DJ for some prior professional service rendered – Kobak headed west. Along the way, he dropped the single at every potentially responsive broadcasting venue he could think of before finally walking through the door of CFOX. There he handed both single and cheque to the DJ, extended Morrow's warm and personal thanks, and hopped back eastward. By the time he arrived back in Hamilton, 'Picture My Face' had been picked up by several stations across the country, all because it had landed in medium rotation first on CFOX. Sometimes, it would seem, even owing money pays off.

The single's recording experience was positive and productive, but what Jack Morrow had in mind for the first album, called simply *Teenage Head*, was something closer to (his) home, something with minimal upfront expenditure and something involving – as it usually did with Morrow – an old acquaintance who was open to cutting a deal.

Gabe Salter owned – or partly owned, depending on whom you're speaking with – a Toronto recording studio called Thunder Sound, which was also part of Inter Global Music, a record label that specialized in quick and dirty re-recordings of hit tunes for the Kresge's and Zellers department store market. Salter and his father, Abe, were, according to most people interviewed for this book, a not entirely unblemished pair of businessmen.

Wherever the truth lies, IGM wasn't exactly the major-label deal the boys had been hoping for. But IGM was also distributed by CBS, so it was better than nothing. And at the time, the band was simply so pleased to be cutting a record that they didn't ask many questions about how that arrangement was made. Looking back, it was probably the best Morrow could do for the band at this point, all factors considered. No major labels were nibbling, no American deals were looming, radio airplay was scarce and the boys, getting tighter and more popular by the day, were playing to jammed houses every night and everywhere. Very likely, his thinking was: get them in the studio, get a hit on the radio, then go grab that pot of gold at the end of the rainbow.

Certainly it was time for some morale juice. The band was growing restive, not entirely enthusiastic about what Morrow had achieved so far. 'You have to understand what IGM was,' Lewis says. 'It was less than K-Tel. It was below K-Tel. They took hit songs, re-recorded them with session artists – that way they didn't even have to pay any licencing rights – and put them out as greatest hits. That was the type of label IGM was. They figured out that they could do that and make a lot of money.'

Before heading into the studio, Frankie Venom sat down for an interview with *Shades* magazine and expressed his dissatisfaction in no uncertain terms: 'The band's not happy with the label at all. There's just no relationship with the company. Look at us. The stage is fucking shit, there's no money, the same fucking clothes, we're not satisfied with the gigs we're getting, we're not satisfied with anything right now. We hate it. I'm seriously thinking of getting into professional soccer or something. It just depends on how the album goes. If it dies, the band'll die.'

The man waiting for Teenage Head in Thunder Sound was Alan Caddy, a full-time sound engineer who might be recording Christmas carols one day, disco the next morning, and he re-recorded Top 40 hits for the department store market in the afternoon. As the band recalls, he had no particular enthusiasm for Teenage Head, no experience or sensitivity to this so-called 'punk' music and very little patience for suggestions he ought to do things any other way than he always had. It would not prove a harmonious recording atmosphere.

'To have an original band come in, playing original songs, not having total control over how everything's done, was very foreign to them,' Lewis says of the studio staff. 'We complained a lot about some of the stuff that was going on, but by that time we were playing live so much we just weren't that aware of the particulars of recording. So I wasn't aware that things weren't going as smoothly and as perfectly as I thought they were. I just assumed again we were in good hands and that everything would be okay.'

The band also assumed that the sheer magic they could muster live would naturally cast its spell in the studio. They knew how good they were, so how could it not? The recording lasted several sessions, interrupted by Morrow's intense schedule of gigging and tours.

For Mahon, the process of making the first album had ample historical precedent: 'There's a ton of examples of bands that come along live, they're playing great, they're writing great and then you get into the studio and you're totally at the control of whoever's working the board. And at that age, none of us knew how to do anything.'

While there were disputes concerning the band's use of its own equipment (Lewis was mortified that he couldn't use his own Marshall amplifier) and entitlement to listen in on their own takes, which occasioned shouting matches over what the band should sound like, *Teenage Head* did ultimately get recorded and released, which meant all those fans – like myself – who'd previously had to go see the band live to hear such killers songs as 'Top Down' and 'Lucy Potato' now had a record they could buy and take home to play.

I did exactly that. I remember taking the bus from my university base in Ottawa to Toronto – road time: five hours – the weekend the album was released, and buying it (along with the Police's second album) at an A&A's a block away from the terminal. I remember rushing over to my friend Jim's place on Beverley Street to give the album a listen, and I remember the strange feeling of murky dislocation that followed. I mean, there it was, coming out of the speakers: all the right songs with all the right words and all the right instruments, but somehow flat, subdued – just, you know, *there*. Jim, who had also seen the band a lot, looked at me and I back at him, our faces slack. The *Teenage Head* album, which we'd anticipated as much as we'd anticipated any album maybe ever, sounded just ... *okay*.

The band felt the same way. The album was a letdown, a sonic sigh where it should have been a primal scream, and it had nothing on the debut albums of such other first-wave punks as the Ramones, Clash, Damned, Dead Boys or, certainly, the Sex Pistols. It missed something anybody who had ever heard the band live had heard, and that was a tightly packed three-minute pop missile of a song, as loud as the sky falling but never so loud that you couldn't hear the sheer craft of the songwriting. And maybe that was it: the band had gone into the studio to be recorded by people who'd never heard them live, so had no idea what kind of sound they were missing when they rolled tape. During the staggered recording process, the band had shown up on time and prepared every day – years of practice and nightly gigging had instilled a hardcore work ethic in these twenty-year-olds – and for the hours Caddy was being paid to produce, he was never less than fully on the job: recording the band according to the manner he recorded just about anything, and he recorded everything in just about the same manner.

'Jack Morrow took credit for production,' Lewis tells me, 'but he didn't produce anything. He was just there. He was trying to do the Phil Spector thing: "I control the recording, I control the publishing, I control the producing."'

Lewis was baffled and disappointed. Compared to the single they'd released, the album sounded almost like a different band. 'The 45 is an isolated piece,' he says, 'and it sounds great. We were really happy with it. That's why when we did our first album and the sound quality was so lacking we didn't understand it. "The 45 sounds great, how come this album sounds muddy?" We

Teenage Head live and outside: Jackson Square, Hamilton.

Steve, born for stardom.

were pretty pissed off. We were told, "Well, that's the way you sound, boys." I remember first seeing it, and thinking, "Yeah, we finally did it." But then I played it and I thought, "This isn't Teenage Head, this doesn't sound like what it should sound like." I thought, "Holy shit, we've blown it."' For Lewis, the band still hadn't quite made it. They had an album out, sure, but it wasn't on Polydor, wasn't on CBS, and *Teenage Head* didn't do justice to Teenage Head.

Certain fans were equally as confounded, Don Pyle among them: 'This perspective may not be accurate – it's totally just about my experience – but I saw things kind of go off the rails for the band really early on. From the day the first album came out. The choices made in mixing the album – it's like the washed-out colours of the album cover art almost represent the washed-out sound that they got.'

On the cover, the band are dressed up like cartoon thrift-shop punk clowns – hats, big sunglasses and slicked-down hair – all popsicle colours and silly finger-popping shimmy-shake. Beneath their comic-book-font logo, Teenage Head looks not only amiably goofy and begging not to be taken seriously, but like a bunch of kids. Or grown-ups trying to be kids. The *Teenage Head* album art suggested a punk-era Monkees.

Steven Leckie remembers seeing the album for the first time: 'That's quintessentially Teenage Head, that they borrowed from the Monkees, not the Beatles. Hence the way they look. They're certainly not selling sex or violence. If you consider that the cover of their first album looks like a children's show, I guess they're selling a good time.'

Nonetheless, many years on, *Teenage Head* has acquired a certain unqualified classic status – especially among the most discerning collectors of vintage punk, of which there are more everywhere and every day. And my ears hear it differently now than they did back then. Back then, I heard it in the context of the band's live sound, an aural bar set so high perhaps no studio recording could reach it, let alone a studio in Toronto in 1979 with no history, experience or even interest when it came to recording this sound. Now that that context has receded, I hear a truly fantastic and utterly essential album. I don't hear the dampening effects of ill-suited studio treatment but the transcendent power of the songs and the band playing them. I used to think it took a pretty piss-poor studio to make a band like Teenage Head sound listless. Now I understand it took a band like Teenage Head to sound amazing no matter what idiot was behind the board.

This Ain't Hollywood owner Lou Molinaro was a little too young to see Teenage Head perform in their early glory, which meant he was one of the many listeners – like the Headstones' Hugh Dillon – for whom the first album was a revelation, the sound of the doors blowing open on possibility. Molinaro considers Teenage Head nothing less than a national pop-cultural milestone: 'I would say the very first *Teenage Head* album is the most important Canadian rock 'n' roll record ever made – more important than *American Woman*, more important than Leonard Cohen, more important than any Joni Mitchell record. Teenage Head changed the whole face of Canadian music single-handedly. Teenage Head were the band that proved you could be young, you could be successful and you could be doing this. They represented everything that was right about being a musician and doing it for the love of music and doing it for the love of entertaining your fans.'

For their part, the surviving Teenage Head players have more than made their peace with the first album. The decades have, if anything, made them proud. 'When it first came out we were heartbroken,' Mahon tells me, 'but the more people got into it, they just loved it for what it was. We're the same. It grew on us.' Upon reflection, Stipanitz is also forgiving, both of Alan Caddy and the first Teenage Head album he produced: 'He knew music, he knew how to engineer music, he knew how music was structured and how recordings were structured. The music itself was far more intense than he'd ever dealt with, so he was at a loss there. At the time we were all disappointed with the way the album sounded, but when I've listened to it recently I'm not disappointed anymore. The songs are honestly portrayed.'

No matter what disappointments simmered at the time, brooding over the record was an only slightly more feasible option than re-recording it. And there was no time for either. The band had to get back to work, and Jack Morrow had a lot – a whole lot – of work lined up.

Machine Head

The Last Pogo was a cheeky dig at *The Last Waltz*, the Martin Scorsese movie depicting that most un-punk of hippie-rock cinematic requiems – the final concert of The Band. The event, the Horseshoe Tavern's last night of punk music, was even recorded for semi-posterity by Colin Brunton, making his first vault from club employee to filmmaker. It was a night to remember under normal circumstances, but a lot of the Horseshoe crowd was not in a normal frame of mind: they were hammered, high, excited and packed into the place like jarred pickled eggs. And when Teenage Head took the stage, they went fucking crazy. An era had ended, and the last sound heard was the final chord wallop of 'Picture My Face.'

In Brunton's movie, the club looks about to explode from the density of the punks, poseurs, band members and out-of-water suburban curious crammed within, and the brief Teenage Head set, shot so tightly that Frankie seems to leap out of the frame as much as he's in it – like lightning channelled through a PA. Then the cops arrive, and there's a riveting moment where Jack Morrow, looking for all the world like a dad who's come downstairs to mediate a teenage basement brouhaha, attempts to get between the cops and the band, and Steve Mahon waves a raised finger in the face of one of Toronto's finest. Not in profane defiance, but to plead the case to play one more song. This is Teenage Head at the pinnacle of the Toronto punk moment, hammering a bent beer cap on a fizzling era.

The day after the Last Pogo, the club was a disaster zone. The kitchen was filled with broken tables and chairs. Beer bottles and shards thereof were strewn everywhere. Stains of all manner were splattered wall to wall. 'It reminded me of Rod Steiger's Al Capone movie,' Gary Topp recalls, 'when he's in the jail yard and they're shovelling coal. That's what the tables and chairs reminded me of – big piles of coal.'

By that point, however, Teenage Head were long gone. Morrow had put them on a train, going east, far from the receding sound of the roaring crowd. All the way east, in fact, to Oromocto, New

Brunswick, where Morrow had booked them, of all things, a one-week gig at a military base. After taking a long train ride out there, and then hitchhiking from the train station to a pizza joint close to the base, the band waited for Mahon to arrive with the truck and equipment. When they finally reached the base, they set up their gear and promptly fell asleep on the stage. It was a long way from the Horseshoe.

On the night of their first performance, Teenage Head played a single set before being pulled offstage and warned that if they kept it up they were likely to be beaten silent by a crowd that clearly didn't dig the sounds. But a commitment was a commitment, and military protocol is military protocol, so Teenage Head was actually paid to *not* play for a week. But they *were* required to show up at showtime every night just so they could be seen not playing by the management that had booked them.

It was a long week in Oromocto. 'They were thinking, "Okay, we can just send this band out like it's a cover band,"' Lewis remembers, '"and they'll go play a week – which we never had done – "plus a matinee on Saturday." We'll go and do the regular routine thing that Canadian bands go do. That taught me a real music-business lesson. That we were on our own. That this industry did not get this at all.'

Fredericton, the next stop on the eastern tour, was a significant improvement, and not just because there really wasn't room for anything but improvement after the Oromocto debacle. It was also the first hint the band had that there were people who really *got* them outside of Hamilton and Toronto. Still, it was cold, far away from home and nobody had any money. After finishing up the Fredericton gigs, they looked closely at the next destination on the itinerary – Richibucto, even further north – and collectively said, 'Fuck this.' They headed back to Ontario.

'I drove home,' Stipanitz says. 'We had a pickup truck with a 110-gallon gas tank in the back. I drove straight home in fourteen hours. In hindsight that was a good experience because we were learning how to be on the road. Find out that you wake up in the morning and there's not much to do but practice. You start to get tight, helps the band get better.'

Frankie contemplates the room. No structure is safe.

And good thing too: from this point on, Teenage Head would be playing and driving and driving and playing relentlessly: five or six nights a week, across most of the country and for the next several years. Under Morrow's hand, the band was everywhere all the time. Richibucto residents aside, if you were in Canada between 1978 and 1983, you had a pretty good chance of seeing Teenage Head. And if you liked them and wanted to share the joy with friends, you also had a good chance of seeing them again, soon. From the day that Morrow took over the operation, Teenage Head toured like a machine. There was arguably no band of their era — or, likely, anyone else's — that played live as much or in as many places as Gord, Frank, Nick and Steve. In the months between the recording of *Teenage Head* and *Frantic City*, their second record, the band consolidated their reputation as the country's most exciting live rock act.

Exciting for them too. Getting out on the road across the country made the band realize not only that they had followers across Canada — and that the record, somehow, had managed to get out there — but that what they were doing could generate frenzy wherever they did it. With few exceptions, Teenage Head shows were packed, prepared to party and crazy. And whether or not the band was aware of it, by the time they were about to go nationwide, they had also helped transform Toronto as a live music venue.

'The great thing about that whole scene was you had to go to clubs to see the bands,' Bob Segarini says. 'Back in those days you couldn't make an indie record in your mom's kitchen with your laptop. You had to actually get into a studio to make a record. And these kids played and they played and they played and they turned places that weren't live music venues into live music venues because people showed up to see them. What started out as an art-college lark turned into one of the most viable and vibrant things in the city.'

Thanks largely to Teenage Head, suddenly there were bars and live music everywhere. You could actually make a living playing music. Segarini used to work six nights a week, he says, as did dozens upon dozens of other bands. The kids created their own circuit, places like Larry's Hideway and the El Mocambo.

And outside the hipster, punk-hip urban centres, Teenage Head connected on the level that was always their bedrock anyway – as a high-energy pop-rock act playing songs that made you want to jump, dance and drink a lot of beer. The punk accoutrements only helped embellish what was really musical spectacle as old as Elvis: rock music as physical stimuli, carnal primal scream and pure, unadulterated fun. Like the Ramones and the Clash, they could have stripped themselves of the punk associations and still rocked like a mother.

In 1992, I asked Frankie Venom when he first realized Teenage Head had made themselves heard beyond Hamilton and Toronto: 'The first time we went out west,' he said. 'When we'd play places like Calgary, Edmonton, Regina, Saskatoon, and it would be sold-out like two, three nights in advance. And these club owners, who got very greedy, were charging like ten, twenty dollars to get into a club. I remember in Edmonton, for instance, we arrived at the club at five-thirty for a sound check, and there were lineups around the block. That's when it hit home. It was like, wow, we're popular, you know?'

This is a key period in Teenage Head's history for a couple of reasons. First, because it was this intensive, nationwide touring regimen that exposed them to people across the country and solidified a legacy that lasts to this day. And second, it compensated for the fact that Teenage Head was otherwise unaided by just about any other form of exposure: there weren't many Canadian TV shows they could appear on, music videos were still to come, the press – last among the population to get past the 'punk' label – was rarely supportive or even present, and their radio rotation was restricted to those stations cool enough to play out-of-the-antique-box Canadian music.

One reason the band didn't get much radio play illustrated just how absurdly conservative mainstream Canada was at the time. David Marsden, then at CFNY, always felt the band was handicapped by their seemingly salacious name: 'I think the biggest problem the band had, and I'm disappointed to say this, and certainly not on any radio station I was involved with, but the majority of them across Canada didn't want to actually say the words *Teenage Head* on the radio.' Marsden's station, on the contrary, was delighted to add Teenage Head to its playlist. 'A lot of CFNY music was about the punk, the edgy – primarily music that nobody else would play. Teenage Head filled every room they ever went into. This was important music. And if it was important music, we thought we should share it.'

The lack of conventional exposure meant Teenage Head had to get their message across as directly as possible: by playing their music to as many people as possible and winning them over, one throbbing set of eardrums at a time. Of all the ways to build an audience, this has to be the hardest and most unlikely, especially in a country as sprawling and sparsely populated as Canada. There may be no more powerful testament to the power of this band and its music than the fact that this is exactly what they did. They played themselves into something like legend.

Treat Me Like Dirt author Liz Worth discovered over the course of research and promotion for her book that there really was only one Canadian band of the era that everybody knew. 'If I meet people in smaller cities like Sudbury,' she says, 'they maybe never

The endless highway: on tour, 1982.

saw the Viletones or never heard of the Diodes, but they had all
seen Teenage Head. That's the one band that, across the board,
wherever you go in Canada, everybody recognizes.'

Whereas under Kobak's auspices, Teenage Head had been an
unlikely local sensation that galvanized an unprecedented independent underground music scene and challenged less accomplished bands to step up their game – the Morrow era was one of
calculated, even cunning, expansion and exploitation. Seeing how
the band could ignite a crowd and draw the same people back
again and again, understanding the exponential growth of that
audience through word of mouth, Morrow put them out there
further and more intensively than they'd ever been before. He
worked them like dogs, and never forgot that, until they're hungry
or tired, dogs love to work. As Lewis puts it to me with grave
understatement, 'We sold a lot of beer.'

And, much more significantly, they converted a lot of future
musicians. 'The first time I saw them would be the Lakeview
Manor in Kingston,' Hugh Dillon remembers. 'Just a dangerous
little shithole. In these shitty little fucking Ontario bars, there were

horrific cover bands who just played regurgitated cover shit. And this band came in with their own shit, their own style, their own lyrics. It was like, you want to write your own songs – Teenage Head wrote their own songs. I didn't want to play covers. If I'm going to cover anything, it's going to be a Teenage Head song.'

In Kingston, Dillon formed (and named) his band the Headstones at least partly in tribute to Teenage Head. In the same city, Gord Downie and future members of the Tragically Hip rarely missed a show. In Vancouver, punk fanatic – and future Guns N' Roses bass player – Duff McKagan saw Teenage Head and loved them. In Edmonton, the Pursuit of Happiness's Moe Berg saw the Head play, and in Fredericton Peter Rowan, future manager of Sloan, saw every show the Head ever played there. Because I was a university student in Ottawa with a family and summer job in St. Catharines, I was in a position to see Teenage Head in Niagara Falls, St. Catharines, Hamilton, Toronto, Ottawa and Montreal. And I never had to wait long either.

Under Morrow, Teenage Head actually drew a regular salary – $400 a week – which meant no worries about day jobs. They were professional musicians whose only responsibility when they woke up at the crack of noon was to make more music. They had a rider that demanded so much booze be provided at every show, and they had staff to carry their equipment, set it up and tear it down. They really had no worries apart from hangovers and getting to gigs on time, which is something they also became famous for: no matter what condition the band was in, no matter how far they'd travelled that day from yesterday's gig, Teenage Head got up onstage and astonished. Among the many common refrains you'll hear from people who worked with or saw them at this time is that they never saw a bad show. Which again, whether attributable to that basement-born work ethic, Morrow's managerial savvy or a happy confluence of both, made perfect business sense: if you knew – like *knew* – Teenage Head was going to put on a smoking-hot-shit show every time you went, why wouldn't you go back again and again? And why wouldn't you tell everybody you knew? By recommending a Teenage Head gig to the uninitiated, you were practically guaranteeing a good time.

The other refrain you'll hear a lot when talking Teenage Head to folk is equally pertinent to their enduring legacy among peers and their timely expansion as a business interest: everybody liked them. And I mean *everybody*. In the course of writing this book, I might have encountered people who felt excluded by the band, left behind or insufficiently recognized, but even these people agreed that they were really nice, decent and humble dudes. Sure, they knew how to party, drew groupies and had their occasional old-school-rock way with a hotel room, but they were never less than nice. Well-raised boys from Hamilton who just happened to make crowds crazy wherever they played.

'They were genuine,' Viletones guitarist Freddie Pompeii remembers. 'A lot of the other bands, they grew to like us too, but still Steven Leckie had a way of turning people off. He would insult people and choose sides and make somebody his enemy. Those guys never did any of that shit. They just played. Like their attitude was, "It's all good, you know?"'

The significance of this is not easily understated. In a business where resentment, jealousy, unpaid debts, systemic mendacity, drugs and alcohol fuel all manner of idiocy, Teenage Head's fundamental decency as a collective proved as transcendent in interpersonal terms as their music was categorically: it floated above everything and seemed to find a way of reaching everyone. In Brunton's documentary *The Last Pogo Jumps Again*, you'll see no shortage of unhealed wounds, still-simmering resentments and never-endingly nursed slights. Part of it comes with the terrain: it was a small scene, a competitive one, a historically under-recognized one, and one that invited a whole lot of passion for very little lasting benefit (materially, anyway). It has also become the last stand of rock 'n' roll music that really meant and stood for something, the final big splash before retreating into the soothing wallpaper of boomer nostalgia. So one can only expect there'd be residual bile built up, and in Brunton's movie it splashes over the rim constantly. If punk rock is like the high school of popular music (and it doesn't help that it took nearly twenty years before bands like Nirvana, Green Day and Blink 182 came along to make it commercial), then the Toronto scene is only more intensely so for being egregiously undocumented, under-appreciated and ignored. Talk about a breeding ground for ill will. And yet, wherever they went, Teenage Head were liked by fans, managers, journalists and fellow musicians alike, and this, along with the crowds they drew and the beer they sold, made them somebody you'd love to see again.

Still, for all their universal likeability, Teenage Head wasn't immune to bad behaviour, and the source of this could be summed up in two words: Frankie Venom. Almost always, when the band stepped in public-relations shit, it was Frank who took the lead. Stipanitz remembers a potentially significant early show in Vancouver: 'We played a club with a live, no-delay broadcast for the local rock FM station. No delay. Halfway through, Frank announced his version of the station's call letters: 'You are listening to radio station C-U-N-T.' The next day Frank went to the station to apologize to the general manager, but our songs were pulled from rotation. After our Vancouver debut, we left the second-largest national market with our reputation intact, but with no industry support. We never did become very popular on the west coast.'

There are other stories. Many other stories. Of how Frank could be cutting and cruel when he drank, or of how he'd deliberately misremember people's names just to mess with their egos. Of how he couldn't say no to anybody who offered him anything, and how he allowed himself to be surrounded by just such people. And he had a temper. The first time that Peter MacAulay, who'd get behind the mike with Teenage Head after Venom died, saw the band in a club called the Hawk's Nest near Kitchener, Ontario, Frank went berserk with his mike stand when the sound system blew out from the band's sheer volume. 'The other guys didn't even blink,' MacAulay says.

Venom's antics aside, Teenage Head couldn't stop playing. It was working like a dream for everybody. Maybe not a perfect dream – Jack Morrow being a character in it – but close enough if your idea of a rock 'n' roll heaven is playing all the time to houses packed with people who love your music. This part of the dream had come true for the band. They were living it.

'We thought it was great,' Venom told me in '92. 'We were happy just to get a nice secure weekly paycheque. We had little cheques with "Teenage Head" printed on them. We were young and naive. Gosh, we were eighteen, nineteen. We weren't interested in the business aspect of it. We just did it for the fun of playing live. We just enjoyed the shows. We didn't care who got paid, when we got paid, who was going to get the money – we just wanted to play.'

While the band was so relentlessly on the road, Morrow was consolidating a home base in Toronto. He rebranded the not-exactly-luxury lodging and liquid refreshment establishment Larry's Hideaway as the Headspace, which became the primary Toronto venue in which to see the band. A one-hundred-room hotel notorious for its cockroaches, brawls, cash-only transacted sexual liaisons and general vibe of advanced seediness, the club nevertheless served its purpose as a place to come and see what, by '79, had become the hottest local act going. Decorated so there was no mistaking this as Head HQ, Larry's became the permanent version of what Morrow, with his banners, slogans, posters, buttons and T-shirts, made of every venue in which his band played: a branded promotional opportunity. Why just play when you can really *play*? 'Jack claimed to be running Larry's,' Al Mair remembers. 'That meant he got a piece of every dollar that came in from any source, whether it was beer sales or room rental or whatever else Jack was selling.'

By the time the clock had ticked down to a new decade, Kobak's contract with the band was about to expire. Their new contract, prepared by Morrow and his lawyer, would terminate Kobak's co-managerial position while retaining him for a number of sundry and labour-intensive purposes for which he would never be paid. For a while he acted as principal booker for Larry's Hideaway and the Headspace, and then formed his own booking company called Teen Agency. These were all busy enterprises, and Kobak estimates he helped find gigs for dozens of up-and-coming acts that otherwise wouldn't have made it as far as the Elizabeth Street Bus Terminal.

'That whole year of 1979 I was booking not just Larry's Hideaway,' Kobak explains, 'I was booking every band in Toronto, and then some, with Teen Agency. And once again, what happened to me? I never collected 10 percent. There were maybe two bands that maybe gave me fifteen bucks or something once.'

When I met with Kobak many years later, he was still struggling to get by. Although semi-successfully repurposed as a dowser – someone who can find buried valuables and dimensional portals with the aid of a carefully altered coat hanger – he has apparently never had any luck making or keeping money. Just about everything he's ever owned he's had to sell, and just about everything he's found he's lost. While I can't presume to do a dowsing job on this gentle and generous man's spirit, I suspect Kobak's primary liability in material terms is the purity of his passion. He sold records not for money but because he loved music and wanted others to do the same. He managed Teenage Head not because he saw a business opportunity but because he heard a noise that needed to be heard. And he got into booking because he wanted to give other deserving bands a chance to be heard as well. What he did he did because he really, truly and deeply cared – and sadly, that's a hardly a profitable proposition.

By the end of 1979, Kobak was forced to relinquish control of Star Records to his cousin Mike Shulga. He owed $25,000 to his record distributor, Records on Wheels, and had a briefcase with $30,000 worth of expenses accrued with Teenage Head. At the end, exhausted, frustrated, demoted and broke, he closed up shop and tried a career in the shiny new field of computers. It didn't exactly take, and Kobak continued to bounce from job to job, almost as peripatetic as the band he helped make, but which was now out of reach and out of control, and about to hit the new decade with a heavy reputation, an actual record label and the sound of beer bottles pounding on tables from coast to coast.

In the beginning, Stipanitz says of Kobak, 'he heard the band and wanted to be the manager. Had no experience but knew and loved the music. He was a believer in the music. He was an integral part of the band back then. He helped make things happen. He was very generous to us.'

Mahon concurs: 'Kobak was great. He had his problems and issues, but his heart was in it completely. And we all felt bad during that transition where we realized that Jack was going to take us a couple of steps higher on the ladder than Paul. Paul had the ability to take us so far and then Jack took it further. But both were very important people as far as the success the band had.'

If this provides small comfort today, and if Kobak felt left behind at the time, it must also be remembered that Teenage Head didn't have the opportunity for much reflection back then: they were not only facing firmly forward, Morrow's machine was driving them that way at full speed. 'Well, what choice did they have?' Don Pyle asks. 'I remember them playing the Rondon Tavern on Dundas. It's like one of the worst drinking holes and flophouses in the city. And it was close to where I grew up, so I would see who was playing there and it was always just crappy bar bands. And I remember Teenage Head. The first time I saw they were going to be playing at the Rondon, I thought, "Oh my god, that's the working Canadian band. You're going to play every shithole bar in order to get a paycheque." And those things kill your soul, you know? In some ways, it elevated them because tons of people saw them, they went everywhere, they played all those little towns that, you know, the Viletones weren't going to: North Bay, Sudbury, Sault Ste. Marie. And they built an audience. It allowed them to keep going, but was killing them at the same time. It was like chemotherapy.'

'I thought they could be monsters,' Al Mair says of his first impression of Teenage Head. 'They were the right act at that time. Just perfect.'

The right time for Mair was, specifically, the fifth year his label Attic Records, then the biggest independent label in Canada, had been in existence. It started in 1974, and by 1979 had achieved something special: it had proven a competitive place for new Canadian acts to go, and it was known for doing business honestly. By only its second year, in fact, Attic signed Triumph as well as Hagood Hardy, who had a double-platinum album in Canada and won *Billboard*'s Instrumental Artist of the Year in the U.S. 'We were kinda hot,' Mair says now.

Teenage Head was on their radar. Mair's partner, Tom Williams, was out most nights at the clubs, and he had been hearing a lot about this new band. He grabbed Mair and they went to check them out at Larry's. 'It was a no-brainer,' Williams says. 'This was a band that had rabid fans, were great onstage and had good music.'

Attic wasn't the only label that wanted a piece of the Teenage Head action. CBS, too, was circling. But the Head, possibly in light of the Diodes' abrupt disengagement by Columbia Records, liked the fact that the more modest Attic would give them the support and attention a bigger label wouldn't or couldn't. They were an innovative Canadian label with major-company connections, small enough to nurture and promote the band intensively, but ambitious enough to kick an obviously hot prospect up to the levels they were so clearly ready for. And their enthusiasm certainly helped.

'They were great,' Mair says. 'Frankie was a star, but his head was screwed on right. He wasn't a Johnny Rotten. He was Frankie Venom. He had the dark eyeshadow, there was kind of a touch of evil about him, but to me it was all tongue-in-cheek.'

Attic also offered a good producer and a decent budget – the latter being what probably clinched the deal for Morrow. And for Attic, in turn, the talented, personable band brought with it apparently solid, forward-looking management with a plan. But as Ralph

Alfonso, former Diodes manager and later an Attic employee, puts it, signing with a record label is a process riddled with romantic self-delusion. 'People have this really strange fixation as to what a record deal is,' Alfonso says. 'It's this fairy tale where suddenly this father-like figure comes in and lifts you off the street, gives you bags of money and overnight makes you a star and you never have to do anything. And that exists to this day, and makes just about all musicians easy prey for disappointment.'

Negotiations began. Morrow had strong ideas about what the band ought to be doing and so did the guys at Attic. They didn't always sync up. 'We'd talk about what the single was going to be,' Williams explains, 'what radio stations had picked up on it, why the fuck was he doing whatever he was doing. Jack and I had a very open relationship and a good one, you know. I didn't trust him for a second and he had no problem with that. Jack knew who he was. I enjoyed watching him. The stuff he could do and the publicity he could get for that band. I don't think he liked the band very much as people – he used to say they were pinheads, and that Frankie couldn't pick his nose on his own. But Jack often looked at all his bands like that. They were a means to an end.'

Teenage Head eventually signed with Attic, and pre-eminent among the promises made, for the band anyway, was the prospect of getting back into the studio to do it right this time. Once again, one surmises that it was the music – and the opportunity to get it on vinyl properly and then tour it to audiences not necessarily hunkered around wooden tables in basement bars and taverns – that excited the band more than anything about the Attic deal. It looked good for the band, it looked good for their music. Why worry about anything else? Let Jack do the negotiating and set the terms, and let Attic get to work making albums and converting the masses. How could anything be wrong with an arrangement like that?

The album that became *Frantic City* – the peak of Teenage Head's commercial and recording career – was produced by Stacy Heydon, a Canadian guitarist who'd spent much of the previous few years on tour with David Bowie and Iggy Pop, a CV that was singularly impressive to Teenage Head.

'I was quite aware of the band,' Heydon says. 'They were gigging at Larry's Hideaway and all those local places. I had been producing a bunch of bands at the time. I was working with Johnny and G-Rays, and I did a live album for Al Mair – Jayne County and the Electric Chairs.'

They recorded at the Kensington Sound recording studio, located above a fish market in Toronto's Kensington Market. Lewis still remembers the stench of the place. He also remembers being wary of Heydon at first, thinking this relatively rookie producer might have been both too inexperienced and too straitlaced. 'We thought he wouldn't get what was going on,' Lewis says, 'but he actually did. He got us at our peak. He knew exactly what to do with us. He taught me a lot about guitar, he taught me a lot about structuring guitar solos, he taught me a lot about song-writing, he helped arrange songs. He really cared.' Though the Head hadn't requested them, Heydon brought in the right session players too: Grant Slater on piano, Walter Zwol to play synthesizer, Rick Morrison on sax. 'Frantic City sounds the way it does a lot because of Stacy Heydon,' Lewis says.

A relatively recent addition to the Attic staff was Lindsay Gillespie, whose past associations with CFNY, Morrow and Teenage Head made him the natural point man for the promotion of Frantic City. 'I got hired by Attic Records in 1979, at the same time the record label was talking to Teenage Head,' Gillespie recalls. 'And I knew what was going on because I was still tight with the management and the band. When Teenage Head got signed, I wasn't part of the deal, but they needed a promo guy who knew the scene so I got hired at the same time. The first record I really got to work on was Frantic City.'

The schedule was tight, the studio smelly and the weather hot, but inside Kensington things quickly clicked. Compared to the recording experience at Thunder Sound, the making of Frantic City wasn't a struggle. On the contrary, it was something of a joy. 'Frantic City took two weeks to record,' Lewis remembers. 'We were never in the studio very long. Not a whole lot of overdubbing, just some background vocals, guitar solos, some sax stuff. Stacy was just very musical and he got the songs too. He didn't have a

95

problem with my amp like IGM did on the first album. I was allowed to bring my Marshall.'

In studying the band live, Heydon came to understand what the band could do well, but also what they needed to do in the studio. It wasn't just a question of capturing the live spark, but of keeping it lit while accommodating the realities of studio recording. 'I remember thinking they were very raw,' Heydon says. 'I liked their energy. Mostly I thought they should tidy themselves up, set off Frankie just a little bit. Which is exactly what I did in Kensington Sound with them – make it a little more legible without sucking the life out of it.

'It's a fine line between sucking the life out of something and letting it live and being completely obnoxious. Working with Jayne County and touring with Iggy Pop, we knew the Sex Pistols and all these guys, they'd hang out on the road with us. I always thought there was magic in it, but it was so mired in muck and shit and drugs and bad musicianship it didn't come out in the wash much. But with these boys, yeah, I think it did. *Frantic City* was a representation of them live, although they could probably never sound as good as *Frantic City* live because I could cheat and make things maybe just a little better than they were.'

One of Heydon's insights concerning younger bands was that they could be instantly uncomfortable in a studio environment for a single reason: they weren't standing in front of blaring amplifiers. They were in a controlled environment and playing through headphones, and this could be as disorienting for a club-hardened live act like Teenage Head as not playing their own instruments. 'Once you strap headphones on guys used to standing in front of Marshall stacks, it's like putting Wayne Gretzky in a roller-hockey rink – he's just an average hockey player.' Heydon had the Head first play every song live in the studio. They laid down each track with the whole band at once and then subsequently started stripping it down from there.

One of Heydon's greatest assets was his understanding of Frankie Venom. 'Frank had that personality and he just didn't give a shit,' Heydon laughs. 'That's what I loved about Frank. He didn't care what anybody thought about him. If he wanted to

The Attic signing. Jack Morrow at right.

drop trou that night, he was dropping trou. Everything and anything went with Frank, and I think that was part of the allure.' While the rest of the band could focus on playing their instruments as well as possible, Venom, so easily prone to studio boredom, was at a loss without an audience wired to his nervous system. But he and Heydon worked well together, a sense of mutual respect greasing the wheels of collaboration. If Heydon asked Venom to repeat a line or chorus, or was critical of his timing or pitch, Venom listened and did as instructed. The self-deprecating Heydon claims he was no more than a bus driver or coach; he had, as he says, 'left his ego in the trunk of his car,' and expected the band to do the same. They obliged. 'It was basically a perfect storm of raw talent,' Heydon says. 'And the will to make it great and the will to work with someone they trusted.'

Frantic City marked the beginning of Teenage Head's most brilliantly lit professional passage: hit records, heavy radio rotation, bigger live venues, lavish press attention — all these and more were headed the band's way almost at the speed of sound itself. Everything seemed aligned. They parted ways with Stacy Heydon having had an incredibly satisfying and fulfilling studio experience.

They fully expected they might work together again. But they never did.

And why not? Did it have anything to do with Jack Morrow?

Asked the question, Heydon takes a deep breath. 'When *Frantic City* came out and started to become a phenomenon, well, let's just say he would have been instrumental with me not having much to do with them anymore. I've never, ever had a rift with one of the guys in the band. Never. And that's why it was just so strange that they would assimilate themselves with this guy and stay with him. I'm sure they lost a lot of support as a result of that.'

Heydon pauses again, carefully assembling thoughts and words. 'I've kind of gotten away from dealing with negative people in my life, and when any negativity touches me I just go the other way like a pinball and I'm done with it. But I'll tell you one thing – I saw potential in that band. As much potential as I've seen in any band I've ever worked with, and that bus was stopped. The brakes were pulled on that bus of productivity somehow, some way. I'm sure this Mr. Morrow had much to do with it, but you know, at the end of the day it's the band who chose to work with him and live by the heat of the flame or whatever.'

Discussions with Al Mair and other members of Teenage Head clarify what Heydon was so respectfully indirect about: Morrow had convinced the band they could get a marquee producer, like Toronto's Bob Ezrin, who had worked with the likes of Alice Cooper and Kiss, especially in light of *Frantic City*'s smash success. Morrow felt they could do better than Heydon, and he pushed that way. Mair pushed back: he thought Heydon had done a superb job producing Teenage Head's album, and he wanted him back. Morrow prevailed, and Stacy Heydon never recorded with Teenage Head again. But Bob Ezrin never did either.

The new decade beckoned. Teenage Head were ready to take the '80s by storm. Everything felt perfect: their new album, their new material, their new label. All they needed to worry about now was moving forward and consolidating this long-overdue convergence of fortunes. Morrow would worry about everything else.

1980: Crest and Break

By June 2, 1980, the machine was humming. Even the weather that day in Toronto – sunny, cloudless, T-shirt-warm – seemed brightened by the fortunes accruing to the band below.

Since its release in March, *Frantic City* had been certified gold: 40,000 copies and counting sold in Canada. The re-recorded single of 'Top Down' had not only effortlessly eased into constant rotation on CFNY, the three-year-old classic-rock station Q107 had picked it up as well. With its clean, radio-friendly sound, Eddie Cochranized boogie riffs and irresistible pop accessibility, Teenage Head's album was the sound of summer coming. Although the album's twelve songs veered from the acoustic embrace of the sweet, sax-buffeted ballad 'Somethin' on My Mind' to the rolling-thunder onslaught of the live staple 'Disgusteen,' and even though it blended original songs with such golden-age twangers as Cochran's 'Somethin' Else' and Vince Taylor's 'Brand New Cadillac' – covered the previous year by the similarly roots-reverent Clash – *Frantic City* cohered seamlessly as an album by a band that knew what it was, knew where it came from and definitely seemed be going somewhere. It even cracked some AM Top 40 lists. The boys in the band were about twenty-two, and they were living the dream of hearing themselves whenever they turned on the radio. When the album went gold, they presented the mayor of Hamilton with it in a ceremony that got extensive press coverage – a classic Jack Morrow stunt that never would have occurred to any of the competition. Punks? Maybe. Solid citizens? Absolutely.

'We got one single from *Frantic City*,' Lewis says, '"Somethin' on My Mind" was the A-side and "Let's Shake" was the B-side. CKOC here in Hamilton charted it. That was probably one of things I'm most proud of, because that was reserved for bands like the Beatles and Creedence Clearwater Revival, to have both songs listed on the charts.'

Up until then, the band had played a lot of high schools. And for a lot of kids, the Head was their first concert experience. And for some kids in particular, their first concert experience was exceptionally memorable. 'I remember one night,' Mahon says, 'I think it was Oshawa. We go to do our first set and all the girls are kind of screaming around the front of the edge of the stage and everything, and all of a sudden I hear Frank stop and "What do you want with that bass player? You're just staring at that bass player. You just want to suck his cock, don't ya?"'

'That's what led to Ontario Place,' Mahon adds. 'Because we'd probably done a couple of hundred high schools in southern Ontario. And they all were believers. Whether they came from Kingston or Belleville or Barrie or Windsor. All they had to do was get on a train or a bus. And they *all* went.'

Nothing had been as big as Ontario Place. A provincial public waterfront theme park perched on the shores of Lake Ontario, the place offered open-air evening concerts free to anyone who'd paid admission to the grounds. The programming was predictably eclectic for a tidy, respectable family place trying to please as many people as possible: folk one evening, jazz another, country and some rock. Ontario Place was accustomed to a casual stream of strolling crowds taking their seats after a day's walking around the park, watching the sunset while tapping toes and rocking sleeping babies. It was not ready for Teenage Head.

It will tell you something about Ontario Place — and maybe Toronto and Canada in general — in 1980, that the facility only moderately promoted the evening concerts, relying largely on signs posted around the grounds to attract people already there. Low-key was the order of the day, so low-key Ontario Place didn't really have security beyond the ticket takers and pavilion staff. It was a place where hell never broke loose nor was ever expected to.

'I'm pretty sure we caused that riot,' former Attic co-chief Tom Williams admits with a chuckle. 'At that point there was someone new at the Ontario Place Forum every night. And local press didn't pay much attention to them because it would go from Teenage Head to Tony Bennett to whatever. But we wanted to make it a special event and make everybody pay attention to it, so we bought a lot of radio time, a lot of advertising.

'Those of us inside had no idea what was going on outside. There were no cellphones then. So the bands were playing and I was standing in that little walkway that went back to the dressing room, and all hell broke loose. We had record company jackets at that time, kinda silk things with the Attic logo on the back, and somebody threw a beer bottle at us. I can distinctly remember them yelling, "Record company faggots!" And we had to run back down to the dressing room. They can put that on my tombstone: "Caused a Riot."' And not only had Attic bought that additional advertising, but at the peak of their popularity and radio airplay rotation, Teenage Head were playing for *free*. There was still even more publicity: Morrow had convinced Attic to hire a float to drive down Yonge Street to promote the gig.

The evening's opening act was none other than Segarini, the band led by the long-time musician, Head fan and new-music booster who'd seen the audience for the Hamilton band morph in two years from basement bars on Yonge Street to this: a virtual sea of people sitting on the lawns rolling away from the stage, eagerly awaiting a show that was still hours away. It was almost as if you had taken all the Ontario clubs that the Head had played at, where their audiences might be twenty-five, fifty, a hundred and fifty people, and bussed all those combined audiences in to Toronto. 'Any guy that's toured in a rock band or played a lot of shows will tell you there are gigs that have a buzz and gigs that don't,' Segarini says thirty-three summers later. 'And you could feel the buzz of this one before you got out of your car at Ontario Place.'

The dressing rooms were under the stage. Although glimpses from the opening of the underground tunnel to the stage confirmed that the gathering crowd was large, no one had any idea how large, or that the situation was getting dodgy: the audience area proper was full, but people kept coming.

'This was back when there was a bottle of Jack Daniel's and a couple of cases of beer in my dressing room,' Segarini recalls. 'I can't remember what they had in theirs, but we were all pretty well lubed all day long. And I think it was Frank's birthday. Out of all the guys, he was the most nervous. Because this was a put-up-or-shut-up kind of gig for him. People were there to see the performing monkey.' Segarini remembers that while the rest of the band was relatively relaxed, tuning their strings and getting ready, Venom sat quietly but intensely on a couch, leaning forward – not morose exactly, but trying his best to focus.

'June second, 1980,' Venom told me. 'My birthday. We had a single on the radio at the time which was basically a love ballad. It was soft with acoustics, it was called "Somethin' on My Mind." And I think it was No. 1 on CKOC in Hamilton. A lot of young kids couldn't see the band because we were basically playing the pubs. So when we played Ontario Place it was free, and obviously open to all ages, so all these young kids who had heard the song on the radio – I think they said there was 15,000 people there – apparently all rushed to Ontario Place to see us because it was the only opportunity.'

Park staff dealt with the teeming overflow as best as they knew how: they closed the gates on several thousand people. When dusk arrived, Segarini took the stage. While Bob Segarini remembers the sound being good and the band playing well, soon into their performance the band heard 'what sounded like booing,' but later understood was a melee erupting on the grounds. Thrown somewhat, the band started to play double-speed, watching as the crowd swelled to such a size that there was no longer space between audience members – they were standing in their seats.

Police arrived to contend with the increasingly unruly crowd. Some in cruisers, some on foot, others on horseback. Pushing ensued. Pushing back ensued. Projectiles got thrown, horses startled, cruiser windows shattered. There was a riot going on.

Venom told me what it was like to first take the stage: 'Because you walked down this tunnel way to Ontario Place to get to the stage, we had no idea how many people were out there. We were backstage for like five hours previous and when I walked out there it was like an unbelievable feeling. Young kids screaming, grabbing at our clothes – for about a minute I couldn't even speak. Just the rush. It was like, "Holy shit." Better than any drug, any alcohol I've ever done. It was amazing to have 15,000 screaming kids just wanting a piece of you. We never had that again, but I'll never forget it. It was fantastic.'

Not a minute and a half into the Head's first song, fans started launching themselves onto the stage. It got louder, crazier. Stipanitz remembers an empty bottle of Black Tower wine whizzing by his head, and Lewis told him later clods of dirt flew by *his* head. (And this apparently from people who were *enjoying* the band.) At one point, a fan almost made off with Lewis's beloved Les Paul, but it was retrieved. There was nowhere near the proper amount of security for the job, nor was the security there prepared to handle such a crowd. The thousands that had been locked behind the gates spilled over.

Nick in the thick of it.

Onstage, the band was oblivious to the rioting, but they were well aware of the ferocious adulation.

'We were capable of pitching a perfect game,' Mahon says, 'and the crowd was there to make sure we did. You couldn't lose. Nobody was on drugs. Nobody had an attitude then, everybody was firing on all eight cylinders. Frank thrived off the energy of the audience. It didn't matter that they didn't pay fifty dollars a seat. We nailed it.'

'I don't think Teenage Head could have planned a better thing to happen,' Segarini says. 'Because it made them instantly not only notorious and infamous, but the subtext of all the national coverage of this thing was very simple: this music and this band had arrived. That this is Beatlemania, only with a negative twist.'

At the time, however, it just felt good to get out alive. There was no time to ruminate over what had happened, even the next day when the headlines screamed 'Punk Rock Riot' and 'Teenage Head Closes Ontario Place Forum.' Because tomorrow was another day, and another day meant another gig somewhere else.

At the Arthur Pop Festival, Frank ascendant.

Here's what Lewis remembers: the next day, the band jumped on a plane, heading west, and were gone for six weeks. Teenage Head was always a nightclub act. Always going to a bar. Straight from the Ontario Place riot to another bar. 'Management didn't present us as a concert act,' Lewis says. 'They were making too much money off of us as a bar band, by playing every night.'

But according to Stipanitz, the day after Ontario Place was one of those rare days off. He distinctly remembers going fishing with Frank: 'After the show, I didn't really know what happened. Frank and I went up north fishing to a trailer and we had no radio or TV. It wasn't until a couple of days later when we came back that people said, "Don't you guys know what happened?" Then we saw the newspapers.'

Stacy Heydon saw the same newspaper photograph of the overturned police cruiser just about the same time everyone else did. 'When they turned that cop car over, they flipped a page in their career,' Heydon says. 'Now, all of a sudden, people are reading in the press that there's a Canadian band people are rioting over – they must be freaking awesome. There couldn't have been a better media push than Ontario Place.'

Across the country, word of the riot preceded Teenage Head and that, combined with the airplay of *Frantic City*, and especially the singles 'Somethin' on My Mind' and 'Let's Shake,' displaying the soft and hard sides of the band respectively, resulted in jammed venues everywhere. While some of those venues were indeed bars, others were larger: universities, colleges, dance clubs. Teenage Head was surging national. Momentum had to be capitalized upon. So what was to be done? Another single, obviously, especially from an album with as much radio playlist appeal as *Frantic City*. But what transpired next was one of those 'buts' Lewis claims always found their way into even the happiest Teenage Head tales.

'So we have our 45 out,' Lewis explains, 'the album's gone gold, everything's great. The next 45 is supposed to be "Wild One." But for some reason Attic Records went to a music consulting agent to figure out what should be next. They went through *Frantic City*, and they said the next one should be "Let's Shake." And I'm like, "Well, no, the *last* 45 was 'Let's Shake.'" "No, it should be 'Let's Shake' with the lyrics changed. More cleaned up." Even though there was no swearing in it, just "too fat and ugly" and "move your ass." And that's what they did. They had Frank go in and re-record the vocals. They made all the words nicer.' Not surprisingly, the re-released single flopped. And there were no further 45s from *Frantic City*.

Mair and Morrow were determined to capitalize on that post–Ontario Place momentum by nudging the band in the direction everyone fervently wanted to see it go: stateside. Mair had wisely brought American industry types to the Ontario Place show, and he followed that up by setting up a series of showcase events in the U.S., one of them at My Father's Place in Long Island, to show the band off and – maybe, hopefully, pray to God – land that universally lusted-after American deal. Never had the goal seemed more attainable or realistic. Although Teenage Head had already made forays into the U.S. – the twin punk pillars CBGB and Max's Kansas City among them – they hadn't done so as ascendant stars.

As Mair remembers, 'We set up a club date in New York, they had a live broadcast of the club date set up, and we had some MTV people interested in possibly putting them on MTV, so everything was really rolling nicely.'

Outtake from the *Frantic* cover shoot: about to explode.

Lewis admits he didn't even know what a showcase *was* at the time they were being planned, and that it's only in retrospect that he's had the chance to fully appreciate just how those gigs, had they actually happened, might have changed his band's destiny. It's one of those what-if scenarios that adhere so maddeningly to the band's history, that can make a guy crazy wondering where all the paths not taken — or simply blocked — might have led.

'I didn't really have any inclination of what those showcase shows meant except that we were going down to the States,' Lewis says. 'We'd already played the places I wanted to play. I wanted to play CBGB and Max's Kansas City. I'd played them. The other places I'd never heard of before. I was still a fan more than I was really a participant. I still dreamed of doing those things that I dreamed of doing when I was a kid. And My Father's Place wasn't a place that was high on the list of legendary venues.'

The night before New York, however, the band played a booze hall in a hockey arena in Palmerston, Ontario. They hadn't had enough rest and the pace was clearly taking its toll. After the show, half of the band returned to Hamilton while Lewis and Mahon, then living in Toronto, got in a van with Gary Frowd, a

Outtake from the *Frantic* cover shoot: like a rocket.

security guard/driver. It's not clear if he was drunk or high (Mahon says he might have been smoking hash, Lewis says he was a coke addict), but Frowd was definitely driving inadvisably fast on the curvy, two-lane highway. 'I just knew we were in bad hands,' Lewis says. 'You've got this band that's doing this showcase, why would you not hire the best, most secure, most reliable people to get this band from point A and back home again, safe and sound, instead of going for the cheap Class C security team?'

It was dark, three in the morning. Lewis remembers worrying that they were going to get in an accident. And they did. The van missed a stop sign at an intersection, went off the road, and Lewis, not wearing a seat belt (there were none in the back), was thrown from the vehicle. 'I was lying on the ground,' Lewis remembers, 'and I thought to myself, "No fucking way. There's no fucking way I've gotten hurt in a car accident. In a stupid car accident."' He tried to stand up and walk and fell right back down. His guitar, he noticed, was lying on the ground too. Mahon's face was banged up but he was essentially okay and he kept yelling, 'Gordie! Gordie! Gordie!' An ambulance came, and, as the shock wore off, Lewis started to feel extreme pain. When he next woke up, he was in an intensive-care ward, all junked up. His back was broken.

But he also had a couple of broken ribs, and surgeons couldn't operate until his ribs had healed.

'I remember hearing on the radio, "Gord Lewis of Teenage Head has been taken to hospital…" and it was like, holy fuck!' Lindsay Gillespie remembers. 'And then freaking out because the timing could not have been worse.'

I heard about the accident almost as quickly as news travelled those days, which is to say the next morning. That it was national news certainly confirms the band's rising status at the time. Six months earlier it probably wouldn't have made the headlines, nor – more sadly perhaps – would it have a year later. But the timing in September 1980, after Ontario Place and *Frantic City*, and just before the New York showcases, meant the timing was perfect for making the national news, but catastrophic for Lewis, the band and all the industry hopes pinned on them. At the time, the crash could be heard coast to coast. It remains possibly the most infamous automotive wreck in Canadian rock history.

Lewis was in a body cast for three months. And then in a brace for another three. The band, however, continued to play, even without him. Teenage Head had been through a riot, and a car crash, and the demand for them continued, unabated. They refused to play New York without Lewis, but Morrow would make sure they'd play just about everywhere else.

The Heart and the Machine

Gord Lewis was lucky to live. He was bedridden for months, and faced extensive physiotherapy to regain mobility. But there was never any question, at least in his mind, that as soon as he was able to get up, pick up his guitar and play again, he would return to Teenage Head.

But it wasn't going to happen quickly. If there was any thought of putting the band, already performing up to six nights a week, on a well-deserved hiatus, it didn't get much traction. Within a day or two of the accident, Morrow was appealing to the rest of the band's sense of obligation to Lewis. The band had to carry on, he argued, so that the bedridden Lewis could continue to be paid while laid up. And besides, there was a shitload of upcoming gigs booked, *Frantic City* was still selling and the band was more famous across the country than ever. The machine might have lost its heart, temporarily, but what machine ever needed a heart to run?

Mahon: 'It just hit me when Jack said that, "We gotta pay Gord. We have to keep playing." So that was like, all right, what else could I do? I was doing fuck all. I was sitting in my apartment.' It might not have been the right thing to do, but framed as a bid to aid a bedridden friend, it certainly felt right.

Stipanitz was also reluctant to carry on without Lewis, but ultimately agreed. 'That accident certainly stopped the momentum,' he says. 'I think we were headed for an American record deal but that put the brakes on all of that. I didn't want to play until Gord was well, but Jack convinced us all that we should. We had to pay the rent. I was naive, and at first I didn't think it was that big a deal: "Oh, he'll be up next week." But when it sunk in that it was going to be months, we reluctantly went back out. And just went through the motions. It certainly didn't sound the same. We always got a lot of energy off of Gord's playing. We fed off each other.'

Stipanitz was also privy to something Morrow had told him, a bit of on-the-down-low info that might have contributed to the drummer's sense of solidarity with the band: Teenage Head's manager had been approached by more than one major label with an interest in signing Frankie Venom as a solo act. No Teenage Head, just Frankie, and Frankie had quietly turned it down: no Teenage Head, no Frankie Venom. He wasn't going to abandon his band for the sake of fame. It was all of them or none at all.

Morrow replaced Lewis with David Bendeth, an accomplished jazz musician, session player and studio recording professional. His resumé, in fact, was irreproachably impressive in just about every area save the one in which he was being enlisted to perform – as a rock guitarist. But there wasn't any time – booked gigs are booked gigs – and Bendeth was available. He joined the band, learned the basics of the songs and within days was onstage as the new lead guitarist for Teenage Head.

'He was completely the wrong guy.' Mahon says. 'Like, oh my god. You're going to pick some jazz player to go in a punk band? He couldn't get the simplest songs. It wasn't like he was playing all the wrong chords or something, and he got through it, but man, we really missed Gordie.'

Morrow had known Bendeth a few years and knew he was a skilled musician. That he might not have been the most appropriate one didn't matter. Bendeth was available and could do the job. Not remotely interested in or acquainted with punk rock or Teenage Head's music, Bendeth nevertheless learned the basics quickly. But he never fully embraced the music, and if there was one thing that drove Mahon, Stipanitz and long-time friend and sideman Dave Desroches crazy, it was the apparent condescension with which Bendeth did the duty. To them, Bendeth was above the music and never let anybody forget it.

Technically, Bendeth's performance with Teenage Head was immaculate: he knew all the right notes to play and when to play them, he grew increasingly comfortable onstage, and he actually developed a camaraderie of sorts with the tempestuous and impulsive Frank, with whom he was always bunked while on the road. But he was no Lewis and he knew it. Even his Stratocaster, to some observers, was wrong: Teenage Head was a Les Paul band. This was Gord's band, Gord's music and Gord's dream. Bendeth was just visiting, and he never lost sight of his jacket on the hook at the door. As soon as Gord could, he'd be back.

If the accident provided Lewis with one opportunity he'd been lacking for the previous three years, it was an opportunity for reflection, and on his return it was evident he'd done a lot of thinking about Teenage Head: about what the band had become and how, and whether the fame that was finally theirs was clarifying or clouding that original dream. These were thoughts that must have been acutely pressing as he watched the machine keep rolling even in his absence. If his dream could carry on without him, maybe it had become something with an inorganic life of its own. Was it running away like that kid who'd grabbed his guitar at Ontario Place? And was anybody going to run after it and retrieve it this time, besides him?

Lewis was ready to slowly reintegrate into the band by the end of 1980, a truly remarkable recovery. At first he'd only appear as a special guest doing a number or two, but gradually he resumed his full position as lead guitar. But maybe not his full former energy – he tended to stand more still while playing, to seem less possessed by the channelled currents of the music's energy than intensely focused on it. But even if he presented differently after the accident, his playing was still unmistakably and blisteringly his. If Bendeth had played Teenage Head's music and played it well, Lewis was the reverse: the music, *his* music, played *him*.

Lewis remembers a distinct change in the atmosphere when he returned to Teenage Head. The rolling on of the machine in his absence had generated something he'd never seen with his band before: a sense of obligation. For the first time, they seemed to be doing this as a job.

'I kept telling myself I was going to get better and join the band,' Lewis says. 'I had no idea I was going to be out of commission for half a year. I knew the band had lost its momentum. I knew things were going to be a little weird, especially when I had to make a gradual comeback. And I didn't feel very comfortable – I felt like an outsider. Frank was the nicest to me. Frank was the one who made sure I got in and out of the van okay, and walked me to wherever I needed to be walked to. He did really did care. He really, really watched out for me.'

Prone to feeling outside of things anyway, for the first time Lewis felt separated from his band. As much, in fact, as he had when he was laid up in hospital. The perceptible drop in enthusiasm, fun and energy in the band could even be seen in Venom, who had begun complaining of boredom, pointlessness and the same-old grinding same-old.

'It really changed for Frank,' Lewis says. 'Frank was a pretty heart-and-soul guy and I think he could see that Bendeth wasn't Teenage Head material and wasn't the guy Frank wanted standing stage left to him. He had to put up with that for three months, and I think he got tired.'

He was, and he wasn't making any efforts to hide it. On New Year's Eve, 1980, City TV's *The New Music* – hosted by future CNN anchor J. D. (now John) Roberts – went to Headspace to interview the band about the Gordless months. Lewis was there, still in his brace and sitting next to Venom, when Roberts asked the singer what it had been like playing without his friend. Venom, with characteristic Frankness, responded, 'It's been good but we haven't been doing the gigs that we should be doing. We're just treading water now. We're not making any waves at all. We're just making the money.'

Lewis returned to a gigging regimen that was almost as gruelling as the one he'd left – at first, he could only stand onstage long enough for a song or two at a time – and he was also staring the next Teenage Head album right in the spindle hole. It was time to get back into the studio for number three, which meant writing new material – with a tired band – on top of re-entry into the live rock orbit and trying to find the old spark.

The third album would be called *Some Kinda Fun*, and the title, behind the scenes anyway, was as ironic as *Frantic City* was genuinely descriptive. Even the cover gave it away: in place of the bubblegum-tinted brightness of the first two albums, with their depictions of the band in a state of high goofball frenzy, *Some Kinda Fun* showcased the band, unsmiling and shot against blackness from slightly above, looking for all the world like four guys about to processed in county lock-up.

The songs didn't come easily – although one classic, the hoser-hedonistic anthem 'Teenage Beer Drinkin' Party,' would here be born – and they returned to working with a producer (former Guess Who recording engineer Brian Christian) who some claim didn't give a shit. It also didn't help matters that Morrow had convinced the band it was time to split with Attic. Album or no album in the works, potential costs of disengaging from a binding legal contract notwithstanding, and the dubious strategy of alienating your (soon-to-be-former) label just as you're working on an album that label will subsequently be left to promote, Morrow and the band went ahead and pressed the separation from Attic.

Morrow's reasoning wasn't his alone. It was largely shared by the band. Frustrated that they hadn't yet broken into the States and worried that their golden moment might be flickering past, Teenage Head was growing bullish on the issue of out-of-country exposure. And it was one of the first questions everybody asked them: When are you going to the States? When are you going to Europe? Why are you still playing these fucking bars and shit in southern Ontario?

It was a climate that infiltrated the *Some Kinda Fun* sessions as well. Stipanitz remembers that the old sense of all-for-one collaboration was gone. He remembers Lewis bringing finished songs to the studio for the first time, a fact that might be attributed to the guitarist's months recovering from the accident more than any deliberate attempt at seizing control, but it felt like that nevertheless. The band was frustrated, tired and uninspired. They weren't connecting with their producer and were pissed with their label. Some kinda fun indeed.

Accounts vary on what precisely transpired in Morrow's negotiations with Attic. According to the band, Attic wasn't doing enough to get the band into the U.S. According to the former heads of Attic, Morrow was making unreasonable demands that contravened their original agreements. Both Mair and Williams insist that getting the band into the States was indeed a priority, but that it would take time, and time was something neither Morrow nor the band were willing to spare. None of this was making the vibe in the studio any better. At one point, relations

Frank, 1979.

between Teenage Head's management and their label grew so tense that Attic had an armed guard posted at the studio door to prevent anyone from stealing the masters. No wonder the boys look so pissed on the cover.

'I don't recall the exact timing of when we decided to let them go,' Mair says, 'whether it was before or after the album came out. But I suspect in hindsight that letting them go had some impact on our interest in them, because we weren't going to have their next album. Maybe we were guilty of not promoting it as 110 percent as we had the first record, but it didn't do as well as *Frantic City*.'

Mair didn't trust Morrow. He was making what the former now calls 'ridiculous demands' and playing games. The album was finished, but he refused to deliver it. And all the money went through Morrow. Though the cheques were made out to the songwriters, they were written to the writers care of his company, ABC Frenetic, and Morrow cashed them. 'Jack just walked over to Larry's and took the money out of the till,' Mair says.

Meanwhile, other questions started to surface, an inevitable by-product of the band's discontent: why hadn't they yet landed an American distribution deal? Why were they still gigging predominantly in bars? What had happened with the momentum generated by Ontario Place and *Frantic City*?

Tensions between Attic and Morrow grew acute. The manager accused the label of shirking its obligation to export the band to America, while Mair and Tom Williams insisted they were doing all they could. The band was a harder sell than they'd anticipated, they claimed, and a gradual move to larger venues and exploitation of the new music-video medium were on the agenda. After several tense meetings in which the label argued its case and Morrow his, Attic finally capitulated and let the band go. After all the days of excitement, glory and promise, Teenage Head and Jack Morrow were no longer worth the trouble.

'We just felt they couldn't take us to the next level,' Mahon says of Attic. 'And they couldn't. I believed it. It's like, "You're stuck in Canada, boys." But as far as Jack goes, I was 100 percent behind him trying to get us into the States. Any Canadian band knew that was a joke in the business. "Come on. Are you just going to just stay a *Canadian* band? You've got to move forward." And when that didn't happen, that's what started that whole "We've got to get off that label."'

Mahon remembers feeling like, well, a cog in a machine: 'Stick them out on the road and keep playing. That's all they can do. They love playing live and that's what they're good at. Just keep them playing. Don't even give them a chance to think about what's going on, you know?'

Tom Williams remembers his last meeting with Morrow. 'Attic was a really good company,' he says. 'A very professional company. We might have been small and scrappy, but both Al and I had worked for major labels. We knew what we were doing. We crossed our T's, did our royalties on time. We never screwed with anybody. We just decided, "This is getting way too messy. We've got other acts. We love this band, but it looks like this band isn't going to stay together in the way they had been, and it takes away from their musical abilities when they've got all that internecine warfare going on." To a great extent Teenage Head was just a working band. They were just a really good, hard-working, punk – if you want to call it that – band. They weren't brilliant guys, so they just needed to keep working.'

Despite the presence of an old-school rave-up or two, *Some Kinda Fun* predictably reflected not only this malaise but Attic's frustration: the album wasn't promoted with nearly the same enthusiasm or aggression as its predecessor, and sales were low.

'Teenage Beer Drinkin' Party' and 'Let's Go to Hawaii' got some modest radio rotation, but apart from that, the album submerged and sunk.

Lewis found himself increasingly being confronted about money. As he and Mahon recall, Stipanitz was especially bullish on the subject of royalties. He'd begun doing some of the math, and it wasn't adding up. How could *Frantic City* have gone platinum while the band – still on their modest $400 a week salary – had nothing to show for it? How could the band be playing as hard as it was, and still drawing the crowds that it did, and not see any more cash?

But then, suddenly, a very welcome distraction from the financial questions – an American deal appeared to materialize. The label was the mighty MCA, and it was interested in recording and releasing a Teenage Head record with a couple of provisions: first, that the recording be an EP instead of a full album, and second, that the band change its name. MCA felt Teenage Head was simply too sexually suggestive, and insisted the band pluralize it: Teenage *Heads*. Desperate for a stateside breakthrough, the band agreed to the name change and went into the studio.

If the band's punk cred had already been compromised by the radio-friendly *Frantic City* – especially the sweet acoustic balladry of 'Somethin' on My Mind' – and the band's unpunkish national popularity, the name change struck many as a final straw. For years, the agreement to change the name in the interest of corporate acceptability remained a sore spot with the band and fans alike, and probably did as much to alienate the original remaining fan base as any acoustic ballads or studio sax musicians.

The matter quickly became moot anyway. A corporate shuffle at MCA ousted the players who'd been interested in Teenage Head, leaving the EP – titled *Tornado*, and produced by none other than Morrow's reliable hire David Bendeth – and the band named Teenage Heads orphaned. They played exactly one American date, in Nashville, as the opening morning act at a weekend music festival. The record was barely released, the band was dropped, and America once again drifted below the horizon.

In this context, it's hardly surprising that the questions being asked by the band concerning money, management and strategy ratcheted up. Nor is it mysterious why Lewis, the source of Teenage Head's original inspiration and vision, would become, belatedly perhaps, a conscientious investigator of how exactly things had got to this point.

Morale was plummeting. Venom was beginning to make his boredom, fatigue and frustration audible in the least productive ways, such as loudly complaining that he was tired of singing the same old songs – the bread and butter that kept the table set – night after night. Stipanitz and he even began quietly kicking around the idea of breaking off and forming their own band. This one wasn't much fun anymore, and for all appearances wasn't going to get fun any time soon. Maybe, just maybe, it was also time to think about dumping Jack Morrow.

'He wasn't doing much for us,' Stipanitz says. 'Our career was stalled. He was never quite honest and open with money, and I'm sure he took a little more than he deserved. But I don't think there was that much that he *could* steal. I often asked him for an accounting and he'd say he couldn't do that. We accepted it for a while, but in the end if you can't be open and honest you need to find someone who can be.'

Heading toward the mid-'80s, the Teenage Head machine was doing some serious sputtering: parts were falling off, repairs were constantly needed and, most distressingly, forward momentum was lacking. The band was still playing to packed houses and salaries were being maintained, but that vital sense of *going somewhere* was gone. The machine was doing nothing more than maintaining its own existence.

'By 1985, we were off of any major label at all,' Lewis explains. 'We just had the live album (*Endless Party*, a vibrant recording of the band's 1983 New Year's Eve gig released by Ready Records), were still playing a lot, still chugging away, but I started to learn a lot about the business. Ignorance is bliss, you know? I started doing a lot of reading, learning about publishing and looking back at what stuff we had signed, and I was like, "What happened? We had a record label but we don't anymore. We still have management but what's the future hold?" I had already found out enough about Jack that I didn't like what was going on. I knew he had to go, that I didn't want to be tied to this person for too much longer.'

Lewis began to follow up on both Stipanitz's and his own suspicions about the money trail. He even went back to Al Mair to query about the paths taken by royalty cheques. What he learned was that everything had been paid out to Jack Morrow's company, as per original contractual arrangement. And that most of that money, even allowing for the customary reductions due to payments to management and staff, was not getting back to the band. There was *a lot* of unaccounted-for cash.

'There was too much conflict of interest,' Lewis says. 'Jack owned too much of us. Like owning publishing and owning management and never providing an accounting of anything. He was ripping us off. I had some meetings with Al Mair,' Lewis adds, 'after I received a statement from the musicians' union for monies I had supposedly received. And I'd never received the money. Al says, "Oh yeah, we have your cancelled cheque right here with your signature on it." And I go, "I never received a cheque. Would you mind sending me a photocopy of the cheque? And do you mind sending me a photocopy of everybody's cheque in the band? With their endorsement on the back?" So I got four forged cheques back. Jack was signing cheques that were written out to us that were going to his office, and that's when I really went, "Okay, this is what's really going on here."'

Lewis served Morrow notice. He was out. But there were other matters of business to attend to. For one thing, Morrow had the master tapes for the first album in his possession, and the band suspected they'd never see them again if they didn't take action. Stipanitz was elected to get them back: 'I snuck into Jack's apartment and found the tapes in his bedroom.' That matter attended, the task remained of serving legal papers to Morrow, which was easier said than done. He had disappeared.

With a brother who was a lawyer, Lewis went looking for Morrow. But Jack was nimble. 'He was gone and no one knew where he was,' Mair says. 'The police ended up finding him working at the CNE, in the Modern Living Building, selling something.' Morrow had returned to his carny roots. And it turned out Morrow wasn't even his real name.

After they tracked down Morrow at the Ex, Lewis confronted him. Lewis remembers him running a fortune teller booth or something, and he went down there with legal papers that would require him to sign off on everything he technically owned and to give up all rights. Perhaps miffed by the burglary of those master tapes, maybe just to stall for time or possibly just being true to his nature, Morrow refused. Lewis had no choice but to sue. But when the court date came around, Morrow didn't. 'Never saw him again,' Lewis says. 'He didn't show up for court. He let it go to the last second. He wouldn't relent. He made us go through every single step, and then finally on the day of reckoning he wasn't even there. Just signed everything back to us. We actually got quite a bit back.'

When Morrow died a few years later, not a single member of Teenage Head, nor any of Morrow's other previous clients, made it to the funeral.

What Can a Poor Boy Do?

With the departure of Jack Morrow, Lewis effectively became the band's manager. Perhaps not technically – the band would have subsequent managers, but none with the influence over the band's business that Morrow had. Lewis made himself far more aware of how business operated and monitored all affairs involving his band. In a way, he had to. If there was any shred of that original dream left, it was only the dreamer who could preserve it. If there was a future for Teenage Head, it was up to Lewis to get it there.

This would be no small struggle. The band was without a label, temporarily without management, and money continued to be a corrosive issue. 'The other guys in the band still don't understand,' Lewis says. 'They still don't get it. Frank went to his grave not getting it. But that's the nature of most of the music business. It happens so fast that you just can't keep up with it. I was trying to run the band, but I was put under the microscope because I was divulging all this stuff as I was finding out what happened.'

Exasperated with the turning of the band's fortunes, Venom was increasingly vocal in his disinclination to keep performing the Heads' hits. His unchecked, hard-partying ways were verging on the uncontrollable. To bolster matters musically, Lewis enlisted his childhood friend Dave Desroches to join the band as rhythm guitar player. Desroches – performance handle Dave Rave – was a gifted musician and songwriter, and his musical taste tilted steeply toward power pop. Gord felt Desroches, who'd already contributed as a musician and sideman to the band for years, was a natural addition. Stipanitz didn't.

'I wasn't comfortable anymore,' says Stipanitz. 'I saw that it was totally getting different. And at that point we divided into different camps. There was me and Frank, and Gord and Dave. Gord arranged for the sessions for the *Trouble in the Jungle* album and brought all the songs in already written. I like writing songs. I don't think it's Gord's fault, because I kind of withheld and withdrew. To be fair, I should have stepped forward and said, "Here are my songs." But at that point I knew Frank was unhappy and he was going to leave the band and go on his own and wanted me to come with him.

'After the album was recorded,' Stipanitz continues, 'Gord suggested we take a month off. It was kind of funny the way this unfolded. Very dysfunctional. I met Frank and I asked him, "Do you want to tour this album, or do you want to start your solo career?" He said, "I think I'd like to leave now." So when we met with Gord and Steve after our hiatus, I said, "I'm going to be leaving the band. I know Frank is going to be doing solo stuff and I'm going to be joining him." Frank said, "Yeah, I'm going to go do something on my own and Nick's going to come play with me." So in the next couple of days I asked Frank if he was ready to start rehearsing with a band and he told me, "Nick, I've changed my mind. I'm going to tour this album with Teenage Head." I said, "Really? Maybe I should join you." And he said, "No, Gord doesn't want you back. He said the only way he'll let the band continue is if you don't return."'

Stipanitz spent a year building hearses for a living. Venom toured with Teenage Head for the same period, then announced he was quitting. He'd had enough. He and Nick formed a short-lived outfit called Frankie and the Vipers – from which Nick was eventually ousted due to disputes with another musician – and Lewis promoted Desroches to be Teenage Head's lead singer. For the first time in Lewis's presence, Teenage Head wasn't the four guys who went back to the basement in Hamilton.

Desroches remembers the period sharply. The band was trying to self-manage, he was trying to figure out how the fuck he was going to stand in for the band's brightest star and there wasn't really a map anymore. Whatever you said about Jack Morrow, he always seemed to have a plan.

'One of the biggest problems we had was the resistance we were getting from the industry,' Desroches recalls. 'Because when Jack left, we thought everybody would applaud. It was the opposite. Everything that had pissed everybody off about the band could be unleashed now. Every agent Jack had ever owed a favour to. It was really stressful. Before, you could always fight against Jack, but the fighting went inside.'

Desroches remembers spending hours on the phone, trying to book gigs, trying to generate press interest, and becoming increasingly familiar with the post-Morrow band's dismal fiscal situation. 'I discovered we were going bankrupt,' he says.

Then there was the looming fact that he'd have to soon step in for Venom. 'When I got the gig as singer, I sweated it for days. I remember sitting in my room in my apartment, literally sick. One night I'd dream the audience was filling Maple Leaf Gardens and everything's "We Are the World," and the next I'm like Bob Dylan and people are throwing stuff at me.' It took a while, but eventually Desroches, already a cult figure for his power-pop ensemble the Shakers, grew comfortable being the Head's lead singer and audiences grew more forgiving, although screams of 'We want Frankie!' confronted him for the first year on the road.

In time, the band even felt ready to return to the studio. The resulting album, *Electric Guitar*, recorded in 1987 and released in 1988, was an under-appreciated and under-released band highlight, a self-produced set of tightly polished power-pop compositions. With the help of fellow Hamiltonian Daniel Lanois as side musician and mixer on some tracks, and the veteran Jack Pedler on drums (he'd join Teenage Head permanently in 2003), it indicated the band was infinitely capable of evolving, adapting and still moving forward. But the album didn't sell well, and despite the collective ego boost that making the album had given the band, *Electric Guitar* failed to herald a brave new beginning. Desroches finally left the band in 1989, after seven years.

Frankie and the Vipers lasted a couple of years, but by many accounts the band was far more dedicated to living the romantically self-destructive rock 'n' roll lifestyle than making or performing music. Stipanitz, meanwhile, found himself drumming for the Tennessee Rockets, an experience he still cherishes for the fact it helped him get the old inspiration back.

In 1992, Teenage Head was offered a tidy sum for a two-show original-lineup reunion, and for a few weeks the original foursome was restored. They played sold-out gigs at Rock & Roll Heaven in Toronto and Barrymore's in Ottawa, and it looked like it might make sense to keep the founding four band members intact again.

At least some members thought so. Not Stipanitz. He told them he'd be happy to play with the band whenever they needed him, but he wasn't prepared to return permanently. Informed that he had to sign on as the Head's regular drummer or hit the road, he left. It was the last time he'd play drums or perform.

In 1995, Teenage Head rallied impressively for the album *Head Disorder*, a pared-down, twelve-song return to punchy hard-pop rock that nevertheless saw only meagre release. A pity, because it's easily the band's best work since *Frantic City*. If Desroches' presence had deftly manoeuvred the band toward an expertly executed power-pop sound, Frank's return pulled Teenage Head back to original glam-punk terrain. It's a truly legitimate and admirable achievement, and another sign of the persistence with which the band, under the right circumstances and with the right players, was capable of being inspired. Meanwhile, the Head continued to perform live wherever it was booked, frequently conjuring the old magic in front of smaller, older, but only intensely more loyal crowds.

Musically, the band never diminished. Mahon and Lewis only grew more formidably synched and tight as musicians and, approaching middle age, became more ferociously forceful. Venom was another story. Although his voice never left him, the years of unchecked substance consumption aged the once lithely beautiful young man into a prematurely puffy and old one, and there was more than one occasion where he was removed from concert venues by emergency medical teams. But where the old Venom shone through was in his dependable return even from those dramatic departures: he was always there for the next show, and his voice always rocked, even if his body didn't.

Stories, sad and similar, apocryphal but imaginable, and too numerous to recount, abound of Frank's last years. You hear how he had to be hospitalized for either collapsing or having a seizure during a performance, only to check himself out and get back to the show. You hear how he would sometimes be pulled out of the van in which he was sleeping in order to sufficiently sober up from a daytime drunk to start the cycle again with that night's show. You hear what it was like to go and collect him from his Hamilton apartment on gig nights, never knowing what shape he'd be in when (and if) he answered the door. And you hear how he never learned to say no. Forever surrounded by people who'd give him whatever form of liquid or chemical distraction he wished, Venom spent his final years playing out the hardcore punk rock string to the end. So you also hear that he was alone in his apartment the morning he called 911 for an ambulance. Stipanitz remembers seeing Venom for the first time in a decade when he took his wife to a Teenage Head show in Toronto. He was stunned. His best friend looked as though he'd aged decades. Shortly after they arrived at Nick's place for a long-overdue catch-up between old mates, Venom plunged through the coffee table and had to be sent off in a cab.

Thank god, then, for 2003. That was the year Lewis realized a long-held dream: recording with a Ramone on drums and a Ramones producer behind the knobs. It had taken some doing to set the sessions up, but arrangements had finally fallen into place. The biggest worry then was Venom: what state would he be in to record? What if he didn't show? And what if he did show but was in no condition to sing? For Lewis and Mahon, it was a legit-imate worry. By the time Teenage Head went into the studio to record the album with Marky Ramone on drums and Daniel Rey producing, Venom already looked like every mile the band had ever covered and then some, and Lewis was terrified this dream project – to record some of the old songs not only properly, but with Ramone and Rey – might collapse like so many others had. But Rey, who'd had experience with such unstable talents as Dee Dee Ramone and Johnny Thunders, knew exactly how to handle Venom. The result – *Teenage Head with Marky Ramone* – is as good and often better than anything the band ever recorded. Not only the most purely punk-sounding recording of the band's long history, but a testament both to Venom's astoundingly resilient vocal capabilities (for a guy as battered as he was) and the endur-ing sonic vitality of their music.

Eight weeks before he died, Frankie Venom agreed to make a cameo appearance at the annual Festival of Friends music event in Hamilton. He'd accepted the offer by the Canadian neo-punk outfit Shit From Hell to sing a couple of songs: 'Let's Shake' and the Ramones' 'Blitzkrieg Bop.' The day was dark and rumbling. Storm clouds threatened, and finally, just a couple of minutes into his performance, it started to pour. Venom looked up, grimaced and threw down his mike stand. 'Fuck this,' he said. 'If I'm gonna die, it's going to be with my own band.' Then he marched off. They were his last words spoken onstage.

Venom's official cause of death was the throat cancer he'd been diagnosed with just weeks before, but anyone who knew or saw him presumed that was just the final cause. He'd been killing himself one way or another for years.

Cancer finally beat Frank in October 2008, months after *Teenage Head with Marky Ramone* was released and weeks before the band was to be presented with a Lifetime Achievement Award by the Hamilton Music Awards. He was fifty-one years old and he was mourned loudly. At a last-minute memorial, musicians, fans and friends turned up in droves, but also bikers, dealers and fellow benders of the bar-propped elbow. For anyone present at any of the early Teenage Head shows or the scene they once crashed and conquered, it was a bracing reminder not only of time's rude passage but mortality itself. I mean, weren't they just twenty-one years old yesterday? Weren't we all? And how could someone with such sheer animal vitality and youthful, carnal charisma be extinguished? And if *he* could be stopped …

Well, Gord Lewis and Steve Mahon couldn't. As Teenage Head, they played on and continue to. In 2003, right around the time of the Ramones sessions, Jack Pedler, who'd first seen the band in the basement of Duffy's Tavern in Hamilton back in the mid-'70s, joined Teenage Head as its permanent drummer. In 2009, veteran fan, band buddy and Cambridge, Ontario, music store owner Peter MacAuley was enlisted in the thankless task of filling Frankie's Converse high-tops, and he does so more than admirably because he doesn't try to be Frank Venom. A gifted showman on his own terms, he sings the songs like the lifelong lover of them he is: not exactly like Frankie Venom, but like somebody Frankie and his band changed the instant he saw them. MacAulay serves the songs and not the singer, and in the process does them both some fine justice.

MacAulay is one of the many people in the Teenage Head support network who got there through fandom. Another is Lou Molinaro, whose Hamilton Club This Ain't Hollywood has not only become a stalwart beacon of the lingering first-wave punk spirit, but has hosted several events called the Gord Lewis Songbook, in which various people hop onstage with the guitarist to perform vintage Head material. Teenage Head has also played the club countless times, and Molinaro – himself a musician and hopeless Headman – claims he opened the joint largely so Teenage Head would always have a home.

As of 2014, Mahon and Lewis were still touring and playing, and Lewis was sitting on a pile of both unreleased old Teenage Head recordings – outtakes, alternate takes, live material and unissued songs – and new songs he'd written over the years. Lewis says he hopes to see all this stuff released someday, that he'd like to record both a solo album and maybe even a new Teenage Head record. But he's being very careful. History has taught him not to get carried away by his dreams.

Five years after the passing of Frank Kerr, and some thirty-five years after I first saw the band, Teenage Head has taken the stage at the El Mocambo in Toronto, a venue they've rattled the timbers of countless times. But this time it's different. Robert Gordon, the storied old-school rock vocalist who rose to punk-era prominence doing eerily authentic late-'50s vocal performances in front of the big-twang traditionalist Link Wray, is singing for the band. It's a deal that's been in the making for four years. As they rip through a note-perfect set of old rock and rockabilly, both Lewis and Mahon look as serious as first-communion altar boys, leaving all the obvious fun to be had by their delighted frontman.

It's not that they aren't having a blast, just that it's a blast these guys – now themselves rock 'n' roll traditionalists of a sort, and carrying a legacy as substantial in itself as Gordon's – are determined not to blow, as if they ever would. As the set plays out in front of an audience ranging in age from eighteen to sixty-eight, the urgency, eros and original danger of these freshly heated chestnuts comes smoking through. The music rings as hot as it ever did, the soundtrack to an adolescence that truly defies age, time and fashion. If real high school is the place you dream of getting out of or mythologize the reality out of, the high school of old rock 'n' roll is one alma mater you can always go back to – and that's because it was never really there. It's the one you fantasize about, the one where you take the stage and blow all the complications of real adolescence, and the ensuing drudgery of adulthood, away.

As they cast careful glances across the stage to each other during the Robert Gordon set, Lewis and Mahon are again a pair of Hamilton high school buddies who heard the call and never stopped answering.

As of this writing, Teenage Head is still making some serious noise. There may only be two original members in the lineup, but live the band delivers those sweet decibels as forcefully as ever. The crowds may be smaller, Venom might be gone and the dream of world domination might be a distant whimsy, but none of that matters in the sheer blast of the moment.

Lewis has preserved his dream, the one that came to him when watching the Monkees and those Beatles cartoons on TV as a kid. It might have taken years of detours, mismanagement, disappointment and slipped opportunities, but the band is now entirely his: he decides when and where to gig, what to play, who will fill in for the missing original members.

Lewis has never quite accepted what the writing of this book has made me more certain of than ever: that Teenage Head has left a legacy in Canadian rock music only that much more amazing for having been made in spite of so much – the period during which they emerged, the country they came from, the industry they baffled, the almost utter disregard of the band by the Canadian cultural establishment. He'll tell you how it still burns him that the band never got a Juno, but I'll tell you that's proof of Teenage Head's transcendent outlaw cred. And Nick Stipanitz will tell you so too: 'Sometimes it's best to run outside the herd.'

Teenage Head didn't need bullshit validation like a Juno. They existed and mattered precisely because bullshit like the Junos needed to be challenged and exposed for the pointless exercise in bland and conservative pop-cultural affirmation that they are. Fuck 'em. But that's easy for me to say. I'm just a fan.

Their time to rise was 1977–78, that now legendary blowback moment in rock music when the music turned against itself – or at least what it had become – and insisted that the original impulses be restored. It was time to get loud again, get dirty again, get simple again. Have some fucking *fun* again. It's as though punk knew this was rock's last chance to matter, so all stops were pulled, and along with some other groups from other places, out from Hamilton roared Teenage Head.

That the Head legacy persists largely anecdotally, without an extended recording legacy or historical documentation, in a country that uneasily regards its pop culture, and in the absence of the common-currency mythology that ensures inviolable legendary status for, say, the Ramones, the Sex Pistols or the Clash, only makes the Teenage Head story that much more remarkable. You really did have to be there to get it, and once you got it, it couldn't be forgot.

Stipanitz tells me about first hearing the news of Frankie's death: 'I heard it on the radio going to work. It was national news. That astounded me, that it got that much press coverage. I still don't fully realize what impact we had and how famous we were because to me we never made it to where I wanted to go. But now I look back and I can see that we were the one-in-a-million that made it that far. The superstars are one-in-ten-million, but we made it to the one-in-a-million mark and I've got to be grateful for that.'

For me, it's more like one-in-several-million, meaning those bands who made a noise so singular and vital it could not be drowned out by anything, who didn't need fame to be enduring, didn't have to conform to be recognized, didn't have to be massive to matter. For me, it all comes down to that first time I heard 'Picture My Face,' as perfect and eternally pleasurable a piece of pop music as I have ever heard. It installed itself permanently in that pleasure centre that only music can access, and it's never left. The simple fact is these guys created great music and performed it – endlessly and everywhere they could plug in – with as much passion and joy as they gave.

If anything, the pure persistence of the band's reputation among anyone who saw them is all the proof you need. Once experienced, you didn't need anything else to tell you Teenage Head was, in the poetic words of Bob Segarini, 'fucking genius.' The truth was ringing in your ears.

Acknowledgements

In the year that I tracked the scorched-earth Teenage Head story, the following people gave generously of their time and memory: Ralph Alfonso, David Bendeth, Moe Berg, Jimi Bertucci, Colin Brunton, Bob Bryden, Dave Desroches, Rolf Dinsdale, Hugh Dillon, David Finch, Lindsay Gillespie, Stacy Heydon, John Kastner, Paul Kobak, Steven Leckie, Al Mair, David Marsden, Lou Molinaro, Peter MacAulay, Jack Pedler, Freddie Pompeii, Don Pyle, Daniel Rey, Lucasta Ross, Bob Segarini, Dominic Solntsneff, Sam Sutherland, Gary Topp, Tom Williams, Liz Worth.

Along the way, these people provided invaluable assistance and feedback on various drafts: Bill Alexander, Stephen Cole, Greig Dymond, the archivally impeccable Gary Gold, and my unaccountably tolerant wife, Carol Maloney.

At Coach House Books, I was tirelessly egged on, back-slapped, encouraged and generally enabled by my x-ray-visioned editor Jason McBride, as well as Evan Munday, Heidi Waechtler and Alana Wilcox. Thank you all for being nuts enough to take this on. And for pretending to be pleased when I submitted an manuscript almost twice as long as expected.

I must, however, reserve special gratitude for the three original members of Teenage Head who gave it all: Gord Lewis, Steve Mahon and Nick Stipanitz. I thank you guys more than you will ever know.

If there are mistakes, ommissions or general violations of the naked truth herein, I take full responsibility.

About the Author

The obsessively inclined Geoff Pevere has been writing about movies, music and all things pleasurably distracting for more than thirty-five years. He is currently a movie columnist with the *Globe and Mail*, and spent a decade writing about the flickers for the *Toronto Star*. He is the co-author of the nationally bestselling *Mondo Canuck: A Canadian Pop Culture Odyssey*, former host of CBC Radio's pioneering pop culture program *Prime Time*, co-host of Rogers Television's *Reel to Real*, and host of TVOntario's *Film International*. He has lectured on movies, pop culture and critical writing at several Canadian universities and colleges. You'll find him in Toronto, which is a city about thirty minutes down the road from Hamilton.

Photo Credits

About the
Exploded Views Series

Exploded Views is a series of probing, provocative essays that offer surprising perspectives on the most intriguing cultural issues and figures of our day. Longer than a typical magazine article but shorter than a full-length book, these are punchy salvos written by some of North America's most lyrical journalists and critics. Spanning a variety of forms and genres — history, biography, polemic, commentary — and published simultaneously in all digital formats and handsome, collectible print editions, this is literary reportage that at once investigates, illuminates and intervenes.

www.chbooks.com/explodedviews

Typeset in Goodchild Pro and Gibson Pro. Goodchild was designed by Nick Shinn in 2002 at his ShinnType foundry in Orangeville, Ontario. Shinn's design takes its inspiration from French printer Nicholas Jensen who, at the height of the Renaissance in Venice, used the basic Carloginian minuscule calligraphic hand and classic roman inscriptional capitals to arrive at a typeface that produced a clear and even texture that most literate Europeans could read. Shinn's design captures the calligraphic feel of Jensen's early types in a more refined digital format. Gibson was designed by Rod McDonald in honour of John Gibson FGDC (1928–2011), Rod's long-time friend and one of the founders of the Society of Graphic Designers of Canada. It was McDonald's intention to design a solid, contemporary and affordable sans serif face.

Printed at the old Coach House on bpNichol Lane in Toronto, Ontario, on Rolland Opaque Natural paper, which was manufactured, acid-free, in Saint-Jérôme, Quebec, from 50 percent recycled paper, and it was printed with vegetable-based ink on a 1965 Heidelberg KORD offset litho press. Its pages were folded on a Baumfolder, gathered by hand, bound on a Sulby Auto-Minabinda and trimmed on a Polar single-knife cutter.

Edited by Jason McBride
Designed by Alana Wilcox
Series cover design by Ingrid Paulson
Cover photo by Don Pyle

Coach House Books
80 bpNichol Lane
Toronto ON M5S 3J4
Canada

416 979 2217
800 367 6360

mail@chbooks.com
www.chbooks.com